*J'adore Paris*

# ISABELLE LAFLÈCHE

# J'adore Paris

## ADVENTURES IN COUNTERFEIT CHIC

Harper Weekend

*J'adore Paris*
Copyright © 2013 by Isabelle Laflèche.
All rights reserved.

Published by Harper Weekend, an imprint of HarperCollins Publishers Ltd

First published in Canada by HarperCollins Publishers Ltd
in an original trade paperback edition: 2013
This Harper Weekend trade paperback edition: 2014

HarperCollins books may be purchased for educational, business,
or sales promotional use through our Special Markets Department.

HarperCollins Publishers Ltd
2 Bloor Street East, 20th Floor
Toronto, Ontario, Canada
M4W 1A8

*www.harpercollins.ca*

Library and Archives Canada Cataloguing in Publication
information is available upon request

ISBN 978-1-44341-333-6

Printed and bound in the United States
RRD 9 8 7 6 5 4 3 2 1

To my dear grandmother Marie, who encouraged me to write.
Your light still shines bright.

"America is my country and Paris is my home town."
—Gertrude Stein

*J'adore Paris*

# Chapter 1

"Welcome back, Mademoiselle Lambert," the French customs officer at Charles de Gaulle Airport says after I've explained that I'm moving back to France. He hands me my passport, and I smile gratefully.

"*Merci, monsieur.* It's great to be home."

For me, moving back to Paris after a year away was, as they say in America, a no-brainer. It means a new job and a new life. I've received an enticing offer: to be Director of Intellectual Property for Christian Dior, a big change from corporate law on Wall Street. Besides, Antoine, my former colleague, now boyfriend, is here. It's exhilarating to finally arrive in Paris with such an enviable position, an exciting new romance, and a new lease on life.

With my feet back on Gallic soil, I head giddily to the luggage carousel to retrieve my bags, beaming with the gushing smile of someone madly in love.

While I wait for my bags, my thoughts drift to the future: spending my days in one of the world's most prestigious fashion houses, working on fascinating legal assignments involving jaw-droppingly beautiful haute couture and exquisitely handcrafted *métiers d'arts*. I just hope to fit in with the fashion crowd; corporate New York, where I spent the last year in an ocean of navy blue suits, may not be the best preparation for cutting-edge trends, but I'm confident that I'll find my place.

It occurs to me that I'm at the exact location of an incident I read about in the news: five masked thieves took down four security guards at the airport's freight terminal, making off with ten pallets of luxury merchandise valued at 500,000 euros. It sounds like something from a TV crime drama. Will my job at Dior involve things like that? It would be worlds away from drafting financial documents for Edwards & White—despite being one of the largest law firms in the world, my former employer was, for me, more like a paperwork factory. I'm ready for a change.

I spot my first piece of luggage—a navy blue Lancel leather satchel—on the conveyor belt and awkwardly wiggle my way to the front of the dense crowd to pull it onto my trolley. I had most of my belongings professionally packed and shipped to France, but my wardrobe I've brought myself. A tiny woman standing next to me gives me a nudge in the ribs as I reach for my fourth enormous bag. This one's a hockey bag I picked up at the last minute at Target, at the suggestion of Lisa, my best friend in the United States. It earns me a few muttered insults and dirty looks from the other passengers, most of whom are dealing with no more than tiny carry-on bags and Longchamp totes.

Embarrassed, I realize that my load could be taken for the luggage of an entire family of six arriving from JFK. In less than a year, I accumulated an impressive wardrobe in New York, thanks to the city's endless sample sales and my weekend visits to Brooklyn flea markets. I've acquired sequined dresses from the 1930s, J.Crew earmuffs in a rainbow of colours, a vintage mauve and chestnut Diane von Furstenberg silk leisure suit (which I've never worn), UGG boots, and a selection of exquisite Dior items I snapped up at a steep discount at an employee sale, not to mention a bright green Kate Spade hat embroidered with the words *I Need a Vacation*. I know some of these accoutrements will stand out in chic Paris, where an understated palette of grey, beige, and navy is favoured, but I've also inherited that fearless New York "tough luck" attitude, and it's liberating. If Parisians don't like it, *tant pis*.

I push my trolley to the automatic doors at the arrivals gate and ask (or rather, beg) a taxi driver for help. He gives me a nasty look and tries to disappear toward the exit, but I don't give up. After a few minutes of sweet talking and the offer of an exorbitant tip, he reluctantly agrees to drive me (cab-wrangling: another skill I acquired in New York). It reminds me that service with a smile isn't this city's strongest suit. Once I'm comfortably seated in the back of the taxi with my bags securely loaded, I instruct the driver to head to Antoine's apartment on rue du Bac, in the heart of Saint-Germain-des-Prés.

The driver rolls his eyes as if my destination is totally predictable. I must look like a stereotypical resident of the bobo neighbourhood I'm moving to, where *bourgeois* meets *bohème*. This suits me fine: I'm looking forward to fitting into the Rive Gauche's chic, artistic vibe. I ignore him; it's best to save my energy for the big hug I'll give

Antoine when I see him later. I just hope he doesn't get home too early and catch me trying to fit all of my clothes into his closets.

We drive past billboards plastered with ads for luxury brands such as Chaumet and Boucheron, and I'm reminded that I'm about to get a taste of this refined world. While the time I've spent practising law—before Edwards & White in New York, I worked for the company's Paris office for six years—has sharpened my legal skills and business acumen, it has also forced me to push aside my passion for art and style for far too long.

As Balzac eloquently put it, *An unfulfilled vocation drains the colour from a man's entire existence.* I'm glad I haven't waited too long to heed his wisdom. Thankfully, Dior agreed to hire Rikash, my invaluable assistant—more like godsend. I couldn't dream of moving to Paris without him; in New York he had become my right arm, left leg, and trusted confidant.

I missed Paris while working for a big American firm. My friend Lisa once observed that the French capital, with its round arches, curvaceous bridges, flowing water, incandescent light, and street names such as rue Madame and rue Princesse, represents a feminine energy, whereas New

York exudes a masculine one, with its towering skyscrapers, rigid city blocks, and raw aggression. As my driver makes a turn onto the majestic boulevard Saint-Germain, and I take in the splendid architecture and the bustling cafés so brilliantly captured in Brassaï's photographs, I appreciate this metaphor more than ever.

To me, New York is like a strong cup of espresso: intense, over-stimulating, and brimming with excitement, whereas Paris is more like a meringue: sweet, airy, and light. I'll be glad to once again bask in all the beauty and charm this city has to offer. *Allez,* bring on the silk pastel dresses, the frilly lingerie, and the exquisite *macarons.* My soul is ready for the change.

I arrive in front of my new apartment on one of the most attractive streets in Paris, and my heart skips a beat. It's located near the Musée d'Orsay, the Louvre, and the Jardins du Luxembourg. Barthélémy, one of my favourite cheese shops, is located only steps away on rue de Grenelle. And knowing that I'll be living so close to La Pâtisserie des Rêves, a heralded dream of a place that offers the best éclairs and lemon pie in the world, makes me grin like a child.

After (over)paying the driver, I start manoeuvring my bags into the tiny elevator of our Haussmannian building. I'm forced to take three separate trips up to the sixth floor, and end up monopolizing the tiny contraption for a solid twenty minutes. I long for the efficiency of those sturdy New York models that can hold three tons worth of people and merchandise at a time. I haul my bags into the elevator, one by one, under the suspicious gaze of the building's concierge, Madame Roussel, a lady of a certain age who, according to Antoine, takes immaculate care of the premises and who clearly doesn't appreciate me dragging my enormous hockey bag along her polished floor. I mutter a sheepish "*Désolée, madame,*" but she ignores me and walks away.

It doesn't matter, because as soon as I open the door, I forget all the trouble I went through to get here.

I plop my bags on the kitchen floor and notice a spectacular bouquet of pink peonies in a vase next to a chilled bottle of pink Taittinger. A note is scribbled on a piece of monogrammed paper:

> *I'm so happy you've finally made it, ma chérie. Make*
> *yourself comfortable, I should be home around five.*
> *I've made reservations for dinner at our special place.*
> *Je t'aime.*
>
> Antoine

I hold the note up to my nose, inhaling the faint scent of his cologne, and feel dizzy with happiness. I look around, taking in the warmth and the love emanating from every corner of the apartment. It's really a gem of a place: a one-bedroom with an office that faces a lovely courtyard and with lots of light. Its decor is mostly masculine in feel right now, dominated by muted neutrals, but I hope to insert a feminine touch here and there: a gold sunburst mirror we picked up together at the Chelsea flea market will look lovely atop the mantle in the living room; a snow white desk I bought at the MOMA store will hold court in our office; and I will scatter some coffee-table books throughout the space. Finally, my beloved Marc Clauzade painting of stylish ladies window-shopping in Paris in the 1940s will look sublime over my vanity in our bedroom.

I imagine having our families and friends over for lively dinner parties and spending weekends reading in front of the fire. We'll support each other and respect each other's personal space.

I decide to pour myself a glass of pink bubbly to help ease the pain of unpacking. I have to do it now; I don't want Antoine to really see the absurd amount of clothes and accessories I've amassed after embracing New York–style retail therapy.

He's mentioned that I should use the closet in the office to store my belongings, since the one in our bedroom is a bit small. When I open the door and discover that the office closet is about the size of a mouse hole, I nearly fall over my hockey bag—*Ah, non! C'est pas vrai!*—while trying to hold on to my Champagne flute. He can't be serious, can he?

I take a deep breath and march into the kitchen for a second glass of Champagne while I devise an unpacking strategy. Miraculously, the alcohol allows me to become *very* creative about storage: I decide it's best to remove Antoine's sporting equipment from the hall closet and place it in the office instead. I then place his collection of sneakers in the *chambre froide*—the pantry—since it's barely being used and has excellent air circulation. Afterward, I meticulously arrange my cocktail dresses, work attire, and shoes according to colour in the hall closet. Convinced he won't mind, I store my handbags, jewellery, and accessories in the bedroom armoire. *Voilà!*

I decide to get rid of the incriminating evidence and throw the shoddy hockey bag into the communal trash.

Proud of the result, I serve myself one last glass of bubbly and take it with me into the bath so I can relax before dinner. Watching my lavender salts melt into the soothing hot water, I envision slipping into a chic black cocktail dress with matching pumps, putting my hair up in a classy chignon, and painting my lips a bright cherry red, courtesy of Chanel's impeccable Rouge Coco.

Unfortunately, even the best plans sometimes go awry. I wake up an hour or so later, naked in an empty tub, looking up at a puzzled Antoine, who is dangling my discarded hockey bag in one hand and one of my Dior platforms in the other.

"Catherine? Are you okay, *mon ange*? Madame Roussel told me this bag belongs to you; she found it in the trash. What's up with all of this stuff, and what happened to my shoes and biking gear?"

*Oh la la, bienvenue à Paris.*

"To us." Antoine raises his wineglass after we're seated at one of our favourite haunts: le Bistrot d'Henri, a quaint, rustic French art deco bistro located near Saint-Sulpice, a short walk from the apartment. We've come here a handful of times during my visits over the last few months, including after my formal interview at Dior three months ago. The low ceiling makes it feel romantic and private, and we've come to know the owner.

"To us, *mon chéri*." I clink back with a glass of water. I've had enough to drink for one day.

After a sobering rearranging of our closets in a more (according to Antoine) useful and equitable way, and a long welcome embrace, we sauntered here arm in arm to celebrate my official move to Paris. In no mood to get formal after a second bout of unpacking, I threw on a comfortable pair of black jeans and a simple cashmere sweater with ballerina flats.

"Sorry for turning your apartment into *Project Runway*," I say, feeling slightly mortified.

"First of all, Catou, you need to remember that it isn't *my* apartment; it's *ours* now. And you don't need to apologize. We'll figure something out. I just wasn't expecting such a massive landing of women's clothing."

I cringe at his words. I went on so many shopping sprees to forget about my very stressful Manhattan job. I vow to avoid this behaviour in the future. Both my spirit and my bank account will thank me for it.

"Besides, I much prefer it when you lie around our apartment naked."

"Ha! That might be okay at home, but I'm sure it won't go over too well at Dior. I need all those clothes; who knows what kind of dress code is enforced there?"

"You'll find out soon enough. And you probably have some kind of employee discount, which means you'll be bringing home more clothes that we don't have any room for." He playfully pokes my nose and signals to the waiter to bring the menu. "We need to implement a new rule: for every new item you bring home, one needs to be tossed out."

"Okay, fair enough. Consider it a *marché conclu*." Moving in with your better half requires a few concessions. "On one condition: that rule also applies to your record and vintage T-shirt collection."

After Antoine orders us the house specialty, a hearty lamb stew that's been cooked for hours, accompanied by potatoes au gratin with nutmeg, I drop the final bomb about my belongings, hoping we can finally change the subject. "The rest of my things will arrive next week," I say tentatively, wishing for a moment I had ordered a glass of red myself. I try to soften the blow. "But don't worry, it's only a few boxes of books and things for the apartment, and I already know where I'll put them."

Antoine's face drops and he sinks back into his chair, but then he surprises me by rolling up his sleeves and moving in for a kiss. "You've already captured my heart, so the apartment is yours for the taking. I consider it a not-so-hostile takeover." He smiles broadly, revealing his boyish dimples. His laughing brown eyes look right through me, and I feel a jolt of lightning through my body.

My head spinning with relief and happiness, I lean forward to kiss him back and run my hand through his thick mane of dark curls. I thank my lucky stars I've met such a generous soul. Although our romance grew slowly out of a work relationship, it's turned out to be a fairy tale.

"Excuse me, *monsieur,* but you should know that I no longer communicate in that type of legal lingo. You'll need to brush up on skirt lengths, colour trends, and shoe styles from now on."

"That's fine. I'm glad we'll have something to talk about besides what goes on at Edwards & White. And your life is about to get way more interesting than mine." He puts on a fake pout.

Antoine had recently been named a partner at Edwards

& White in Paris and was responsible for overseeing high-profile legal matters, such as a major industrial privatization for the government. But still, it isn't high fashion.

"I'm really looking forward to my first day," I say, digging into my lamb. This delicious comfort food's aromas and flavours remind me of my childhood in the south of France.

"I bet Rikash is too."

My assistant was busy moving the entire contents of his apartment overseas and taking intensive French lessons at the Alliance Française in New York.

"Absolutely. He's been working hard on learning the language of looove." I purse my lips mockingly. "We've made plans to get together next week, before our first day. I'm pretty excited to see him in Paris."

"He's such a hoot. I'm sure you'll have a blast working together at Dior. They have an amazing legal team."

Antoine has a background in intellectual property, and Dior has hired his firm as outside counsel in the past. He's become fairly knowledgeable about their business. In New York, I assisted him in drafting Dior's U.S. anti-counterfeiting policies and procedures—by far my favourite assignment, for several reasons. However, I'd earned my new Dior position without any help from him.

"Have you had any dealings with the Dior legal department besides Pierre Le Furet?" I ask, curious about my future colleagues.

"No, he was my only contact there, but I'm sure you don't have anything to worry about. They surely can't have anyone as crazy as Bonnie Clark." My former New York boss makes Patty Hewes, Glenn Close's character in *Damages*, appear as innocent as Little Bo Peep.

"I hope not." I feel my stomach turning just thinking about her.

He sees my sour expression and changes the subject. "I'm so glad we have a weekend to ourselves before you start. I wish we could've gone away somewhere for a bit of sun and surf, but I'm way too swamped with work right now."

I smile, reminded of Antoine's fun-loving personality, which I only got to know after we got close. I discovered he likes surfing, snowboarding, and listening to live rock 'n' roll—just the right amount of cool *pour moi*.

"But I do have something that will make up for it." He pulls two pieces of paper out of his back pocket and places them on the table. They're tickets to see Roy Hargrove, one of my favourite jazz musicians, play at the New Morning, a renowned club in the 10th arrondissement.

"*Oh mon dieu!* Antoine! You're the best!" I stand up to hug him.

The restaurant owner drops by to see what all the fuss is about.

"Antoine just surprised me with tickets to an amazing jazz concert." I hold them up. "I'm so excited!"

"Ah, you know how to treat a lady, don't you, *mon cher.* You two make such a great couple." He looks around the small room. "Didier, bring these two *tourtereaux* a dessert once they've finished their meal. It will be *sur la maison.*" He winks.

Antoine smiles at me from across the table, and I'm convinced that moving back to Paris was the best thing I've ever done. It's now with a sense of relief that I can say that I willingly gave it all up: the chance to make partner at Edwards & White, a fat share of the firm's profits, and an eventual corner office. I'm ready for a personal renaissance. After all, life should be made up of unexpected twists of fate, *n'est-ce pas?*

After our meal, we take a stroll so that Antoine can show me a few of his favourite neighbourhood landmarks. He puts his striped cashmere scarf around my bare shoulders as we walk past an English pub called The Frog & Princess.

"This is a great place for having a beer after work. I come

here sometimes with friends and colleagues. And I love its name—it reminds me of us."

I give him a peck on the cheek. "It looks like some of those sports bars in Manhattan. I guess it must attract English-speaking expats."

"Yes, exactly. Lots of Americans and Brits come here."

"I'm going to stay away from this place for a while. I'm looking for a change of scenery."

After heading north toward the boulevard Saint-Germain, we turn onto the tiny passage de la Petite Boucherie, which leads us directly to one of the most charming and tranquil squares in Paris.

"Oh! Place de Furstenberg!" I gush, darting into the elegant square, with its tall trees and wrought-iron lamp-posts. It's like a scene from a classic film. The simple oasis is surrounded by chic design boutiques and antique shops.

"Gorgeous, isn't it?" Antoine takes my hand and leads me toward the centre, pointing toward an elegant building skirting the square. "That's the Eugène Delacroix Museum. Delacroix lived and painted there until his death."

I look on admiringly. Antoine's mother owned an art gallery and passed on her love of art and her expertise to her son.

"In his old apartment and studio, you can find a few of his watercolours and a self-portrait of him dressed as Hamlet," Antoine adds.

"I'd love to come back here with you and visit."

"Of course, *ma chérie*. Now that you live here, we'll have plenty of time for that. But for tonight I wanted to show you one of the most romantic places in the city. I'm so happy to be here with you."

He grabs me by the waist, lifts me up, and kisses me tenderly while I slide back to the ground. Except that my feet are nowhere near the ground and my head remains floating in the clouds.

# Chapter 2

"So, dah-ling, what will you be doing with so much free time on your hands?" Rikash gives me a mischievous smile and takes a sip of his cocktail. We're relaxing at Le Dali restaurant in Le Meurice hotel the afternoon before our first day at Dior. The crowd is a mix of fashionistas and suits. "A thirty-five-hour work week and forty days of vacation per year will be quite a change of pace from your days in New York. Aren't you worried about getting bored?" He crosses his legs elegantly, revealing his purple-striped Paul Smith socks and shiny new Italian shoes.

"Are you kidding? I'm so happy to be back to a more relaxed schedule. I might cook for myself once in a while, rather than eating out of a cardboard box every night."

"You can say that again. My stomach is still recovering from years of indigestible takeout food. You see I've ordered the Meurice Tonic, a one hundred percent green cocktail made to detoxify and energize the body. You should order one for yourself, pussycat. I bet it also does wonders for tired complexions." His emerald green eyes sparkle against his delicate bronzed features.

"Thanks, but I'll stick to my glass of Burgundy." I twirl my glass and take in the sublime surroundings: there's an incredible fresco of nymphs floating across the sky covering the entire ceiling, numerous vintage Louis XV chairs upholstered in cowhide, and gorgeous crystal chandeliers. In the adjacent room, there's a wood-panelled bar where a grand piano holds court, surrounded by a flock of old stools. I imagine someone playing Cole Porter's "I Love Paris," a fitting piece to underscore my return to France.

"Speaking of complexions, the hotel spa offers a glacier regenerating treatment, and I think we should try it." He wrinkles his tiny nose. "You're now back in the land of *esthétique*, so I shouldn't need to remind you how seriously French women take beauty rituals."

"Glacier regenerating? It sounds like the cover story for the latest issue of *National Geographic*." I laugh, my head tilted toward the gorgeous ceiling. Rikash often coaxes me into trying crazy treatments to improve the texture of my skin or the tone of my buttocks. Often, they amount to nothing more than expensive pain and suffering.

"Pumpkin, nature gives you the face you have at sixteen, but it's up to you to deserve the face you have at fifty."

"Yes, but I'm only in my thirties."

"My point exactly. This type of treatment is meant to keep you in that decade forever."

"Okay, let me know when you've booked it." I'm aware of the satisfaction it gives him to advise me on such matters. Rikash, a long-time New Yorker, takes his wrinkle-reversing treatments very seriously.

He leans forward to touch my scarf with his long, delicate fingers. It's silk.

"What's that pattern?" he asks, his eyes narrowed into two tiny slits.

"It's Fifi Lapin; you know, the fashionista rabbit. You must know the blog."

"Fifi Lapin?" He stares at me with a look of horror. "Don't tell me you have a French rabbit around your neck. That's so un-Dior. Please don't wear that at work. Or in my presence." He waves his right hand in mid-air.

"Really? I happen to like this scarf; the pastel colours suit my complexion. And Fifi is adorable, *non?*"

"Dah-ling, the best thing for your complexion is a lot of loving, not some silly rabbit."

I decide to change the subject. I won't win this argument. "I haven't been here in ages. It's stunning." I take a sip from my crystal goblet and look around.

Rikash is living at the luxurious Meurice while he searches for the perfect Paris apartment.

"Did you know that Orson Welles and Franco Zeffirelli stayed here?" Rikash studied cinema and makes documentaries in his spare time. In addition to his other extracurricular activities.

I know that one of the hotel's most famous guests was Salvador Dali, who at one time spent one month every year on these sumptuous grounds. In fact, there are a few Daliesque touches in the restaurant: a chair decorated with women's feet and a lobster on a telephone.

"So, how's lover boy?" Rikash says slyly. "He must be ecstatic that you've finally moved here—he can go back to his billable hours now that you're by his side."

"Antoine's great, and he's been so sweet. He picked up

tickets for a jazz concert last weekend. Other than that, we've hardly left the apartment. It's been pure bliss."

"I'm sure it has." He raises his eyebrows lasciviously. "I'm really happy for you. Mae West said it: *A hard man is good to find.*"

"Rikash, we do engage in other activities."

"I really don't understand why," he says, adjusting his new Dior cufflinks.

"Come on, there's more to a relationship than just the physical."

"Like what?"

"We stay up late cooking, drinking wine, and watching old Godard films. It's so romantic."

"Oh dear." He covers his mouth as he fakes a yawn. "If I were you, I'd be giving a whole new meaning to the term '*amuse-bouche.*'"

I shake my head. "You're a riot. I'm sure you'll have your share of fun here. There are lots of great nightclubs and cafés where you can watch the beautiful people."

"Of course, dah-ling—this is Gay Paree. I've already checked out a few places, and I don't mean the cafés." Rikash was always months ahead of me when it came to knowing what was new and hip in New York. Why would things be different here?

"It sounds like your French classes have already paid off."

"Yes, dah-ling, but as you know, my best communication skills are non-verbal."

"Right. I'm not sure why I even bothered mentioning it. Maybe Antoine and I could join you at a club some time."

"Sweetie, going to a nightclub with your boyfriend is like going to a *boulangerie* with a baguette under your arm: it's totally pointless." He waves his hand in the air dismissively. "But you're both welcome to join me at the gallery opening I'm going to tonight in the Marais. I hear *le tout Paris* will be there."

He waves to a dashing gentleman walking by in a sharp tailored suit and horn-rimmed glasses. Seeing Rikash hold court in the lobby of one of Paris's most luxurious hotels confirms that he's a work of art all his own.

"No, thanks. I want to turn in early; we have a big day tomorrow. Speaking of, shall we go over some of our new responsibilities at Dior? It's important that we start off on the right foot. We're meeting with Sandrine first thing tomorrow morning."

Sandrine Cordier is Dior's general counsel and my

new boss. We first crossed paths in California while I was attending an Edwards & White conference. From what I've observed so far, she's well respected, intelligent, and incredibly chic.

"Good idea." He's immediately all business. In a professional setting, Rikash's ethic is second to none; called to duty, he's all about getting the job done. In addition to being a tastemaker extraordinaire and a good friend, he's a pro at organizing my schedule and keeping my computer humming and my correspondence up to date. I hope to be able to hand him some more challenging responsibilities at Dior.

"We'll be handling a few high-profile matters, including the anti-counterfeiting project we started in New York, but on a more international scale. Also, Dior has started launching lawsuits to fight the sale of fake products online. We'll probably be involved, so we should get up to speed."

"It sounds exciting. But how will we manage without the resources we had at our disposal at the law firm?"

"Sandrine said we can count on other lawyers to help out, and can bring in outside counsel when we really need to."

I raise my hand to signal to the waiter that I'd like another glass of wine. After looking me straight in the eye, he turns and walks away. It's a bit of a shock; despite its abrasive edge, America is still the land of "We aim to please." I wonder how Paris manages to attract so many visitors when they're often treated with such disdain. I belt out, "*Monsieur, s'il vous plaît,*" to remind him who's footing the bill for this expensive aperitif, then turn back to Rikash.

"Does that mean Antoine, and Edwards, will continue to receive work from Dior?"

I take a deep breath. Antoine and I have not yet discussed this. Despite the fact that he and my former employer have handled Dior cases in the recent past, I feel uncomfortable sending new legal work to my boyfriend. I don't want to be accused of nepotism my first week on the job. But more importantly, I've vowed to keep my professional and personal lives separate. My involvement with a firm client in New York ended in disaster. I'd been working on an initial public offering for Browser Inc., a technology company, when the CFO—whom I was dating—asked me to participate in a securities fraud. I turned him in. The case is under investigation by the U.S. Securities and Exchange Commission, and I still feel emotionally bruised by the fallout.

I need to address this with Antoine soon, but I've been brushing the issue under the carpet.

"Well, umm . . . maybe . . . umm . . . sort of."

"I guess that means no."

Rikash knows me so well. My eyes water a little, and I give him a smile. "I still haven't really recovered from what happened in New York with Jeff—"

He cuts me off by raising the palm of his hand in the air like a traffic cop. "No need to explain, I completely understand. How are you planning to break the news to him?"

"After a satisfying Ménage à Trois." I raise my glass and wink.

He nods approvingly. "Ooh, that's my girl."

"Don't kid yourself—it's the name of our favourite red wine from California."

He rolls his eyes. "Ah yes, of course."

# Chapter 3

"We're going to be late!" Trying to hail a taxi in four-inch heels at the height of Paris's morning rush hour is not easy. After meeting at Le Meurice again for a quick espresso, we're heading off to our first day at Dior's headquarters on avenue Montaigne in the 8th arrondissement.

"Don't worry, sweetness. Punctuality is the virtue of the bored. Besides, we won't be late; this is Paris, remember. Sandrine is probably stuck in traffic, in a public transit strike or in some sort of demonstration."

"I hate being late. We should've ordered a taxi in advance for this morning." I'm anxious.

"Believe me, I tried, but apparently you can't reserve a taxi between 8 and 10 a.m. in Paris. It's some new rule they enacted to add to the inefficiency of the transportation system."

"We could rent some Vélib' bikes." I point to the public bike service that has drop-off stations at the city's most popular intersections. "Antoine uses one almost every day to get to work."

He looks at me like I've just suggested we crawl to our destination. "You must be joking. I'm trying to make it to my first day on the job, not six feet under. Besides, I'm not in the mood to wrinkle my suit. It's Dior Homme, and it's new!"

"Okay, okay." In New York, you can roll out of bed and into a cab, but here, taxis are more difficult to come by at this time of day.

As I do my best to flag one down, a car drives by us with its windows open. The driver is screaming at the top of his lungs while hitting the gas: *"Bordel de merde, que faites-vous dans le milieu de la rue? Tassez-vous bande de naz!"*

Massively cleaned-up translation: "Get out of the way, you idiots!"

A sustained honk follows.

Rikash runs into the middle of the street, waving his Hermès attaché case over his head and shouting, "Fuck off, you freak!" He finishes up by giving the driver the supreme insulting gesture, *le bras d'honneur,* meaning "up yours" or something a lot less elegant.

This is where the Old World meets the New, the two cultures colliding with grand fanfare thanks to the internationally shared stress of getting to work on time.

"What a jerk," he says, gliding his delicate hands over his pleated trousers to remove any creases.

We finally manage to get a ride. On our way to avenue Mont-aigne, I feel a frisson of excitement. High-profile intellectual property work, a famous couture house, and hobnobbing with the biggest names in fashion: the idea makes me giddy. This is the first morning in a long while that I'm actually looking forward to going to the office.

My daydreams are interrupted by Rikash tapping me on the shoulder. "This is absolute madness!" His nose is pressed against the window. He is mesmerized by our progress around the Arc de Triomphe at rush hour. The French follow the rule that cars must give way to traffic coming onto the roundabout, but since there are twelve entrances, the only way it actually works is by constant hoots of the horn.

"A total recipe for disaster." Rikash shakes his head. "You need to have four pairs of eyes to navigate out of this place."

He puts one hand on the door handle and one around the passenger's headrest, as if holding on for dear life.

The next moment, his gaze zeroes in on a handsome young man in a tailored suit swooshing by us at top speed on a scooter. His tie is flapping in the wind, and his dirty blond curls are sneaking out from under his helmet. He successfully avoids colliding with three cars by engaging in a dangerous slalom manoeuvre, then disappears into the morning traffic.

"Wow, who was that helmeted man? He was hot."

"And a bit suicidal." I take a quick peek at my watch to make sure we're still on time.

"This means something. It must be a metaphor for how French society operates." He peers out the window as if looking for the right words to describe what he's just seen. "It's complete disarray in Jean Paul Gaultier."

# Chapter 4

"*B*onjour, madame. Bonjour, monsieur. Welcome to Dior." A lithe brunette in a slim black skirt, simple turtleneck, and towering heels welcomes us into the foyer. "Madame Cordier will be here in a few minutes. You may take a seat in the salon."

The offices are decorated with neo–Louis XVI furniture and are dominated by grey, Mr. Dior's favoured colour when he opened the famous couture house on avenue Montaigne back in 1947. The design is even more stunning than I remembered: both chic and understated, with lots of open space—the apex of luxury. The silk curtains dressing the windows fall to the floor like ball gowns, delicate silver vases holding pink roses have been artfully placed throughout the room, and grey and white settees and oval-backed chairs provide artful seating areas.

The offices are abuzz with pretty young things running about purposefully. Most of them are wearing tasteful knee-length black dresses and barely a trace of makeup. I see a lot of hair slicked back in neat ponytails or chignons. There isn't any bling on display. This rarefied space exemplifies class, elegance, and luxury. I peer down at my outfit and sigh with relief: the navy blue Dior suit I picked up at an employee sale in New York and the new Repetto pumps I found last week at Les Galeries Lafayette—replicas of the ones Brigitte Bardot wore in *And God Created Woman*—are perfect.

Rikash nudges me in the shoulder as we walk past a giant framed advertisement for Lady Dior handbags. I can't help giving him a huge grin. He knows how much this job means to me.

After a few nervous minutes on our part, Sandrine arrives. She makes quite a grand entrance, descending the imposing staircase from the upstairs offices while skimming a jewelled hand along its wrought-iron railing. She's so elegant in a mauve silk blouse with a large bow tie collar, a charcoal grey A-line skirt, and a pair of charcoal grey booties adorned with straps and buckles. A chunky metal-coloured bracelet from Dior's most recent jewellery collection—I recognize it from magazines—completes her look. This is such a far cry from the conservative work attire I've been used to (at the law firm, wearing an open-toe shoe was the equivalent of showing up for work in your bra), and so much more in line with what I've been dreaming about, that I need to hold myself back from jumping into her arms.

"*Bonjour, les amis.*" Her voice is like music and she's the picture of refinement when she stops before a glass case holding a New Look–inspired two-piece ensemble of pink taffeta.

She greets us with a warm embrace instead of a handshake, and I'm taken aback. In the world of corporate law, keeping your distance is the norm. No one wants to seem too touchy-feely; it's taken as a sign of weakness.

"Catherine, I'm thrilled you're finally here. I have so much work for you." She lifts one of her cuffed hands in the air to indicate the piles of paperwork waiting for me. "And you must be Monsieur Rikash. I've heard so many great things about you!" She points a ringed finger at his lapel.

A deep fuchsia rises in his cheeks. It's the first time I've ever seen him blush. Amazing.

"Don't pay any attention to what you've heard about me, especially the parts that are true."

She responds with a large smile. "*D'accord*. Shall we go upstairs?"

We follow her up the staircase and into a brightly lit office, where piles of manila folders are placed on her desk beside an elegant vintage lamp. A vase filled with red roses sits on top of an antique secretary, and photographs of Sandrine with a handsome man are scattered throughout the space. A large painting of an elegant older woman is hung on the wall facing the desk. Sandrine catches me staring at it.

"That's my grandmother. She was an acquaintance and client of Mr. Dior."

Rikash is practically drooling in front of the tableau. I imagine him hitting the floor and launching into a sun salutation in veneration of Sandrine's grandmother.

"Please have a seat." She crosses her legs and I see a hint of black lace stocking. "I'm so happy you're here. I've been swamped since your predecessor, Mr. Le Furet, left us."

"He seemed to manage a heavy workload. I could tell by the number of matters he sent to our firm."

"Yes, he did. But he decided to retire in the south of France," she adds, staring out the window with a faraway look in her eyes.

"Lucky him. It's a beautiful region. That's where I grew up. My mother still lives there."

"*Ah bon?*" She looks distracted. "Yes, it's lovely, indeed." She turns back to us alertly. "I was impressed with the memo you prepared for us on American anti-counterfeiting laws in New York. It was well written and thoroughly researched."

"Thank you." It's the first compliment I've received in a while about my work, and my heart swells with delight. In New York, receiving a *bon mot* about your efforts was about as common as spotting a polar bear in the Sahara Desert. Rikash reads my mind and winks conspiratorially. "It'll be interesting to see whether the proposed U.S. legislation meant to protect the copyright of fashion designs will be enacted. France is ahead of the game in that regard." I've done my research.

Historically, unlike in the United States, fashion designs have received copyright protection under French law. Case in point: in 1994 a French court found that the American designer Jack Lawrence had copied the style of an Yves Le Grand dress too closely, and awarded a substantial sum to the French designer. This may change in the U.S., however; similar legislation is being proposed.

Sandrine smiles widely. "Your experience will help you manage the matters we have waiting for you. We're about to commence a lawsuit against the website eShop concerning the sale of fake merchandise on their site. This issue has become of critical importance to Dior, and we have decided to become more aggressive. Your timing is perfect."

"How long has counterfeiting been a problem for Dior?" Rikash asks, captivated.

"I'm afraid it's been an issue for as long as the company has been in existence. There's a record in the company archives of an incident in 1948 where a woman who had ordered a custom-made Dior ensemble came across another woman wearing the same outfit in a nightclub. There was an investigation by the French police that lasted over six years. The result was the arrest of a group who had bribed company seamstresses for patterns to copy."

"Has it gotten worse over the years?" I know that counterfeiting has long been a problem for luxury companies, but if huge sums of money are spent fighting it, why hasn't it tapered off?

"Exponentially. Although we've seen a slight drop in

our brand's fakes on the market, counterfeiting has steadily increased in all areas of retail. We certainly can't ease up on our efforts against it, because as soon as we do, the fakes come flooding back."

I think about how the market for luxury goods has sky-rocketed in recent decades. Today, women of all ages and income levels long to own designer accessories to dem-onstrate their individuality and, paradoxically, a sense of belonging and awareness of the latest status symbols. For many women, being caught carrying a no-name bag is inconceivable. But how many of us can afford the bags toted by Hollywood starlets? I wonder whether women who buy fakes would even be interested in the real thing if the copy weren't available. But I decide to keep that to myself.

"I read in *Le Monde* yesterday that Dior won a rul-ing against a big Internet browser promoting ads for fake goods," I say.

Sandrine seems delighted that I've kept up to date and gives me a warm smile. "Yes. I'm glad you mentioned it. You'll be involved in that lawsuit."

"You can count on us to keep up the fight." Rikash grins.

"I love your attitude, Rikash," she says warmly. "I'll have my assistant, Coralie, take you to your new office so you can settle in. Before you get started on work, though, you must have a tour of the archives and the atelier. It's important that you immerse yourselves in the Dior culture—and it might be fun, too."

"That sounds perfect." I'm weak in the knees at the thought of visiting the Dior atelier and seeing *les petites mains* at work. The "tiny hands" are the expert seamstresses who add the fine embroidery to ball gowns and create the delicate lace that makes a couture cocktail dress a red-carpet classic. I've read many articles about these genius craftswomen, who, unlike the star designers, work in anonymity, but I never imagined I would actually meet them.

Coralie, a petite blonde whose locks are swept up in a *soigné chignon*, leads us down the hall to an office with an adjoining alcove. Two modern glass desks are lined up side by side facing rue François 1er. Delicate framed vintage illustrations by René Gruau line the walls, and a bouquet of red tulips is perched on a bookcase. Grey leather in-trays and Montblanc pens are sitting on both desks.

"Little welcome gifts from our perfume collection." Coralie points to two Dior gift bags overflowing with light pink tissue paper. "Oh, and please don't make any plans for lunch. Sandrine is taking you both to Ladurée." It's an iconic

French tea salon, renowned for its gorgeous baroque decor, exquisite pastries and world-famous *macarons*. Ironically, an outpost had opened on Madison Avenue just as I was leaving New York.

"This is totally dreamy!" Rikash exclaims as soon as Coralie is out of earshot. He grabs my arm and kisses me on the side of the head. "This is so exciting! I feel like Gene Kelly in *An American in Paris.*" He does a little twirl and sprays some of his new Fahrenheit cologne all over our office.

"We'll have lots of hard work to do, don't forget." But I can't contain my excitement either. "And wait, this is just the beginning."

I want to pinch myself. For the first time in a long while, reality has become better than my wildest dreams.

"I know, dah-ling. We will totally paint this town *rouge.*"

# Chapter 5

"Brain cells come and brain cells go, but fat cells live forever," Rikash chants as we exit the tea room on les Champs-Élysées. "That Saint-Honoré was totally sinful. I bet I put on five pounds in one sitting."

"Why can't you just enjoy it? You're in a different place now, so stop counting calories. Besides, you'll walk it off."

As I say this, it hits me that we're in a nation of contradictions. Despite our passionate love of food, the French are obsessed with maintaining their figures; all you need to do is walk into a local pharmacy to see the evidence. There are aisles of slimming gels, diuretic pills, and water with supposedly "eliminating" virtues. But I have yet to meet anyone capable of resisting a bite of a Saint-Honoré cake made with puff pastry, caramel, and whipped cream or a *religieuse* pastry filled with thick custard and topped with delicate, pretty icing (truly a religious experience).

"That was kind of Sandrine to take us for a lovely lunch, *non?*" I ask.

"Yes, it was. I'm just not used to finishing a meal with a ton of cream puffs. And I haven't seen many Reebok Sports Clubs around here."

Rikash's observation is spot-on. New Yorkers set their alarms for the middle of the night to sneak in a gruelling workout before work, but the French don't punish their bodies that way. People here just eat more moderately and burn off calories doing pleasurable things like walking to and from the metro, shopping, and love-making.

What's more shocking to me is spending two hours in a restaurant at midday. I've become accustomed to the American way of doing lunch: gobbling up a sandwich in front of my computer. I need to reacquaint myself with the idea of taking my time—no easy task.

Sandrine rushed off to a meeting after lunch, so Rikash and I decided to stroll back to the office.

"The Saint-Honoré cake is a part of French culture. It's been baked on special occasions for over a century. It's named for the saint, of course, but also because the shop that first made it was on rue Saint-Honoré."

"All right, it scores extra points for that—it's my favourite street in Paris." He winks. "I thought our lunch was very educational. Can you believe that counterfeit perfumes contain antifreeze and urine?"

"Crazy, right? That information almost killed my appetite." I grimace.

"It gives a whole new meaning to the term 'eau de toilette,' doesn't it?" he adds as we meander along the majestic Champs. "I guess it's not half as bad as Lady Gaga's perfume. I heard a rumour that it smells like blood and semen." He puts two fingers in his mouth in a gagging gesture.

"It makes our work even more important. This isn't just about lost profits; we're dealing with people's health. Some of this fake stuff is toxic."

"No kidding. I'd freak if antifreeze were dabbed onto my delicate temple."

We take in the beautiful store windows lining the boulevard, and Rikash shakes his head. "So I hear that sales only happen twice a year in Paris. Who decided *that*?"

I chuckle. Rikash won't have quite as many opportunities to hunt down bargains at sample sales here. "The government regulates *Les Soldes*. The sales happen twice a year to encourage tourism during the slower months. But that's not the worst of it: most shops outside the tourist areas are closed on Sundays. Good luck with *that*."

"No!" He stops dead in his tracks. "Are you kidding me? What do people do on Sundays?"

"Go to museums, spend time with family."

"Hmm. That's an interesting concept." I can see him trying to wrap his mind around what I've just said.

"Actually finding a drugstore open on Sunday when you're feeling under the weather can be a challenge. You'd better stock up on necessities."

"No kidding. Thanks for the heads-up." He looks like I've just informed him that the country is at war. It hits me that I'll miss the convenience of having a Walgreens on every street corner, open at all hours of the day and night.

We're about to cross toward avenue Montaigne when Rikash guides me wordlessly into a shopping arcade. I raise my eyebrows inquisitively, and he responds with a tilt of the head. "Follow me. I have something to show you." He's sporting a childlike grin that makes me *very* worried.

Past some touristy children's boutiques and a few shoe shops, we make a sharp left and enter a place I never dreamed existed: Luxe WC, a luxury emporium dedicated exclusively to accessories for the bathroom. Chrome toilet paper holders shaped like tree branches sit next to scented candles and expensive air fresheners. You can even use the shop's own facilities if you're willing to pay a steep fee.

"Only Parisians could come up with something like this," I marvel. "How did you find this place?"

"I accidentally came across it last weekend. You need to see this." He takes me to the back of the shop, where he pulls aside a silk curtain to reveal *la crème de la crème* in accessories: a replica of Marie Antoinette's cabinet at Versailles, on sale for 8,000 euros; shower curtains encrusted with Swarovski crystals; and a black padded toilet seat that looks suspiciously like the quilted motif of an authentic Lady Dior handbag. "It looks like we may have found our first anti-counterfeiting mission," he jokes.

One of the first things we learn during our tour of the company archives is that none of Christian Dior's collections failed, either critically or commercially, during his lifetime (he died of a heart attack in 1957). Style had been at a standstill internationally during the Second World War, and Paris had lost its title as the world's fashion capital. When Dior emerged with the New Look in 1947, he re-established the city as a centre of sophistication and possibility.

Completely enthralled, we spend several hours in the archives' rich historical space, getting lost in time and vintage photographs. There are countless albums showcasing the collections Yves Saint Laurent, Gianfranco Ferré, and Marc Bohan created for the couture house after Dior's death; a Cecil Beaton portrait of Dior in his mansion at boulevard Jules Sandeau; shoe design sketches by Roger Vivier; black-and-white photographs of the first Dior shows; and splashy pictures of more recent runway events, including those by John Galliano.

Dior had always worked with celebrities and the entertainment world. Marlene Dietrich reportedly told Alfred Hitchcock, before accepting a role in the movie *Stage Fright*, "No Dior, no Dietrich!"

The records note that, in his autobiography, Christian Dior thanked psychics who predicted his success with women. This makes me smile; a psychic I visited during my time in the Big Apple recommended I abandon the practice of law to pursue a more fulfilling career in fashion. A coincidence? I don't think so.

Before we leave the historical treasure trove, Rikash points to some recent advertisements for diamond-encrusted cellphones bearing the company's signature cross-hatching. He whispers that these devices go for a whopping 25,000 euros apiece. I make a face. They're clearly not made for forgetful types like me, and I find them a little too flashy. I feel these gadgets symbolize wasteful excess, something that contradicts the very idea of refined elegance, but I realize that for some—in fact, for many—inaccessibility is synonymous with luxury.

I leave the room, wondering what ring tone I would choose for the blingy gadget: Marilyn Monroe's "Diamonds Are a Girl's Best Friend" or the Beatles' "Can't Buy Me Love"?

We make our way toward the haute couture atelier to meet the real stars: *les petites mains*. The house contains two different ateliers: *le flou*, where flowing dresses and delicate blouses are created, and *le tailleur*, for the more structured, tailored pieces. Each atelier has its *première*, the first seamstress, who is traditionally dressed in black and manages the group, and two *secondes*, who direct a group of about twenty seamstresses and a handful of apprentices. I look on as one of the supremely talented ladies joins two pieces of fabric using *point de chausson*, a method inspired by embroidery. She's surrounded by candy-coloured Cinderella dresses made with yards of gorgeous silk and princess-like tulle. I'm mesmerized: it's inspiring to watch a skilled artisan work at her craft with such precision and patience, especially in a world where immediate gratification rules the day. Clearly, these artisans elevate a piece of clothing to a work of art.

"The house of Dior has always celebrated women," Antoinette, a *seconde* in the *flou* atelier and our tour guide, advises us.

My eyes well up a bit: being here is like living a childhood dream.

Later, as we're settling into our office, a high-pitched female voice blasts along the hallway. Rikash and I scurry to the door to take a peek. An imposing flame-haired woman is rushing down the hall with a harried-looking young man right behind. He's wearing a close-fitting grey suit and oversized black-rimmed glasses, and is taking long strides down the hallway in an effort to keep up with her.

"Have we booked all the flights to Shanghai?" she barks.

"*Oui.*"

"Ordered the five thousand pink roses?"

"*Oui,*" he says, nodding repeatedly.

"Signed the contract with the DJ?"

"*Oui, madame.*"

"Have the fittings been done with all the models?"

There's a brief silence.

"*Non,* we're still waiting for Ruby to show up from New York. Her flight was delayed."

"We're behind schedule! Call the atelier immediately and let them know."

The young man stops and fishes around in his trouser pockets to locate one of several communication devices he appears to be carrying.

"*Allez,* what are you waiting for? Call now!" she commands, then turns on her heels to descend the grand staircase at breakneck pace.

The assistant's shoulders droop, and he sighs audibly before placing the call. Seeing the bewildered look on our faces, Coralie rushes over to explain.

"That was Laetitia. She heads the public relations and special events department. Dior is hosting a major show in Shanghai next week, and the entire company is in a frenzy."

"Who's the poor chap working for her?" Rikash asks with a look of pity.

"Xavier, her assistant."

"It looks like Xavier could use a little Xanax," Rikash says. "She reminds me of someone we used to work with in New York. Bosses can be tough sometimes." He taps me on the elbow.

I shudder at Rikash's reference to Bonnie: she'd made my stay in New York a living hell.

"Yes, Laetitia can be a bit demanding." Coralie smiles conspiratorially but kindly. She then disappears behind her desk, obviously trying to steer clear of office gossip.

"Thank goodness we don't work for Laetitia. I don't think I could take another diva, especially now that I'm sharing an office with one," I joke.

"Ha! Very funny. You know you can't live without me, so don't even go there." He pokes me with his fancy new pen.

"At least Laetitia is barking about fashion shows and roses, not prospectuses and public offerings."

"And Xavier can bark at me anytime—especially in my boudoir."

"I didn't think a French hipster was in your palette." I think back to a few of Rikash's New York conquests. I remember a lot of muscled shoulders, rock-hard buttocks, and square jaws.

"Dah-ling, you should know by now that I'm just like any great painter: I like to dab my brush into the full range: acrylics, watercolours, oil paint—"

Sandrine appears in the doorway. "Okay, it's time to meet the brains behind our department: Frédéric Canet, Dior's assistant general counsel. He's my right-hand man and will provide you with all the background information you need."

She gestures for us to follow, her costume jewellery clinking as she sashays down the hall. We follow her to a large corner office. Inside, papers are strewn everywhere and books litter the floor. Diplomas from the Sorbonne, Oxford, and Yale are framed on the far wall. I'm taken aback: this is completely different from the rest of Dior's headquarters. This looks more like a lawyer's office. A tall man who looks like a cross between Jeremy Irons and Vincent Cassel sits at the desk, wearing a conservative suit and glasses perched on the tip of his nose. He's reading a document the size of the Magna Carta.

As I glance up at the impressive collection of accolades, I'm reminded that prominent French companies tend to hire and promote only those who've attended the world's top schools. Will I move up the corporate ladder with a law degree from l'Université de Provence and a one-year exchange program with Pepperdine? I'm not sure, but I'm prepared to do whatever it takes.

"*Excusez-moi, Frédéric,* but I'd like to introduce Catherine Lambert and her assistant, Rikash. They'll be taking over Pierre's files." She slides her manicured hands down her hips and winks at us.

"Ah yes, you mentioned that." He looks up momentarily to stare us up and down before going back to his document. "I hope they're prepared for battles more fierce than the Napoleonic Wars."

Rikash looks at me with raised eyebrows. It's obvious that we've caught Frédéric at a bad time. He looks like he would rather be sweeping the streets of Paris than exchanging pleasantries with us.

Sandrine approaches his desk. She gently but pointedly pulls the document out of his hands and puts it in a file folder, signalling that it's time to play nice with the new kids. "You need to discuss counterfeiting with them. It's our new priority, remember?"

Frédéric removes his reading glasses, crosses his legs,

and gives us an annoyed look. "Okay, where shall we start?"

"From the beginning, *mon cher*," she answers breezily while walking toward the door.

"The beginning? I thought you said they had lots of experience." He avoids making eye contact with either of us.

Frédéric's demeanour brings me back to my days at Edwards & White, where I met a lifetime supply of over-bearing types. It's worrisome, but I tell myself I can handle it. This is no time to let myself be intimidated.

"They do, but a little refresher never hurts, now does it?" Sandrine waves to us, then closes the office door, leaving us speechless in front of Frédéric's massive desk.

I feel like a baby kitten that's been left beside a coyote. I try to maintain my composure, but my sweaty palms threaten to give me away. I'm grateful to have Rikash by my side.

Frédéric takes a deep breath before launching into a professorial soliloquy. "As you probably know, the retail industry loses approximately thirty billion dollars world-wide every year from the sale of counterfeit merchandise. Clothing and fashion accessories account for at least seventy percent of all counterfeit goods. The numbers are simply astounding."

I see from the corner of my eye that Rikash is nodding like a good student, taking in the teacher's every word. I try to do the same as Frédéric continues.

"The good news is that French laws are in our favour: purchasing fake goods is considered illegal here and, unlike in North America, buyers can be subject to stiff criminal penalties: three hundred thousand euros or three years in jail."

I'm familiar with international counterfeiting laws, but this is clearly new to Rikash. He twists in his chair, silently mouthing "Oh my god" in my direction. I'm sure he's thinking about the fake Gucci belt he bought on one of our last brunch dates in lower Manhattan. It could have landed him in jail here.

"However, the problem isn't so much with the buyers— the public is slowly becoming more educated in this area— but with the players distributing the goods. It's become the preferred source of funding for organized criminals who also deal in narcotics, weapons, child prostitution, and human trafficking, and even have connections with terrorism. Some say these organizations use their distribution channels to move fake goods, and it's becoming extremely difficult to track them down."

Although our work here is sure to be exciting, something tells me there might be speed bumps ahead. It's one thing to handle white-collar criminals in the lofty world of mergers and acquisitions, but battling organized criminals? I hadn't really considered that.

"Why is it so difficult to track them down?" Rikash manages to squeeze in a question.

"They're attracted to piracy because they can remain anonymous. Counterfeiting rings usually operate as cash businesses. They lease manufacturing equipment from third parties and generally don't maintain reliable paperwork. Counterfeiters can move merchandise, hide assets, destroy evidence, or disappear without leaving a paper trail. And any profits made in this type of market are difficult to trace."

"So how do you manage to eventually find them?" I ask, intrigued.

"We do it through surveillance. We have over fifty private investigators on the ground, working with informants. Once we have reliable information, we let law enforcement know and we attempt to seize the goods. Your predecessor, Pierre, was good at managing all this. And this is where your first assignment comes in." He finally looks me straight in the eye.

"You want us to get some leads?" I ask.

"*Non, non, non.*" He shakes his head, removing his glasses.

Despite his curtness, I try again. I don't give up easily. "Perhaps you'd like us to contact some of your private investigators to discuss upcoming seizures?"

He shakes his head again, but this time with a condescending smirk. "No, but keep going, Mademoiselle Lambert. You're getting close."

His attitude is starting to get me hot under the collar, but I keep my cool and continue to play his game. "Set up a meeting with local law enforcement?"

"Almost there: you're burning!" I sense he's taking pleasure in this game of cat and mouse.

Rikash jumps in. "Perhaps if she's burning, that means she's gotten pretty close to hell." He nonchalantly crosses his legs, with the satisfied look of a fighter who's just given a knockout punch.

Frédéric smiles broadly, happy to have met a willing adversary. "Bravo, Rikash! You've figured out what your mission will be."

"Really?" Despite his bluster, Rikash now looks totally confused.

"You're both going on a raid tomorrow morning to observe some seizures and arrests. You'll be accompanied by three gendarmes and a private detective. So, yes, I guess you can call it getting pretty close to hell."

I nearly fall off my chair. I knew that my responsibilities here would involve dealing with law enforcement agencies, but I wasn't expecting to be sent on a raid my first week on the job. This is a far cry from my visions of sitting in the front row at couture shows, next to the editor-in-chief of *Elle* magazine.

I peer over at Rikash, who's as white as a sheet.

Like the winner of a boxing match after the referee has counted to ten, Frédéric rises to his feet triumphantly. "Here's the seizure warrant. The police officers will meet you here tomorrow at seven sharp. You might receive some threats along the way, but don't worry about it—it's pretty routine."

"Threats?" I croak, dumbfounded.

"Unhappy vendors can get a bit violent. One of your predecessors had his knuckles broken with a lead pipe."

Rikash now looks as though he might faint. "But you don't understand. I don't like pain. I cry when I get a facial."

My head spins. How could Sandrine not have mentioned this at lunch today? Did she purposely avoid telling us?

"I'm sorry, it's just that Sandrine didn't mention we'd be going on raids so soon. I'm afraid we've been caught off guard."

"Sandrine isn't the one making this decision; I am. There's no better way to learn the ropes," Frédéric says curtly. Then he smiles. "By the way, Catherine, you should forget about wearing high heels tomorrow. I think jeans and sneakers will be more appropriate. Just in case you need to run for your life."

# Chapter 6

*C*hampagne *makes you feel like it's Sunday and better days are just around the corner.* Marlene Dietrich's famous words come to mind as I wait for Antoine at the Hôtel de l'Abbaye, a charming and romantic *hôtel particulier,* a townhouse of a grand sort, in the heart of Saint-Germain. We had agreed to meet here after work to celebrate my first day at Dior. What I wasn't expecting, however, was to be ordering a bottle of Champagne to calm my jittery nerves. After a few sips of pink Taittinger, I start to relax and admire this dainty, delectable space. The tiny bar at the back of the lobby adjoins a lovely courtyard. I take a deep breath and remind myself of why I moved back to Paris: first and foremost, to be with the man I love; second, to pursue a career in a field I'm passionate about. So what if my first day wasn't exactly what I expected?

"Hello, *ma chérie*," Antoine arrives and moves in for a kiss. I stand to greet him but can barely muster a smile.

"Why the long face? What happened on your first day?"

"We got an unexpected assignment."

"Oh?" He takes off his suit jacket and places it on the back of the antique settee.

"Rikash and I are going out with the local police tomorrow. Let's just say that's not what I imagined for my first week."

"What do you mean?" He takes a seat next to me as the waiter pours him a glass of bubbly.

"We're going on a raid to bust counterfeiters and confiscate their merchandise."

"Really? That sounds amazing! I wish I could be a fly on the wall to see you guys in action."

"I don't know about that. It seems a bit scary. Apparently, a former colleague got his knuckles broken doing this."

"Are you serious?" His expression changes from jovial to concerned. "Who told you that?"

"Frédéric, one of the top dogs in our legal department."

"Was it—the broken knuckles—a one-off? Or does it happen all the time?"

"I have no idea. He didn't say."

"I knew most luxury houses were active in doing raids. I just didn't realize the risks for the people actually carrying them out." He takes a sip of Champagne, then stares into his flute. "I'm sure you have nothing to worry about if the police are accompanying you, Catou." He rubs my shoulders and kisses my cheek. His tender gesture lifts my spirits. "You need to trust Sandrine and Frédéric."

"You're probably right. Anyway, I can hardly wait to see Rikash riding around town with the police. It should be a day to remember."

We order some smoked salmon appetizers and enjoy our aperitifs.

"So, how was your day?" I ask.

"Same old, same old; just billing my life away while thinking about you." He takes my hand in his and kisses it gently. "But let's not talk about work. Save your energy for your big raid, *mon amour*." He feeds me a bite-size canapé and whispers in my ear. "And I have a good idea about how to help you relax before your big day." He kisses me on the nape of the neck, and my worries about what awaits me tomorrow magically disappear.

# Chapter 7

"You know I'm only doing this for you, love," Rikash declares between bites of almond croissant as we wait for the gendarmes to arrive at the office. "Spending the day dressed down in a filthy police truck isn't exactly what I had in mind when I accepted this position."

"Yes, I know, and I really appreciate it. I'm sure this is a test to see what we're capable of. After today, we'll be back to pushing paper."

Sandrine explained during lunch yesterday that we'd be responsible for maintaining an evidentiary chain of custody for all Dior trademarks. Clearly, there will be lots of paperwork involved.

"Dior is renowned for its New Look, but this is a bit

much, don't you think?" He points to his ripped jeans, fleece sweater, black motorcycle jacket, and dirty Diesel sneakers.

"I think you look sexy. Maybe you'll charm one of the gendarmes," I say, trying to pierce his sombre mood.

He immediately perks up. "Ooh, you're right. Men in uniform!"

I'm wearing a pair of khaki combat trousers, a grey sweat-shirt, hot pink Marc Jacobs sneakers, and my red glitter Miu Miu sunglasses. Nothing too conspicuous, I tell myself.

Frédéric shows up in our office a few minutes later with three middle-aged men in full police dress. All are of medium height and on the burly side. Rikash's face falls as he catches a glimpse of the men we'll be spending the day with, and he gives me a thumbs-down.

"Catherine, Rikash, please meet Sergeants Larivière, Ruppert, and Mazarin."

"*Bonjour.* Very nice to meet you. We're looking forward to our first raid." My voice is brimming with faux enthusiasm.

"The pleasure is ours, mademoiselle," Larivière replies. He gives Rikash a friendly nod but keeps a comfortable dis-tance. "Frédéric told us about your time in New York. I'm sure you'll be prepared for some of the characters you will encounter today."

"Yes, it was quite a jungle." A smile crosses my face. I'm not referring to the crowds on the streets of Manhattan but rather to the atmosphere at my former office: it was about the survival of the misfits.

"Sergeant, can you give us an idea of the role you expect us to play today?" I ask.

"*Absolument.* We will need your assistance in identifying the fake goods to make sure they're in fact replicas of Dior merchandise. Once they've been duly identified, we can seize them. The vendors may try to flee, so we must act quickly. Afterward, we will rely on both of you to inventory everything and make itemized lists."

"What do you do with the seized merchandise?" Rikash asks.

"We have it destroyed in a secure facility," Frédéric answers.

Given the huge amounts of money involved in producing, distributing, and camouflaging the copies, I'm taken aback to learn this.

"We need to wait for Chris, our private investigator, before we can set out," Sergeant Larivière says, staring at his watch. "He's apparently received top-notch tips about where some of the vendors will be today."

Rikash sighs, staring at his iPhone. He's obviously looking for a distraction before we go off on our very unglamorous mission. To make matters worse, Laetitia and the PR team are massed in the hallway outside our office, discussing guest lists, runway set-up, and Champagne for the Shanghai show. I stare down at my casual outfit and feel completely out of place. I remind myself that it's only a test to see what I'm capable of, and that things will get more glamorous soon.

Just then, a dark and handsome man appears in the office doorway. He is tan and fit and looks straight out of a Calvin Klein ad. He's wearing a Burberry trench coat and dark jeans, with bright red Converse sneakers.

Rikash looks up and nearly drops his phone.

"Hi, everybody. Sorry I'm late. There was some major traffic on the way from the airport." His accent is American.

After he shakes Frédéric's hand and greets the three gendarmes, he walks toward Rikash and me. "I'm Chris. You must be the new team members. Welcome aboard." He flashes a Colgate smile.

"Hellooooo, so nice to meet you." Rikash darts forward to shake Chris's hand. "You can't imagine how thrilled we are to be going out on a raid."

It's amazing how the presence of an attractive male will rev up Rikash's enthusiasm. I shake my head.

"Fantastic. I heard you guys worked in New York for Edwards & White," Chris adds cheerfully. "I did some work for them a few years ago. Great firm, isn't it?"

"Oh yes, we absolutely loved it!" Rikash is now shamelessly lying to this handsome stranger. I discreetly pinch his left arm to signal that he should stop.

I move forward to shake the investigator's hand. "Catherine Lambert, and this is my overzealous assistant, Rikash. But you can call him HRH. It's short for *His Rikash Highness*."

Rikash is silent for a moment before bursting into laughter. To my surprise, everyone in the office follows suit, including Frédéric. Pleased that I've managed to break the ice, it occurs to me that we might be in for a highly entertaining day after all.

"How did you get into this business?" I ask Chris once we've settled into the undercover police truck. The backseat windows are blacked out, so there's nowhere to look but at each other.

"I started working in L.A., my hometown, as a general investigator but got a break when a big sporting goods manufacturer asked me to go after some counterfeiters. Now I have hundreds of clients in the retail industry."

"How fascinating." Rikash gives him sweet eyes.

"It is, actually. I have forty agents working for me in cities all over the world, but I still like to get my hands dirty, especially for my most important clients."

"That's impressive," I say enthusiastically. "We're thrilled to be learning the ropes with someone as knowledgeable as you."

"It's great to see you interested in playing such an active role. Your predecessor, Mr. Le Furet, didn't go on raids much. He preferred to remain behind the scenes."

"Sorry to interrupt," Larivière says, "but we need to tell the driver where we're going."

"Yes, of course. Porte de Saint-Ouen," Chris says. "A large shipment of fake goods was due to arrive there early this morning."

"Where do you get your tips?" I ask, intrigued.

"Some come from the clients, others from law enforcement officers who've seen something shady. But most tips actually come anonymously from other counterfeiters competing for territory. It's like the drug trade: mercenary."

I close my eyes and take a deep breath, trying to relax before we get to our destination. I know we're heading to an unsafe part of town and need to calm my nerves. I see Rikash checking out his hair in the driver's rear-view mirror. My phone vibrates and, startled, I jump from my seat. I peer down and see a text message from Antoine wishing me good luck. This soothes and energizes me: I'm ready for action.

Chris is now leaning forward, looking keenly ahead through the windshield. "Okay, I see them," he announces. "Let us out a few blocks from here."

I crane my neck to look out the driver's window as we pass the vendors, a half-dozen men and women in puffy black coats standing behind a large table loaded with bags, scarves, perfumes, and belts. The driver casually eases the truck to a stop a few moments later.

"Okay, are you ready?" Larivière asks. "Here's the plan. Catherine, you and Rikash will get out on the right side of the truck, cross the street so that it looks like you're coming from the metro, and then head back to the table to verify the merchandise. I trust that you're well versed in Dior's product lines. We'll wait for you to report back. Whatever you do, don't be nervous; the vendors will sense it straight away and know something's up."

"Okay, no problem." My heart is pounding in my chest as if I'm about to apprehend a serial killer.

We hop out of the truck and follow Larivière's instructions. Rikash pretends to chat on his phone (with Chris, of course, as if arranging a date for tonight). It's hilarious and helps me relax. As we approach the vendors, I'm feeling a little more at ease. Surprisingly, a major adrenaline rush washes over me, and I approach the table with confidence.

"*Bonjour.*" I look the first vendor straight in the eye. He's wearing baggy jeans, a black windbreaker, and a black and white bandana covered in double CCs on his head, an obviously fake Chanel scarf. Instead of greeting us, he takes a puff from his cigarette and blows the smoke right into our faces. Horrified, Rikash takes a step back and waves the smoke away.

I look down at the merchandise on offer: Miss Dior Chérie perfume in plastic bottles, shoddy-looking versions of Dior saddle bags, and a few acrylic scarves with "Dior" poorly printed in large bold characters. I've just picked up one of the bottles when a young woman in tight jeans and a black leather jacket scurries toward us from across the street while letting out a bird-like whistle. The man in front of us reaches under the table, then proceeds to slide most of the merchandise off the table and into extra-large garbage bags. Some items fall to the ground. He lunges forward and wrestles the perfume bottle out of my hands. Rikash manages to grab a few discarded items from the street. We've identified the goods but we've lost the vendors: they've all run away. Without saying a word, we dash toward the truck.

"We have some of the goods," Rikash announces to the team, out of breath. "But the vendors disappeared. How did they know? Did we do something wrong?"

"No, they have spotters on street corners with two-way radios. They probably recognized the truck. You did a great job, guys," Chris declares, staring at his phone. "I've just received another tip about more vendors nearby, from the same group. Now that we know they have our stuff, it'll go faster next time."

Although I'm disappointed that we didn't really complete our first raid, I'm relieved that it's over. I give Rikash a high-five.

We arrive at our next location, a few blocks away, and I'm ready for action. Without waiting for instructions this time, I jump out of the truck, with Rikash close behind. We cross the street and nonchalantly walk to the corner, where some vendors are scattered, littering the street with their fake goods.

A young man in a leather jacket addresses us. "Bags, you want bags? Louis Vuitton, Chanel, Dior?"

Rikash winks at me; we're in business. He confirms that they're in possession of counterfeit Dior goods by rifling through the stacks of bags, picking up a copy of a Lady Dior bag, and holding it in mid-air for everyone to see.

I sneak a hand behind my back and make the okay signal with my fingers. Within seconds, Chris and the three gendarmes have run to our side. I pull out the seizure warrant, and some of the men standing nearby flee the scene.

The man in the leather jacket is now fuming. After swearing at us for five minutes, he hands over a black garbage bag overflowing with scarves, purses, and belts. A young woman in a sweatshirt is standing beside him, biting her nails nervously.

"It looks like the tip was good," Rikash confirms.

"Where did you get this?" Chris demands, holding up the fake merchandise.

The young man remains silent.

"Do you understand my question? Where did this come from?" Chris points to the bag.

"I don't know," the vendor finally says, staring at the sidewalk. The woman says nothing.

Chris shakes his head.

"I'm not buying it, but it doesn't look like we'll get any more information out of these two," Larivière says gruffly.

"The next time we catch you with this stuff, you're going into the truck, got it?" Chris points to our vehicle.

The vendor responds by spitting on the ground.

As we prepare to leave the scene with three large bags, the vendor impatiently gestures to the woman next to him. She fumbles through her purse and pulls out an expensive-looking camera, which she points at Rikash and me. We try to look away, but she's shooting like the paparazzi.

Chris taps me on the shoulder. "Don't worry. It's pretty routine. They like to share pictures of anti-counterfeiting agents among their group so they won't be caught off guard next time. Essentially, this means you did a great job. Congratulations."

There's a sinking feeling in the pit of my stomach. I imagine my picture being broadcast over the Internet and getting into the hands of every counterfeiter in this city. Why not take out a full-page ad in *Paris Match* to get a head start?

Rikash puts his arm in mine as we walk back to the truck. "I know I possess model-like cheekbones, but I prefer to get my picture taken by a professional."

"No kidding. I didn't like that one bit. Who knows where those pictures will end up?"

"It's okay, dah-ling, we'll be fine. We simply can't drive through this part of town anymore without starting a riot." He pats me on the back before letting out a startled cry. "Oh no! I just stepped in dog poo!"

I can't help but laugh as he pulls his sneaker up to look. "I'm afraid that in Paris, it's as iconic as the Eiffel Tower."

He looks shocked. "No, really? You mean a nation of such sophistication doesn't pick up? That's gross!"

"At least you stepped into it with your left foot. In France, that means good luck."

He stares at me incredulously. "Are you kidding me?"

"No, I'm not. But I guess any way you look at it, *mon ami*, we're now in the *merde*."

# Chapter 8

*B*eing copied is the ransom of success. Thus declared Coco Chanel, a one-time rival of Christian Dior.

I think back to our raid while having a cup of coffee in my office. I'm pleased with the result of yesterday's operation. We managed to seize a decent amount of fake merchandise and perhaps discouraged those sellers from hawking Dior goods in the future. According to Chris, busting the smaller vendors is important: seizing their products can get us one step closer to the ringleaders. But the replicas were of such shoddy quality, I'm convinced Mr. Dior must be turning in his grave.

I look out our office window. I'm having a hard time shaking the look of anger on the vendors' faces. I wonder again where those photographs of me will end up. Despite Chris's words to the contrary, my intuition tells me I should be worried.

Sandrine stops by and snaps me out of my reverie. "Bravo, Catherine. I hear things went smoothly for you and Rikash yesterday," she says, beaming with pride.

"Yes, they did. I was a bit nervous at first, but I think I eventually got the hang of it."

She puts a small bouquet of coral roses on my desk. They're daintily tied together with a raw silk ribbon in the superb way only French florists can manage. "A little gift to reward you for your efforts."

I inhale the delicious perfume. "They're divine, but it really wasn't necessary. I simply followed Frédéric's directive." I'm surprised by her thoughtful gesture. I've received more gifts during my first week at Dior than in my entire seven years at Edwards & White.

"Yes, I understand that Frédéric asked you to accompany Chris and Sergeant Larivière." She fingers a rose petal. "I hope it wasn't too intense for your first week. He likes to initiate colleagues with a baptism by fire." She smiles reassuringly.

"Best way to learn. Besides, I've been subjected to it

before. What doesn't kill you makes you stronger, *n'est-ce pas?*"

"Absolutely." Sandrine sits down on the ledge of our office window. "Before I forget, there's a counterfeiting museum in Paris. It's a real gem, and not far from here. It also happens to be on my way home. Would you like to stop in there after work with me?"

"I'd love to." What a nice offer. My colleagues in New York weren't always so generous with their time.

"And how's Rikash doing?" She changes the subject. "He seems to be fitting in nicely. All the ladies in the atelier love him. He's such a charmer."

"Yes, he is. I'm sure he can out-charm the savviest counterfeiter. His skills will come in handy." I say this in jest, but it might just be true.

"You're right, he was a great hire." She twirls a gold cocktail ring on her middle finger.

Rikash walks into the office wearing a sharp navy blue suit and a cobalt blue shirt. He's carrying the morning paper under his arm.

Sandrine looks up. "You look very chic today."

"Well, it's great to be back to cashmere. I don't think I can handle wearing fleece for more than a day."

"You did a fine job handling those counterfeiters yesterday," Sandrine says.

He responds with a grin and throws the European edition of *The Wall Street Journal* on my desk. "Have you heard the news? The U.S. Department of Homeland Security just shut down eighty international websites selling fake merchandise."

"That's fantastic!" I exclaim.

"Apparently, the seized domains were registered in the United States, but the operations were based in China. This is a major win for our industry." Rikash smiles and removes his jacket.

Sandrine's bracelets clink together as she grabs the paper from my desk. After speed-reading the article with the focus of a hawk, she rushes out of the office, pausing just briefly to utter, "Thank you, Rikash."

"She looked surprised," I say, looking at the door.

"Perhaps she was caught off guard by the news. I don't know why; it's all over the Internet."

"Maybe."

"Don't worry about Sandrine." Rikash adjusts his vintage cufflinks. "I would rather you focus on more important matters, like helping me get that gorgeous private investigator into my lair. Any suggestions, sweetie pie?"

"What if he's straight, Rikash? Or, heaven forbid, not interested?"

He sighs audibly. "First of all, you should know that my gaydar is pretty accurate. And even if I'm wrong, I get a kick out of seducing straight men; it's a personal hobby of mine, and frankly, I'm very good at it. And, honey, 'not interested' is not part of my vocabulary. Never has been, never will be."

"All right, I get the point. But just remember that you don't want to cause any drama with someone who works for Dior."

"Look who's calling the kettle black. Need I remind you that you once seduced a firm client and have now moved in with a firm colleague?"

Ouch. *Touché.*

"If you don't mind, I'd rather forget that former client. And just so we're clear, I moved in with a *former* colleague. That's different."

"Whatever. What's important is that I employ the right seduction tactics with Chris."

"If you want my opinion, it's all about using a subtle touch; scaring a bird is no way to catch it."

"Well said, *mon ange.* I like the way you think."

"Why don't you call him? You could ask him what we

need to do with the inventory of seized goods. You'll know pretty quickly if he's interested."

"Good thinking." He picks up his phone and dials Chris's cell number, as excited as a child about to speak to Santa on Christmas Eve.

His youthful enthusiasm makes me smile. I wish I were so carefree. I guess all those years working in a law firm have stripped the innocence away. Can I get it back?

Rikash's face lights up when Chris answers, and he begins to pace, cellphone in one hand and the other in his trouser pocket.

My own cell rings and I see that it's Antoine. Given that he rarely calls this early in the day, I pick up right away. To give Rikash some privacy, I tiptoe out of the room and take the call in the hallway, greeting Antoine with, "Bonjour, *mon chéri.*"

"Guess what? The acquisition I've been working on for the last month just closed. That means we can go away this weekend to celebrate your first raid." He's excited.

"Sounds wonderful. Where are we going?"

"I can't tell you. It's top secret." I can barely hear him. There's traffic and loud sirens in the background.

"Where are you?"

"Place de la Madeleine, walking by a giant billboard for a Dior perfume called Poison. That got me thinking of you."

"So you think about me when you see a scantily clad bombshell selling Poison? Should I be happy or worried?"

"You should be *very* happy. Imagining you in the same outfit gets my pulse racing."

"So what do you plan to do about it?"

"You'll find out this weekend, *ma chérie*. Going back to the office now. *Bisous.*"

Elated, I walk down the hall and spot Frédéric rushing into Sandrine's office. He nods and gives me a not-so-cold smile. Could it be that my raiding skills have earned just a tiny bit of his respect?

To give Rikash a bit more time to talk to Chris, I head down to the lobby. I take a seat in the reception area to peruse some fashion magazines while Laetitia, Xavier, and what must be the entire PR team run back and forth in front of me. I hear the words "show," "Shanghai," and "Champagne" repeatedly. I can't help but feel envious, imagining the team dressed to the nines in this season's Dior collection, jetting off to exotic locales for fashion shows and celebrating at the hottest nightclubs while I load cheap copies of their accessories into the back of smelly police vans.

Laetitia catches me watching them and walks over. "I don't believe we've formally met. You're the new lawyer from New York, right?"

"Yes, Catherine Lambert. Lovely to meet you." I extend my hand.

She responds with a steely shake. "You're French, not American?"

"Yes. I only worked in New York for a short time. Before that, I was with a law firm here. I'm really happy to be back." I try to show a bit of *égalité* and *fraternité*.

"I'm sure they'll keep you busy up there. Frédéric is a slave driver, and so is Sandrine. *Bonne chance!*"

Clearly, she doesn't have much time for small talk. I bet the seamstresses in the atelier and the designers are running around like mad too, perfecting the last-minute fittings. I wish I could catch of glimpse of the spectacle, but it's not really my business.

I'm flipping through a copy of *W* magazine when a picture of the president of Longuerive, the watch company, catches my eye. He's sitting at the wheel of an enormous steamroller and looks to be crushing hundreds of watches. The photo caption reads: "Longuerive president Jean-Marie Doucet leads an initiative to destroy 1,000 counterfeit watches confiscated from street vendors in Los Angeles."

My mind races. According to Frédéric, we have a sizeable inventory of seized fake goods sitting in a warehouse. What if we destroyed the fakes publicly? It might create some media buzz. I'm convinced it would be a first in Europe. I run back upstairs, sit at my computer and start typing away furiously.

Rikash hurries back when he sees me, clearly dying to talk about his exchange with the hot investigator.

I hold up my hand. "Please save it. I'm in the middle of something, and I don't want to lose my train of thought."

"Oh, aren't we important? Okay, suit yourself, but don't come looking for details later."

"I'm sure I won't have to."

He responds by sticking his tongue out.

I ignore him and keep writing my memo to Sandrine and Frédéric:

> Dear colleagues,
> After reading about an initiative taken by the president of Longuerive Watches in Los Angeles—the public destruction of a thousand fake watches, with the help of a steamroller—it occurred to me that Dior could stage

*a similar event here in Paris. This would likely attract*
*important media attention and bring public awareness*
*to our ongoing anti-counterfeiting efforts.*

   *Given that the fashion industry is accustomed to*
*using shock value to generate media buzz, and that this*
*type of action has already been successfully undertaken*
*by a fellow luxury brand, I think this would comple-*
*ment our work in this area.*

   *I would be delighted to take the lead in organiz-*
*ing such an event and look forward to receiving your*
*thoughts.*

                             *Kind regards,*
                               *Catherine*

I weigh the pros and cons of pressing the Send button.
In New York, one is usually lauded for taking initiative, but
here I wonder if it will look like I'm pushing the limits of
my authority. I think back to some of the moments in my
career when I've been assertive and thought creatively. It
has usually worked out well. What do I have to lose? I press
Send and stare at my computer for several minutes, hoping
for a positive response.

When none comes, I get nervous. To distract myself, I go online to do some additional research about the Longuerive event. Journalists from all over the United States have called it a gutsy and inspiring move. This helps soothe my anxiety.

Finally my inbox dings to indicate that I've received a message from Frédéric.

> To: Catherine Lambert
> CC: Sandrine Cordier

> Dear Catherine,
> Thank you for your message.
> This is a bold and interesting proposal. I will defer to Sandrine for final approval in this matter.

> F.

I exhale in relief. "Yes!"

"What's up?" Rikash asks, standing so close behind me that I can almost taste his Eau Sauvage aftershave.

"An idea popped into my head, and Frédéric likes it."

"Oh? What's the great legal mind up to now?"

I turn my computer screen toward him so he can read the message.

"Ooh, way to go tiger. You're on fire. I see that my amorous conquests are helping you excel at your job. That's music to my ears."

I reposition my screen, hoping for a message from Sandrine that doesn't come. Satisfied that I at least have Frédéric's support, I turn to Rikash.

"Okay, I'm all ears. Tell me everything."

After a leisurely walk, Sandrine and I arrive at the Musée de la Contrefaçon on rue de la Faisanderie, a quiet residential street in the 16th arrondissement. As soon as we enter the attractive *hôtel particulier,* we're greeted by a distinguished-looking man who I learn is the museum director. "Ah, Madame Cordier! Always a pleasure." Sandrine bats her eyelashes.

After introductions are made, we begin our tour. Sandrine tells me that the museum was established in 1951 by L'Union des Fabricants, an organization of local manufacturers, to educate the public about the perils of counterfeiting.

We walk toward some glass cases. More than three hundred items are on display, the counterfeit pieces paired with the authentic originals. Of course, there are luxury items such as leather handbags and couture dresses, but a wide array of household goods are also showcased: laundry detergents, pens, tools, Peugeot hubcaps, toys, and games.

Sandrine points to a pair of Swiss Army knives with a grin. "It's not always easy to tell the difference between real and fake, *non?*" A red card inscribed with the word "*authentique*" is placed in front of the original. She's right: the copy looks identical. The fake packages of Marlboro cigarettes are also convincing, given away only by the absence of health warnings.

I admire the way Sandrine moves from display to display with nonchalance and grace, exuding that special made-in-France sexiness. During our walk here, we kept our conversation professional, but she was still animated and warm. It's so different from American women, who seem to share intimate details about their lives with any female colleague willing to lend an ear. I make a note to follow Sandrine's lead; restraint and discretion are far more attractive than over-sharing.

I'm disappointed that she hasn't brought up my destruction proposal, but decide she just hasn't read it yet. Looking around at all the fake stuff on display, I truly believe that my plan could be a great marketing coup for Dior.

"Catherine, come here. You must see this!" She signals for me to follow her to another room. "It's the highlight of the museum." She giggles like a young girl. "Take a look. It's the oldest counterfeit object in France. It dates from the first century BC." She presses her gloved finger against the glass. "At the time, Greek and Roman wines were considered the highest quality, and this is a fake wine stopper made by a Frenchman. He's imitated the mark of Marcus Cassius Caius."

"Clearly, we're not dealing with a new problem." I smile.

"No, counterfeiting has been a nuisance since the beginnings of commerce. The methods are far more sophisticated today, obviously," she says, gesturing to the cracked piece of pottery with its worn inscription. Her expression becomes serious. "The fact that we have an entire museum dedicated to this issue highlights how seriously our government takes it."

"Thank you for bringing me here, Sandrine! It's been eye-opening." I mean it. And I feel like we're colleagues now.

"It's my pleasure, Catherine." She puts her hand on my shoulder and guides me toward the exit.

As we approach the coat check, the museum director leans forward as though he can't help kissing Sandrine goodbye. He whispers something in her ear, and she tilts her head back like Carole Bouquet in the Chanel television ad from the 1980s. Glamour, class, and intelligence are a powerful and alluring mix, I'm reminded. And there's nothing fake about that.

*Chapter 9*

I've agreed to meet my mother at Café de Flore, her favourite Parisian haunt. This quintessential Left Bank café is intimately linked with Paris's rich artistic and cultural history. Jean-Paul Sartre, Françoise Sagan, Serge Gainsbourg, Miles Davis, and Juliette Gréco have been patrons, along with another chic anti-conformist: my mother. Today, it's a popular meeting place for artists, business types, and fashionistas. Sonia Rykiel is a regular and even has an item on the menu named after her: Le Club Rykiel, a club sandwich made without bread or mayonnaise.

I sit at the back of the room on one of the red Moleskine banquettes and do some people-watching before she arrives. Elegantly-put-together ladies are lunching with companions, and a handful of men are sitting alone, reading newspapers. It all reminds me that there's a whole world happening outside the practice of law. In the last few years, I've missed out on many carefree moments. I resolve to make up for it.

Just as I signal for the waiter to bring me a glass of water, I catch a glimpse of *maman* walking through the front door. She's wearing a striped Gerard Darel dress, with a black patent leather Chanel bag across her chest and open-toe gladiator sandals. As she makes her way to my table, a few men swivel their heads to get a better look at her. I smile.

"What do you think?" She extends her arm and places her wrist in front of my nose. "I just tried this on at Le Printemps, but I'm not sure."

"What is it?" I jerk my head back in reaction to the strong smell. "It's a bit on the strong side, *non?*"

"Osez-Moi! by Chantal Thomass. I'm trying to add a touch of spice to my life." She takes a seat.

"It's very . . . sensual. I'm sure Christophe will like it." My stepfather. "Maybe you should leave it on for a while and see how it reacts to your skin."

"You're probably right, *ma chérie.*" She asks for menus, even though I already know what she'll be having. She's ordered the same thing for the last twenty years: a lemonade and the *salade de haricots.* "So, how are things with Antoine?"

"Fantastic. He's taking me out of town for the weekend to celebrate my new job. He's such a sweetheart."

"Maybe he'll propose?" She lowers her sunglasses and looks me straight in the eye.

Her voice is kind, but I know that getting engaged isn't necessarily her idea of a good time. My mother's definition of a spouse is someone who'll stand by you through all the trouble you wouldn't have had if you'd stayed single. Although she's happy now with Christophe, that was not always the case with my father.

Before answering, I order a hearty croque monsieur and the Flore Cocktail: a delicious mix of Grand Marnier, cognac, Champagne, and red berry coulis. When the waiter departs, I say, "Don't worry, *maman;* we're not there yet."

"I'm just looking out for your best interests. Anyway, I'm glad you're liking your new position at Dior. I always knew you'd be ten times happier working in fashion." She takes a sip of her drink.

"Yes, you were right about that. The world of counterfeiting is fascinating." I refrain from telling her that one day's work involved liaising with three gendarmes and getting my picture taken by criminals. There's no need for her to worry.

"I was thinking about you the other day. I read an article about fake hiking equipment and baby formula. Can you believe that counterfeiters would copy *that*?" She shakes her head. "It's far more dangerous than a fake handbag, isn't it?"

"That's why it's so important to put a stop to it. And I won't tell you what goes into fake perfume; it would kill your appetite."

"*Oh mon dieu.*" She places her manicured hand over her mouth. "I can only imagine."

After our meal, we order espressos and the legendary tarte Tatin to share before we head over to the Musée des Lettres et Manuscrits for an exhibit about the French writer Romain Gary. On our way out, some of the lunching ladies, a few of the solo gentlemen, and even the waiters stop us to say goodbye to my mother.

Once we're outside, we walk past the lovely Fragonard shop, where pretty perfume bottles, dainty pillows with French embroidery, and colourful home accessories are artfully placed in the window.

The museum, located in a gorgeous Haussmannian building, houses an important collection of historical documents related to figures from French history ranging from writers to politicians. I've always loved seeing the handwritten notes of Marcel Proust, Gustave Flaubert, and Antoine de Saint-Exupéry.

A young woman at the entrance hands us a brochure about the current exhibit as we stroll inside. Gary was a diplomat, a compulsive writer, and a passionate lover. He was married to the actress Jean Seberg, and committed suicide a year after she did.

A few minutes in, my mother pulls a vibrating cellphone from her coat pocket. She peers at the tiny screen and whispers, "So sorry, *ma chérie,* but I must take this."

She rushes out into the museum's courtyard. I assume the call must be urgent if she's willing to interrupt a gallery visit to take it. My mother isn't a slave to her phone like the rest of us. Concerned, I follow her outside, keeping my distance to give her some privacy. After a few seconds, I hear her talking about lampshades, wall coverings, and bedspreads. She sounds excited, her numerous bracelets clinking against one another as she moves her arms animatedly. Clearly, there's nothing to worry about. I go back inside.

She eventually catches up with me. "*Désolée*. It was a new Parisian client. I just had to take it." She puts her phone away. "I've got so many new projects in the works, I'm in a bit of a tizzy."

I want to remind her that she once chastised me for taking a conference call during dinner, but decide to drop it. I'm thrilled to see her design business thriving; she's worked so hard at turning a hobby into a source of fulfillment and income.

"No problem, *maman*. I understand."

"I just hope I can give all of my clients the attention they deserve." She looks a bit worried.

"Well, I'm here now. I can help you, if you need me," I find myself blurting out, despite the fact that between work and Antoine, my schedule is pretty packed.

"Really? That would be fantastic, Catou. I would love your advice on a few things. Can you join me for some shopping next week?"

"Of course. I'd love to." After all, my interest in her business is genuine. "Shall we?" I point back toward the exhibit.

"*Ah oui*, I want to read about Romain Gary's mother. Did you know that his famous book *La Promesse de l'aube* was written as an ode to her? Perhaps you should write a book in my honour. God knows you'd have lots of material." She winks.

My mother was a beautiful bohemian.

Born Camille Berthelet, she looked, and dressed like, Brigitte Bardot. She paraded through the streets of Paris in long, flowing skirts and oversized sunglasses, and with a carefree spirit. She read Simone de Beauvoir's novels and essays, became part of the women's liberation movement in the 1970s, and rubbed shoulders with the literati while spending her days at Café de Flore and Les Deux Magots.

My father first laid eyes on her during a business trip to Paris. Freshly promoted to a managing director position on Wall Street, he was, while a generous soul, her complete opposite: dead serious, ferociously ambitious, and sartorially conservative. He worked hard to woo her, marshalling his dashing smile and his passionate love of poetry.

They spent afternoons at Buttes Chaumont Park, a sprawling, romantic garden where Parisians head for picnics and naps in the sun. Together, they read Baudelaire and Rimbaud, and sipped chilled white wine. After a long-distance courtship that lasted over a year, they were married, and my father orchestrated a transfer to Paris to begin their life together.

Years after his death, my mother confided in me that she had never planned to marry. As a girl, her heart had been set on becoming a painter and living a nomadic existence rather than becoming a wife and a mother. But my father had been relentless in his pursuit of her, and she genuinely loved him. Plus, her parents were pressuring her to settle down.

Once, in my twenties, I was looking after my mother's house while she was away on vacation, and I found a journal she had kept during the years of my childhood. There were difficult-to-read passages in which she wrote about fighting depression and feeling stifled by domestic life. She expressed frustration about the challenges of raising a child with a husband who travelled all the time. She clearly fought loneliness and had some regrets about forgoing the artistic life. Although I felt guilty reading something so private, it answered questions I'd long had.

There had always been clues of her artistic self in our home: piles of fashion magazines and art books, unopened tubes of paint, untouched canvases and brushes. When

I asked her why she never took up her paints, she just shrugged and answered "No time" or "Feeling uninspired" or "I need to take care of the family."

My father once announced out of the blue that my mother would be going away alone to do some painting. I remember crying and tugging at her skirt as she packed her bags and loaded up her car. After reading her journal, I realized she'd needed to leave us temporarily to maintain her sanity and rebuild her sense of self.

It was only long after my father died that she finally found her calling. She studied interior design in Paris, moved to the south for inspiration, and finally picked up her paintbrush.

I now understand why my mother kept insisting that I look for another job when I practised law at Edwards & White. She knew that, deep down, I wasn't happy, and that my passions lay elsewhere. Having suppressed her dreams for so long, she feared that I would also suffer the consequences of an unsatisfying career choice.

After all, *maman* knows best.

*Chapter 10*

I t is said that Cleopatra had the sails of her barge soaked with perfume before she set off to seduce Mark Anthony; that Madame de Pompadour, one of Louis XV's mistresses, spent millions of francs a year on aromatic elixirs to keep her lover entranced; and that Marilyn Monroe slept in nothing but a few drops of Chanel Nº5.

The French have always been known for their *expertise* in creating fine perfumes, thanks to the culture's celebrated cadre of "noses." The house of Christian Dior shares in this heritage. Back in 1968, Christian Dior hired Serge Lutens, then a photographer and stylist, to create a cosmetics line that became one of the most successful in history.

Working for a high-end company like Dior, one might

forget that there's a whole other world of fragrances out there. The drugstores in New York are filled with perfumes carrying the names of Hollywood actresses, pop singers, and reality show starlets. When I saw women pick one up, I wanted to wrestle the bottle out of their hands and throw it away. As Mr. Dior put it, *A woman's perfume tells more about her than her handwriting.* So who are you if you wear fragrances by Britney, Cher, or Fergie? Curious, Uninhibited, or Outspoken.

Although I've faithfully worn Dior's J'Adore for years, I'm looking to diversify my portfolio of scents, so I'm heading over to Parfums Serge Lutens, an opulent boutique set in the arcade that encloses the Jardin du Palais Royal, the rose-lined garden that adjoins the former royal palace. My weekend away with Antoine is coming up, and I'm in the market for something new and provocative.

Picking out a fragrance at Lutens is not a task to be taken lightly. All of the fragrances made there take their scent cues from everyday objects—sugar, for example, or a freshly peeled orange—and contain unique and untraditional ingredients.

Once inside, I pick up a bottle of Bas de Soie ("silk stockings"), and its exotic notes transport me to the Far

East. I imagine Antoine holding me in his arms and try to guess what he'd like best. He's not into citrus or flowers but goes more for woody and peppery musks. After testing a half-dozen perfumes, I decide on À la Nuit ("a toast to the night": could the name be more perfect?), an intoxicating blast of white jasmine, and leave the boutique feeling a frisson of excitement.

Before heading home, I stop at one of the oldest restaurants in the city, Le Grand Véfour, for an espresso. Also located in the arcade of the Jardin du Palais Royal, it boasts a long and storied list of former patrons: Simone de Beauvoir, Jean-Paul Sartre, Jean Cocteau, Colette, and even Napoleon and Joséphine have dined here. It has a special place in my heart because my father brought me here as a child and sometimes bought me their exquisite *mousse au chocolat*.

A treasure house of eighteenth-century decorative arts, the dining room is lined with delicately engraved mirrors and velvet upholstery. As I take in the sumptuous room, I'm reminded of Cecil Beaton's famous remark. *We are all French*, he wrote, referring to the respect we all have for beauty and refinement. I sit back with my coffee, reminded again of how lucky I am to be back in this sublime city.

*Chapter 11*

Aubervilliers is a suburb of Paris located just north of the Périphérique, and has become a major hub for the wholesale garment industry. Chris has received a tip about a shipment of counterfeit Dior goods scheduled for delivery to the city's Haie-Coq neighbourhood, and I've agreed to accompany him on a last-minute raid. What a life: yesterday I was taking in the jewel-like Jardin du Palais Royal; today, back to the streets.

The majority of the vendors in this district import goods from China and run an honest business selling garments, shoes, and accessories to retail clients from Belgium, Germany, Spain, and Eastern Europe. The wares are mostly run-of-the-mill no-brand handbags, costume jewellery, sunglasses, and the like.

Rikash is, unsurprisingly, chagrined to miss out on spending time with Chris, but has secured an appointment for a hard-to-obtain beauty treatment with a local American plastic surgeon. He was torn, but decided his face took precedence. I covered for him.

"The police will meet us there," Chris says as soon as I step into a black sports car he's rented to get us there quickly.

Once we're on the highway, I start to feel a rush. "I'm excited about doing this again," I tell him. "I really enjoyed myself last time."

"Are you sure? You seemed a bit nervous when we left the scene."

"Let's just say that I didn't appreciate getting my picture taken, but I'm over it now. This job is so much more fun than what I used to do."

"Good. I wouldn't want you to feel intimidated by those goons. They're just playing tough. And it's been great having you and Rikash around."

My idea about publicly destroying the counterfeit Diors comes to mind. Since I haven't heard back from Sandrine,

I decide to share the idea with Chris. After all, he's been working with Dior for a while.

He frowns for a moment after I explain my idea. "It might be a tough sell," he admits. "Dior can be old-school when it comes to this kind of thing. I'm not sure senior management will go for it."

"Right," I sigh, reminding myself that I'm no longer in New York, where anything goes—or just about.

"I admire your guts, Catherine. Le Furet would never have suggested something like that. He was pretty conservative." Chris takes a swig from his extra-large Starbucks.

He changes gears as we turn onto the exit ramp for Aubervilliers, and his fingers brush unexpectedly against mine. I feel an electric current run through my body. I grip the door handle, trying to steady myself and figure out what just happened. Is the attraction fuelled by the excitement of the raid? I brush it off and stare out the window in silence, focusing on making our mission go as smoothly as it did the first time. I have to admit, it's not easy.

We arrive at the market, and I'm astounded by the number of stalls and vendors lining the wholesale shopping complex.

"There are now thousands of vendors here, and the number is increasing every year," Chris tells me as we walk toward Sergeant Larivière.

"Mademoiselle Lambert, it's a pleasure to see you again." Larivière shakes my hand. "So glad you could make it." He gets down to business. "Okay, you see that trailer with the Czech Republic plates?" He points to a large brown van.

Chris and I nod.

"That's the vehicle we've been told contains the fake Dior merchandise. Apparently, the owner of the van owns that shop over there. Shall we?"

Chris takes the lead and enters the store, where two Asian men are standing behind the counter. Bags of every shape and size are scattered on shelves, and piles of scarves have been arranged haphazardly in a hanging display near the shop's entrance. Seeing a police officer, the two shopkeepers run to greet us.

"Can we help you?" one asks.

"We have a warrant to look for counterfeit Dior merchandise," Chris responds bluntly as Larivière flashes his badge.

"No, no, no. We don't sell Dior here. We have no luxury brands."

"We want to look in that truck." Chris points outside. "It's yours, right?"

One of the men shakes his head, but Chris holds out his hand. "Hand over the keys," he demands. "Otherwise, we'll force it open."

The man nearest us reluctantly pulls a set of keys from his trouser pockets. His hands are shaking slightly.

"Okay, let's go," Larivière commands.

Chris unlocks the van and, after digging around in the back for a few minutes and pulling out a dusty old carpet, emerges with several large black plastic bags. He throws them on the ground and we begin to fish through them. As we've been led to suspect, there are scores of counterfeit items: handbags styled after Dior's famous saddle bags and Lady Dior bags, as well as thousands of watches. The vendor was right in one sense—there aren't any brand labels attached to the goods—but it's irrelevant; they are still illegal copies of Dior's designs.

The vendor tries fervently to defend himself. "I import bags, that's all! I don't know the difference between designer and no designer."

The other man points to the watches. "See? There are no labels or brand names."

Chris shakes his head. "These are illegal copies, and we have the authority to confiscate them."

"You need to speak with my lawyer!" one of the men barks, looking peeved and pulling out a cellphone.

Chris looks at me. "Okay, Catherine, you handle this. It's all yours."

The man hands me his cellphone after explaining the situation—in Chinese, I think—to the person on the other end.

"Hello?" I grab the phone.

"Listen, lady, my clients aren't guilty of anything," a raspy voice insists. "There are no brand names on the goods, and they had no intention of violating the law."

"It doesn't matter," I say flatly. "They're infringing Dior copyright, and we're entitled to seize all the goods. I'm afraid a judge will have to decide whether or not you're right about this." I hang up and see Chris and Larivière looking at me approvingly.

The vendors glare at me and the phone's owner throws it to the ground. It looks like not letting myself be intimidated is paying off.

"Bravo, Catherine." Chris pats me on the back like a proud coach. "You've already become an expert at taking charge and keeping a straight face in front of these thugs. Way to go!" The intimate gesture makes me a bit giddy.

"You're turning into a real pro," Larivière concurs.

"Thank you, gentlemen. Police raids are new to me, but I did get a little practice dealing with thugs in my previous professional life—you'd be surprised."

# Chapter 12

"Are you going to tell me where we're going?" I tug at Antoine's sleeve after we get into his vintage seafoam-coloured convertible. The quirky car used to belong to his mother, and we both love it.

He takes my hand and kisses it gently. "Not yet! But here's a hint: it's sophisticated, just like you, *ma chérie.*"

"I hope I packed the right clothes. I wasn't sure what to bring, and you didn't give me many hints."

"Based on what I've seen at home, I'm sure you have everything you need." He pokes my arm teasingly. "Besides, we'll be spending most of the weekend under the duvet, so you won't need much."

I think of the bottle of À la Nuit tucked into my overnight bag and shoot him a sly grin.

We turn onto the highway heading west, and this throws me off. I've assumed he's taking me south, maybe for a surprise visit to my mother's house or to Saint-Tropez. I guess the bikinis at the bottom of my suitcase won't see the light of day, but I don't care. I'm happy to be with Antoine, no matter where we go.

"Okay, I have no idea. I give up!" It's been a stressful week, as first weeks typically are, so I'm happy to kick back and let Antoine lead the way. I untie my hair and open the window to feel some fresh air on my face. After a few minutes, I feel myself unwind, letting go of the tension in my shoulders. Before I know it, I'm drifting off.

"We're here—Monaco of the North." Antoine's voice wakes me and I find his chin nuzzled into the back of my neck. I lift my head to see half-timbered houses with exposed wood framing and smell the tang of sea air.

"We're in Normandy? What a lovely surprise!" I pull

him in closer for a hug, inhaling the woodsy scent of his cologne. I'm dizzy with happiness.

I can't tell exactly which town we're in. I visited Normandy as a child with my parents and vaguely recall colourful beach umbrellas, sailboats, and platters of fresh seafood. Since my mother's move south, I've spent most of my vacations there, and I haven't visited this region much in recent years.

"First stop: the Christian Dior Museum," Antoine announces. "We're in Granville, his hometown. I thought you should get better acquainted with this place."

I'm touched by his thoughtfulness and kiss him tenderly. Rikash and I saw pictures of Granville in the company archives. Also, Dior has recently released the Granville, a large, hand-stitched leather handbag with the house's signature *cannage* motif, to great commercial success.

"What a wonderful surprise! You're definitely worth switching continents for."

He takes me by the hand. "Let's go, *mon amour*. We have some studying to do. And you'd better take notes—there'll be a test later."

I grab my straw bag and hat—both vintage, of course—and we scurry hand in hand toward Les Rhumbs, a magnificent nineteenth-century villa overlooking the English Channel and the site of the museum. As we make our way onto the grounds, my senses are stimulated by the stupendous view of the water, the sound of crashing waves, the smell of roses, lilies of the valley, and pine trees. We stroll through the gardens and read the signs explaining the property's history: it was designed in emulation of an English park by Madeleine Dior, Christian's mother.

To my delight, there are twelve olfactory terminals set up in the garden to educate visitors about Dior's perfumes. I stop in front of the sign for Miss Dior, and Antoine snaps my picture.

"Did you know that Dior's father ran a fertilizer business here in Granville?" Antoine asks as I read about the origins of the perfume.

"Really? How do you know?"

"I did a bit of research. What's ironic is that, back in the day, the people of Granville would say "It smells of Dior" when they were complaining about the fertilizer odours wafting through town." He grins. "Hard to believe, *non?*"

"Times have changed, haven't they?" I giggle.

I look out toward the horizon and fill my lungs with fresh air. I've always loved gazing at the sea, as it reminds me of life's infinite possibilities. It occurs to me that, less than a year ago, I thought my future was all mapped out on Wall Street, but I ended up dead wrong, professionally and romantically. Today I feel confident that I'm on the right track. When I look at Antoine, who's shooting the view with a camera, my heart swells with delight. My life feels pretty perfect right now.

"I think you'll definitely want to visit the house. The brochure says there's haute couture on three floors. You don't want to miss *that*." He seems as excited as I am about discovering this place. It's obvious that Antoine takes pleasure in making me happy, and that puts me on top of the world.

The house is in the Anglo-Norman style, its roughcast pink exterior enlivened by bay windows and a veranda conservatory. It sits on the edge of a cliff and braves the gusty winds. I feel like I'm stepping back in time.

We walk onto the veranda, where a stunning giant star is sketched on the mosaic floor. I learned in the company archives that its pattern has appeared in many Dior designs.

"So, is Dior planning to retain Edwards & White on litigation mandates?" Antoine abruptly asks as I'm admiring a pink taffeta evening dress on display on the second floor.

"Word on the street is that Dior is planning to sue eShop. I'd love to get involved in a case like that."

My mood shifts from elated to grim. His work is important to both of us, but does he have to raise this now and ruin our idyllic moment? I sigh. "Antoine, to tell you the truth, I haven't talked about it with anyone yet. It seemed inappropriate to bring it up during my first week, when I'm trying to make a good impression."

I know he can see from my expression that I'm annoyed, but he pushes his point anyway. "Catherine, I get that it's been a stressful week, but I'm under a lot of pressure to bring in new business now that I'm a partner. And you worked in the Paris office; you know who I'm competing against. They're a pretty driven bunch."

His curt tone puts me on edge. "I thought we came here for a romantic weekend," I say, my raised voice attracting disapproving glances from a few fellow visitors. "Obviously, you had other intentions."

Confused and upset, I turn on my heels and head for the nearest staircase, racing down to the tea room at the heart of the garden, where Antoine, who has run after me, catches my arm.

"Catherine!" he huffs, out of breath. "I'm sorry. Please

wait. The pressure is getting to me. Don't storm off like that." His eyes are beseeching, like those of a wounded puppy.

I exhale audibly and look away. Older women sipping tea at a nearby table frown at me. Antoine looks so sincere, and it's obvious they're taking his side.

"All right, but no more shoptalk, okay?" I wag my finger. "We're here to have fun, not be stressed out about work."

"Okay, it's a deal." He pulls me closer and kisses me. "I'm sorry, Catherine. I love you." The ladies whisper under their elegant hats, and I notice that they're now smiling.

We spend the rest of the afternoon taking in the view while eating pastries off English porcelain. The delicious baked goods are named for Dior haute couture collections from the past. I'm officially back in heaven.


"What's our next stop?" I ask as soon as we get in the car.

"I'm not sure I should tell you. After that scene in the museum, you deserve to wait."

"Ha! You started it, mister. You really need to loosen up. What are you anyway, a lawyer?"

"No, I'm the personal assistant to a high-maintenance Dior executive."

"Sounds good to me. I'll need you to execute a few orders for me later." I raise my eyebrows.

He smiles over at me. "Your wishes shall be my command."

An hour or so later, the scenery begins to look familiar. We're entering the quaint seaside town of Deauville, with its lovely architecture, its majestic port filled with yachts, and its bustling market. My parents brought me here during one of our last family vacations before my father passed away. We drive along the main street, taking in its quaint shops and cafés. Antoine stops in front of the majestic Hôtel Normandy Barrière, gets out and throws the keys to the valet.

"We're staying here?" My heart skips a beat as I step onto the hotel's stunning front lawn, which is lined with rose bushes and bougainvillea and offers a stunning view of the ocean. The white fairy lights hung throughout the garden give the grounds a magical feel.

"Nothing but the best for my *princesse. Allez,* let's go!"

I can barely hide my excitement as we pass through the hotel's grand wooden entranceway. We receive a warm welcome from the staff and head up to our elegant room, which is decorated with striped wallpaper, Toile de Jouy bedspreads, and vintage furniture. A bellboy arrives with a bottle of Perrier-Jouët Champagne in a silver ice bucket, crystal Saint-Louis flutes, and a platter of oysters.

As Antoine unpacks, I sneak into the washroom and retrieve my essentials from my bag: a Chantal Thomass black satin nightgown, matching vintage Dior pumps, ruby red lipstick, and my new bottle of À la Nuit. I dab the fragrance onto my wrists and behind my knees and ears, then take a look in the mirror. I'm satisfied with the result: Catherine Deneuve in *Belle de jour,* just about. I strut back into the room and take an authoritative tone. "Are you ready to execute orders?" I give Antoine a pout à la Bardot.

He drops his bag and answers with a salute. "Yes, commander."

# Chapter 13

"How about having breakfast in bed?"

"Yes, please," I answer, throwing my head back onto one of the heavenly pillowcases. As I'm rolling around in the soft bedding, luxuriating in the down pillows, Antoine slips a tiny grey pouch into my hand.

"What is it?"

"Open it!"

I untie the delicate strings, and a dainty gold ring with the word "*oui*" inscribed in raised letters slips out of the pouch.

"Antoine! What did you do? This is from Dior's fine jewellery collection!"

"I know. Do you like it?"

"*OUIIIIIIIIII!*"

"It's to symbolize our commitment and your move back to France." He slips it on my finger. "*Je t'aime, ma chérie.*"

My pulse quickens as I gaze at the ring, such a thoughtful gift. It's the first time a man has declared his feelings for me in such a romantic way, and my eyes well up. I think back to my conversation with my mother and smile. I guess she has a sense for these things; while this isn't an engagement ring, she wasn't too far off.

I kiss him back passionately. In moments, my Chantal Thomass nightgown has somehow slipped off. Antoine gently caresses my thighs and nibbles at my scented pulse points. Although it's now close to mid-morning, the inebriating effect of À la Nuit is still potent.

*Oh my.*

On Sunday morning, I slip into a Saint-James striped top, a pleated vintage navy skirt, a cream fedora, and blue Tretorn sneakers. I haven't lost my appreciation for the American preppy look I got a taste of in New York. We venture out for a stroll on the beach, and I feel like Anouk Aimée in

*Un homme et une femme.* Afterward, we stop for coffee and hot croissants at Dupont, a delightful bakery in the heart of town and a perfect spot for people-watching. I feel drunk with happiness every time I look down at my hand and catch a glimpse of my ring; it's a loud yes to commitment for the whole world to see, and I feel blessed.

On the drive home, we stop in Giverny, the village where Monet spent most of his life. We visit the famous gardens, take pictures in front of the lily pond, steal kisses in front of the roses, and admire the paintings that fill the old house.

Back on the highway, we talk about our plans to redecorate our apartment. "The first question should be, where will we put all those clothes while we repaint? Perhaps we can give them away to charity?" Antoine teases.

"*Ah, non!* Not a chance, mister."

"Maybe we could make an offer on the villa in Granville?" he jokes. "It would accommodate at least half of your shoe collection."

"Forget it. The commute would kill us both. The less expensive solution would be to build a walk-in."

He stares at me with furrowed brows. "I guess that means I'm losing complete control of my apartment."

I lift my left hand and show him the *oui* ring on my finger. It's a bit of a risky move, but it was his idea.

He smiles tenderly. "Catherine, I've been meaning to apologize for ruining our first day in Normandy with all that office talk."

"Don't worry, it's already forgotten."

"It's just . . . I'm a partner now, and they expect me to drum up some clients since I'm going to be getting a share of the firm's profits." He shoots me a sideways glance.

I tilt my head back on the headrest and take a deep breath. I know where this conversation is heading, and it's not how I want our romantic weekend to end.

"Mmm-hmm. Yes, I know. I worked there, remember?"

"But you don't anymore. And your new role at Dior could really help me. I haven't heard from anyone in the legal department since Le Furet left the company. He was my only contact there, and now you're my only hope."

Oh boy. Put on your seatbelt, Catherine, this is about to get rocky. "Haven't we gone over this already? Do you want to start another argument?"

"No, of course not. I just want you to understand that things are difficult for me right now. A lot of multinationals are starting to outsource legal work to firms in India. There

120 *Isabelle Laflèche*

was an article about it in *The Economist* last week. And you know who I'm up against; you spent six years in that office. I'm just trying to make sure we have bread on the table."

I remain silent and curl my lip, then respond emphatically. "I'm sure *that* is not a problem."

He sighs with exasperation. "Catherine, you know Dior means a lot to me professionally. Can't you put in a good word on my behalf? I don't think I'm asking for a lot."

Doesn't he get that I'm not ready to recommend him to my boss after only one week? For the sake of keeping the peace and to avoid any potential road accidents, I grit my teeth and say, "I'll see what I can do. I can't promise anything, though."

# Chapter 14

The next morning, I sit in our office perusing fashion blogs and the latest Dior catalogue before Rikash arrives. I need a few minutes to collect myself and prepare for the day. I left our apartment early this morning in part to avoid another argument. Although I love Antoine dearly, sometimes I need time alone to figure things out.

A few minutes with the blogs gets my mind off this weekend's less pleasurable moments. I'm particularly fond of *Making Magique,* which chronicles a stylish young American's adventures in Paris, *My Little Fashion Diary*, and *Tales of Endearment.* The motivated young women behind these sites bring me back to my carefree younger days.

As I look through Dior's upcoming ready-to-wear collection, the words of Voltaire spring to mind: *It is fancy rather than taste which produces so many new fashions.* I lobbied for my job at Dior because of my passion for fashion and beauty, but I'm not blind to the industry's main objective: getting you to part with your hard-earned dollars. Marketing campaigns make you drool over, and pine for, things like a "limited edition" handbag with a two-year waiting list—and your bag may or may not still be fashionable by the time you get it. It's a bit sad, but one of our industry's goals is to create irrepressible urges for things you never knew you wanted, never mind needed.

How many people can realistically afford a Hermès Birkin with an $80,000 price tag? Although I certainly don't condone the sale of fake products, perhaps it's this very inaccessibility that drives the demand for fakes in the first place. After all, it's human nature to want things we can't have.

A few years ago, I attended a conference in Paris and heard a talk by an internationally acclaimed interior designer. He ranted against the luxury industry, claiming that today's youth was wasting their money chasing the new "it" fashions. People would be better off investing in art, a designer chair, or even real estate, he said. Looking at the catalogue before me, with the five-digit price tags next to some handbags, part of me believes this to be true.

After all, in the words of Karl Lagerfeld, *Elegance is a physical quality. If a woman doesn't have it naked, she'll never have it clothed.*

According to a study done at Stanford University, one of the best things a man can do for his health is to be married to a woman, whereas one of the best things a woman can do for her health is to nurture relationships with her girlfriends.

Perhaps that's why I'm so happy to hear a familiar female voice burst out of my cellphone this afternoon. "How's my favourite Parisian?"

My dear friend Lisa and I attended law school together in California for a year and reconnected when I transferred to the New York offices of Edwards & White. I miss our chats, our shopping sprees, and, most importantly, our mutual support. I do have some friends in Paris, but most of them are married, have children, and have moved to the suburbs, so our lives don't intersect as much as they used to.

"Lisa! So happy to hear from you. How are you?"

"Things are great. Work is crazy, as usual, and Charles and I are busy planning the wedding. I hope your mother is still okay with us having it at her beautiful home?"

Lisa had asked if she and her fiancé could get married at my mother's property in the south of France. Given my mother's workload, I realize now that organizing Lisa's wedding might be bit of a stretch, but I keep that to myself. Knowing how much this means to Lisa, I'll gladly pitch in; after all, it will give me an excuse to shop on someone else's budget.

"Let me know if there's anything I can do for you here in Paris. My mother will take care of the decor and flowers."

"That's wonderful, but it isn't why I called," Lisa says, suddenly serious.

Given her tone of voice, I figure it can't be good news. "*Ah bon?* What's going on?"

"It's about Jeffrey."

I feel my insides becoming as tight as a knot. I've put thoughts of my ex-boyfriend at the back of my mind, in a place only my subconscious visits, usually at night. But I knew I would hear about him sooner or later. I was the one who reported his wrongdoings to the Securities and

Exchange Commission, and some follow-up was inevitable.

"Okay. What about him?" I'm frozen in my chair, breathless.

"I guess you haven't read the papers yet? He was indicted this morning. It's all over the *Journal*."

At the time of his company's initial public offering, Jeffrey requested that I illegally transfer shares into an off-shore bank account in his name. He was the chief financial officer of the company, I was acting as legal counsel on the deal, and we were dating. I subsequently sent a letter to the SEC, then got him to repeat his outrageous request on tape. I have visions of Jeffrey appearing in front of a grand jury in handcuffs, unshaven, flanked by members of the NYPD, all the while cursing me over and over.

"I didn't realize it was today." I feel silly for not having paid closer attention to the case. I've been so ashamed about the whole mess that I've purposely avoided hearing anything about it.

"The article mentions that he lost his job, had most of his assets frozen, and had his passport confiscated. I guess that's what you call karmic payback," Lisa says.

It suddenly occurs to me that my letter to the SEC might have been leaked to the press. I ask, "Does the article mention anything about my letter?"

"No, don't worry. Your name isn't mentioned. I know you don't like to talk about it, but I thought you should know."

"Thanks, Lisa, I appreciate it. But I'll feel much better when that part of my life is behind me for good."

"Maybe we'll be able to celebrate that at my wedding," she says.

I certainly hope so.

"There's somewhere we need to be right now," Rikash calls out. His hands flutter around his head, and he wipes his brow with a silk polka dot handkerchief before whisking me up from my chair. I give him a curious look, but he's silent until we reach the elevators.

"Photo shoot," he says, after pressing the call button.

"For what?"

"You'll see."

"We need to wait for the light," the photographer declares

to no one in particular. We've just entered a huge white room filled with fashion assistants, makeup artists, hair stylists, and a contingent from the Dior publicity team. "The light just isn't right." The photographer shakes his head and darts around the room, camera in hand, pointing to the tall windows that look onto avenue Montaigne. After a few moments of this, he comes face to face with Rikash and flashes him a grin. Rikash reciprocates, and some predictable flirtation ensues.

"Hello, I'm Rikash," my assistant says, extending his hand. "We're the party poopers from legal." He points in my direction. "This is my colleague Catherine Lambert, chief pooper."

I nudge him in the ribs and manage a tight smile. I still have no clue why I'm here. To make matters worse, my floor-length cherry red vintage skirt and blue-and-white-striped sweater are garnering looks from the black-clad fashion crowd here. I stand out like Minnie Mouse in a house of horrors. I decide to ignore it; they'll just have to deal.

"Jean-Michel." The photographer gives Rikash sweet eyes. "I was happy when I saw you walk in, but now I'm not so sure." He laughs. "Please come in. We're just getting started." Jean-Michel claps his hands and everyone in the room freezes. "*Allez, on y va!* Get ready!" He points to the window. "The light is perfect now."

A few assistants rush to adjust the lighting umbrellas. A model who looks to be in her teens is dressed in a bizarre outfit involving fur, black lace, and neon green underwear. Her dress is completely see-through, every inch of the racy undergarments exposed. She stands in front of the camera, suggestively licking a pink lollipop. She looks like a young woman who's seen way too much for her age.

I lean toward Rikash. "What's this shoot for? The latest resort collection?" It's the only explanation I can think of for the barely there get-up.

"No, it's for our new anti-aging moisturizer," he answers with a straight face.

"That doesn't make any sense." I shake my head. "Why is she dressed like Lolita if they're taking close-ups of her face?"

"Sweetie, it's not about making sense, it's about making an impression." Rikash sprints onto the set to fix the model's bra strap, saying, "Sorry, Jean-Michel, but I really hate to see an undergarment worn wrong."

"*Non, non, non!*" A loud voice thunders from the side of the room. I crane my neck to find out who's interrupting and gasp to see someone I recognize—but only from magazines. It's Wolfgang de Vrees, Dior's famed designer. He's a rock star. He's leaning against a table near the makeup station, observing the shoot like a hawk. I've read about him. His entourage includes European royalty, politicos, and Hollywood starlets. He's known to be exceptionally talented, hugely competitive, and notoriously difficult to work for. He rarely sleeps and survives on a diet of sunflower seeds and Diet Coke, though rumour has it that for some reason he also eats paper (yes, paper!).

He pays no attention to what critics or editors have to say about his work. Why would he? His annual salary is in the millions, and he is revered like a god. I just hope Rikash doesn't get an earful from him for interrupting the photo session.

He points toward Rikash, shouting, "Who are these intruders?"

"They're from the legal department," Jean-Michel answers flatly.

Wolfgang raises his hands to the ceiling, exclaiming, "Lawyers? God, what a bore! Who invited them?"

Rikash glances my way, his shoulders drooping like a shrinking violet. His cheeks are flushed, and I can tell he's embarrassed. He slinks to the back of the room, and I pat him on the shoulder.

No one has dared to answer Wolfgang's question, so he continues his tirade. "Can we continue without any more interruptions, hmm?"

Jean-Michel obliges and the photo session begins. It's a whirlwind. Assistants and stylists take turns teasing the model's hair, adding eyeshadow, plumping the girl's cleavage, adjusting her skirt, and changing her shoes (for a facial moisturizer . . . it makes sense, *non?*) After an hour of this, the team takes a break and I finally ask Rikash about our role in this charade. "Why are we here?"

He just whispers, "You'll see."

There's a lot of work waiting for me on my desk, and I'm growing impatient. I hope Rikash didn't drag me here just so he could flirt with the photographer. "I don't want to wait and see. I want to know now," I snap. "In case you aren't aware, I have counterfeiters to arrest, lawsuits to win, and designs to protect."

"Whoa, calm down, sweetie." He encourages me to breathe. "If you must know, the publicity team asked us to be here because they intend to significantly modify some of the photos."

I'm surprised. I know photos are routinely touched up with Photoshop to make a model's lips plumper, erase fine lines, or narrow a waistline, but why ask a lawyer? It must be something major.

"How significant are the changes?" I ask Rikash. "Oh wait, let me guess: 'You'll see,'" I say before he has the chance. He rolls his eyes skyward.

I decide to wait this out. Now I'm curious about how they'll alter Lolita's image.

Once the shoot is over, the model departs and we're left with Jean-Michel and a few senior members of the marketing team. Wolfgang has disappeared too, presumably to avoid further contact with members of the legal profession.

"This is what we'd like to do." Jean-Michel shows me his computer screen. "We want to make her face wrinkly and publish before and after photos to show what can happen if you don't use our product."

He places the model's picture next to a digitally altered version that makes her look at least fifty years older. The contrast is mind-boggling.

I now understand why they wanted us here. "Okay, first things first. Have you told the model that you're doing this?"

The photographer and his team remain silent and stare blankly at each other.

"I guess that means no." I'm trying to act like a team player, but something tells me that playtime is about to be cut short. "What does her contract say? Does anyone have a copy handy?"

It's a few moments before anyone answers. "We don't have a copy of it here," the publicity director says, "but she signed our standard waiver."

"I don't think you should publish these photos without her written authorization," I say. The group seems disappointed. "She could sue us for unauthorized and improper image manipulation. It's happened before." I've done my homework in this area.

"This is where our reputation as party poopers comes in," Rikash says.

"Are you sure?" Jean-Michel asks. "If we make them look too young, we get shot down by the Advertising Standards Board, and if we make them look old, we get sued. We can't win." He shakes his head.

I want to say that he wouldn't have any problems if he simply portrayed models realistically, but I keep it to myself. I already feel like the school principal calling an end to recess.

"Yes, I'm afraid so," I say firmly. "She could claim that the retouched image might adversely affect her modelling career. I realize this isn't what you wanted to hear, but I'm just looking out for the company's interests. Let's get her approval in writing, okay?"

After an awkward silence, the publicity director agrees. "She's probably left the building by now, but we'll try to figure something out with her agent."

"Send me the contract. I'll take care of it." I might as well be cooperative, I figure.

I turn to leave the room, Rikash following close behind. As I turn to wave goodbye, I catch him mouthing "Call me" to Jean-Michel.

He lifts his toned shoulders innocently. "Sorry, hon, I really can't help myself. I was born this way."

Back in our office, I return a few calls and emails. Before long, I receive a copy of the model's contract from the publicity department. Her name is Yulia Mintovia, and she's from Bulgaria. I speed-read through the preliminary details until I reach her date of birth. She's just turned fifteen.

I know models start young, but Yulia is barely pubescent. The Council of Fashion Designers of America has established a series of guidelines aimed at promoting young women's health in the fashion industry, including a recommendation that models be at least sixteen years old. Unfortunately, girls of Yulia's age are still prevalent in the industry.

Because she's a minor, I check whether the contract is co-signed by a parent or guardian but find no additional signature. This brings into question whether the contract is actually binding. I make a note to discuss this with our publicity director.

I wonder where Yulia lives and, more importantly, who looks after her. I've read stories of young models disappearing in new cities, falling prey to prostitution rings or to drugs and alcohol.

I finally find a clause about Dior's use of the photographs resulting from the shoot. Our standard release allows the company to use Yulia's image in any way it chooses, but I find a sentence buried in the agency's agreement that requires written permission to be sought for significant alteration. To be on the safe side, I quickly draft a document that outlines what Dior intends to do with the photos and email it to Yulia and her agent. I also request that the documents be co-signed by a legal guardian.

Within moments of sending the message, I receive a reply from Yulia: *No problem, I'll sign the document. Were you the lady wearing the red skirt today? Can I call you?*

I look down at my outfit and sigh. My vintage ensemble was definitely noticed by the fashion crowd, but in the right way? *Yes, that's me. What would you like to talk about?*

Mere seconds pass before I receive her response: *You are a lawyer, right? I need help. Can we meet somewhere outside your office to talk?*

I think about it. She's technically a company supplier, and our interests could conflict down the road. I could end up in hot water if we run into any problems with her pictures. But I come up with a plan: *Send me the signed document first, and then I'll meet you. Okay?*

Something is telling me this is the right thing to do.

I meet Yulia after work at one of my favourite Parisian haunts: Angelina's on rue de Rivoli. Their hot chocolate is world-famous, and their mont blanc dessert, a meringue confection topped with a chestnut purée and filled with crème chantilly, is simply divine.

The tea room's decor is typical Parisian elegance: marble-topped tables, gold-framed mirrors, and gilded ironwork. We sit at a table by the window, where we can watch Parisians hurry home.

After placing my decadent order, I snap my menu shut. Yulia orders only a Diet Coke. Up close, she's beyond stunning. She has piercing green eyes, high cheekbones, long lashes, a small freckled nose, and skin as smooth as silk. She has a delicious mane of ash blond hair and looks ten times more beautiful without any makeup. She has an Eastern European accent, but speaks French impeccably. She looks impossibly cool in a faded grey T-shirt and jeans: I think they're by Zadig & Voltaire, a popular local label. Peering down at my rather untrendy ensemble, I feel as old as my vintage skirt.

Several of the coffee drinkers around us are staring at Yulia. I guess models today really are as famous as movie stars.

"You're missing out on something pretty amazing," I say, pointing to a tray of desserts one of the waiters is carrying by. "You can have a bite of mine, if you want." I smile. "So, what do you want to talk about?"

"Immigration," she says nervously. "I have immigration problems, and I can't afford a lawyer." She bursts into tears and lets her pretty head drop into her hands. "I can't go back to my country. Please help me."

I reach for her hand and offer her a tissue. "Tell me a bit more. Maybe I can do something."

Models tend to have no problem getting past the velvet ropes at nightclubs, but getting across a border is a different story.

Yulia blows her nose, then takes a deep breath. "My visa is expiring soon, and I can't renew it because of my stupid roommate." She scowls.

"Why? What did your roommate do?"

She hesitates before continuing more quietly. "One night we had a party and the police showed up. They found some weed in the kitchen. They interrogated me, and now I'm having trouble renewing my papers." She stares down at her sneakers.

Yulia's story reminds me of something I read about Patti Hansen's early modelling days in New York, where she admitted to embracing the party scene a bit too much. I've always thought this was part of a model's rite of passage. But given that Yulia's a minor, things could get tricky.

"Is your roommate also a model?"

"Yes, and I hate her!" She's so angry all of a sudden. She looks up and her eyes narrow.

"Really? Why?"

"She stole money from me," Yulia snaps. "I owe my agency, and I need help." She wipes her eyes and puts the tissue in her backpack.

"I promise I'll try to help you." I pat her tiny hand reassuringly. "Why do you owe money to your agency?"

She sighs. "Our apartment costs eight hundred euros a month, and I owe nine hundred for my plane tickets from Bulgaria to Paris and five hundred for the photography tests they did when I first arrived. I can only withdraw a hundred euros a week as pocket money—it has to cover all my living expenses. These debts are killing me."

It looks like some agencies are running a racket, hitting these young girls with huge charges before they've even landed in Paris. It's a far cry from "I don't get out of bed for less than $10,000 a day" supermodel fees, but it's their reality.

"I see. I'll make a few phone calls tomorrow and see what I can do about your visa. But first, you must do one thing for me: try this."

I place my hot chocolate, with its side order of whipped cream, in front of her. She pushes it aside, but I'm persistent and slide it back in front of her. It's non-negotiable. Seeing that I'm not going to back down, she smiles, then reaches for the cup and takes a tiny sip, leaving a moustache of whipped cream under her pretty nose and a wide grin on her face.

"You see? That wasn't so hard."

She grimaces, but then reaches for a fork to take a bite of my mont blanc.

"It looks like we have a deal, *ma chérie*."

Françoise Sagan once said, *There is a certain age when a woman must be beautiful to be loved, and then there comes a time when she must be loved to be beautiful.*

During my awkward teenage years, when my self-esteem was at an all-time low, my mother was relentless in her attempts to make me lovable. Although I was by no means plump, I did carry a few extra pounds for a few years, and she thought it in my best interest to lose them. She was spoiled by nature with a rabbit-fast metabolism and a dreamy figure. I, on the other hand, inherited more of my father's genes, including a more naturally round physique.

I suffered from the same body image issues that most teenage girls do, feeling a little inadequate around more popular girls at school, but never resorted to extreme measures to keep myself thin.

When I turned sixteen, my mother put me on strict diet of *salades cuites,* raspberries, grapefruit, and Contrex water. No cheese, no pastries, and no *chocolat.* It was painful, but it worked: I lost fifteen pounds and never gained that weight back.

I still hear my mother's voice in the back of my mind when I'm trying on a bathing suit. Although she only wanted to help, to this day, I'm a little self-critical about my body, though I work hard to quell negative thoughts and accentuate the positive.

Now that I'm back in France, I have my mother close by again, noting any sign of new curves. Many Parisians diet to the extreme, surviving on salads, cigarettes, and coffee, looking as tiny as the Smart cars they drive. I'm not willing to do that—not anymore, anyway.

In New York there was an openness and acceptance that I don't find here. In most circles there, you can pretty much eat whatever you want whenever you want to and look the way you choose. Standing out is not only tolerated, it's encouraged; there's less pressure to fit into a certain mould.

Working for the fashion industry, where being thin is a prerequisite, certainly hasn't helped silence insecurities, but I'm doing my best to quiet my inner critic and feel comfortable in my own skin. Today, though, as I walk home from the metro, I realize that my meeting with Yulia has brought back some of my inner conflict. I begin again to question, as I do from time to time, the fashion world's ideal of thinness. I'm reminded of the Brazilian model who died a few years ago of anorexia. She was twenty-one years old, five feet eight inches tall, and weighed just over eighty pounds.

Designers seem to seek out emaciated figures to present their collections: the clothes just look better on those frames, they say. But obviously, the sought-after skinny look is part of the big illusion machine, the powerful engine that encourages women to remain dissatisfied with what they have and what they look like. Much as we all love fashion, we need to keep looking for a remedy for our dissatisfaction, too. Although it can take years to find, it's priceless. It's called self-love.

I agree to meet my mother at Merci, a design store on boulevard Beaumarchais in the 3rd arrondissement. As I walk into its gravelled courtyard, I'm greeted by a charming vintage red Fiat, its open roof filled with flowers and plants. It puts me in a good mood. The large loft space reminds me of interior design shops in Soho. Around me, I see an eclectic array of accessories: delicate silver jewellery, coloured pencils and notebooks, perfumes by Annick Goutal. One corner has been designed to look like a literary café, with second-hand books on sale for only a few euros. I picture myself cracking open a novel while sipping lemonade for hours here on a rainy day.

Upstairs, furniture, lighting fixtures, and kitchenware are artfully arranged. Another area offers designer clothing and accessories. I see my mother descending the main staircase, engaged in a lively conversation with a woman beside her. She waves for me to join her.

"Come, *ma chérie*, you must meet the brains behind this wonderful shop."

She introduces me to the elegant woman. "This is my

daughter, Catherine. She works for Dior," she adds proudly in a loud whisper.

"It's lovely to meet you." I extend a hand. "You've created a store that's tasteful and original."

The owner smiles gratefully and shakes my hand before disappearing to assist other customers.

"All the proceeds go to a charity that helps children in need," my mother says. "Isn't that fantastic?"

"Impressive. What a generous idea."

My mother then takes me up to the home wares section and begins to bombard me with questions. "What do you think of that sofa and that chair? Would this lamp go well with this cushion?" She's like a sniper firing at lightning speed. It's giving me whiplash.

She walks briskly to a wooden table covered with colourful dishes and begins to load her shopping bag with plates and matching tea cups. Then she dashes toward the sale section and proceeds to examine a display of striped cushions.

"Okay," she says, sliding her glasses to the tip of her nose and peeking at her watch. "We need to leave here in five minutes. We have an important rendezvous at Flamant, the furniture store, then we need to run to Caravane. You know, the boutique where Inès de la Fressange shops?" She's out of breath after all this activity.

Whoa, that's one full agenda. So much for enjoying a cup of coffee with a good book in the store café. Accompanying my mother shopping in Paris makes chasing counterfeiters around town look like a walk in the park. I now understand why her client list is growing: not only does she have a good eye, she's extremely passionate about her work. I'm just a bit worried about her frenetic pace.

"The way you're going about sourcing is a bit exhausting, *non*?" I ask tentatively. "Isn't there a more efficient way to shop for your clients? How about doing it online?"

"I do find some things on the Internet," she allows. "L'Heure Bleue, one of my favourite antique shops in Paris, has gone entirely digital. But there's nothing like picking something up in your own hands."

My mind spins, trying to think of ways to help her save time and energy. I look around at the shop's young clientele, and it hits me. "How about hiring a student to do this for you?" I venture as we approach the store counter.

"*Oh non.*" She shakes her head while juggling her purchases. "*C'est pas possible!* You know my clients hire me because they trust my taste. That can't be delegated, *ma chérie.*"

"Okay, whatever you say." I tried. "If you don't mind, I'll go fuel up with a quick espresso while you pay. I'll need it to keep up with the schedule you have planned."

Before I even make it to the café, my mother is at the counter, chatting up sales clerks and handing out business cards. I have to admire her. If she's taught me one thing, it's to follow your dreams; clearly, they know the way.

# Chapter 15

"Ready for Shanghai?" Laetitia marches into our office with two envelopes in her hand. She places them on my desk.

"Excuse me?" I open the envelopes and am surprised to see plane tickets bearing my name and Rikash's.

"Sandrine can't make it on the trip, so she's sending you and Rikash in her place. She wants a lawyer on site in case anything comes up."

"Wow, this is unexpected," I say, stunned.

"You better drop what you're doing and head to the store for a few outfits. You're leaving later today." Her look implies that what I'm wearing would be better suited for a trek in Nepal.

"Okay. When are you leaving?"

"A few hours after you." She tilts her head sideways, then laughs. "I need to take care of the most complex and controversial aspect of the show: the seating chart. It can get nasty." She turns on her stilettos purposefully and disappears into the hallway.

I want to pinch myself. This surprise invitation to one of the most anticipated fashion events of the year has my blood pumping. Sandrine's so generous. She makes my previous boss look like the Wicked Witch of West. I immediately dial Rikash's cell to share the news.

"I know why you're calling, sweetness. Xavier just texted me. I was so juiced up, I almost fell flat on my face in the metro."

"Did you know that we're leaving today?"

"Yes. I'm on my way to pick up a few things from the menswear collection. You better go shopping too, *ma chérie*, if you want to make a good impression in *Vogue Paris*."

The thought of getting my picture taken again sends shivers up my spine, but at least this time we're talking fashion photographers, not criminals.

"Okay. Can you meet me in the Dior boutique in forty-five minutes? I'd like you to help me choose a few things."

I've grown accustomed to having Rikash by my side when I'm picking out outfits for special occasions. His grand sense of style complements my more conservative tendencies.

"That's perfect, dah-ling. It will give me time to attend to the manscaping."

"The what?"

"You know, a bit of man grooming. I need to clean up the superfluous fur. There's a men's spa up the street."

I roll my eyes. "Okay, see you later."

I phone Antoine to let him know about my last-minute trip, but my call goes directly to voice mail. I leave him a message, hoping he won't be upset that I'm leaving on such short notice.

I then email Lisa, whose firm has an established immigration practice. She might have a contact in Paris who can help Yulia. I also text my new young friend to let her know that some help should be on the way soon.

Then I have a flash of inspiration: perhaps while I'm in Shanghai I can visit the areas where fakes are sold. I email Chris, letting him know about my trip and asking for his Shanghai investigator's contact information.

As soon as I fire off the message, I rush down the hallway

to ask Coralie about the protocol for borrowing clothes for company events.

"Take whatever you like—it's one of the perks of working here." She barely turns her head as she types away furiously. I guess everyone is swamped before the big event.

I want to poke my head into Sandrine's office to thank her for this generous gesture, but her office door is closed, so I grab my handbag and head downstairs. If my employer wants me to play dress-up on company time, who am I to refuse?

The majestic Dior boutique adjoins the office on avenue Montaigne. I stop in front of its tall windows and take in the amazing display: breathtaking ball gowns and Lady Dior bags in every colour of the rainbow. I feel like a little girl peering into a candy store. It makes me appreciate the French term for window-shopping, *lèche-vitrine,* which literally means "lick the windows." Frankly, if no one were around, I think I might press my lips to the glass.

I enter the store and am blown away again by its decor: modern design combined with the traditional Dior elegance. Whimsical phrases such as "Look good," "*J'adore,*" and "Orchid in the land of technology" are etched on mirrored glass throughout the front parlour, and there's a private *salon d'essayage* where one can try on items with the help of a personal assistant. A portrait of Mr. Dior is hung over a marble mantle in the midst of the stunning ready-to-wear. I have to imagine he would be happy there.

To my delight, the boutique stocks home wares like delicate hand-embroidered placemats, cherry-patterned porcelain, and pretty, heart-shaped drinking glasses. I examine the display while waiting for Rikash. Shopping in this historic establishment continues to be a superior experience: no wonder Wallis Simpson, the Duchess of Windsor, spent so much time in the private salon. It dawns on me that there's a big difference between the American and European shopping experiences. As Mr. Dior noted, women in America spend enormous sums of money buying in volume but often achieve little luxury; European women, on the other hand, take pride in purchasing a few well-crafted items that they might pass on to a daughter.

Glancing at my watch, I decide to get started without Rikash. I make my way to the ready-to-wear section and advise the gracious and gorgeous sales assistant of the purpose of my visit.

She lights up as she reaches for a pen and paper to jot down the items I decide to borrow. "You're so lucky to be invited to the show in Shanghai!" She heads to one of the racks. "This silk resort dress just came in yesterday—it's sublime. It would be perfect for the occasion."

She points to another dress, this one made of light pink butter-soft plissé leather with scalloped details. "This one would look stunning with your complexion," she says, her ponytail swinging from side to side.

Of all the gorgeous pieces she shows me, it's an antique rose floor-length gown with flowered embroidery that stops me dead in my tracks. I imagine a French actress wearing this to a premiere at the Olympia. The assistant sees my reaction and immediately says, "Gorgeous, isn't it?"

I nod but stay silent. Surely luxe items like this are off limits to employees.

"You should try it on."

"Thank you, but I don't want to waste your time. I'm sure someone famous will want to wear this at the show."

She stares at me incredulously. "You're going to Shanghai! Try it on!" She insists, and I head to the fitting room.

"So, you're from Paris?" she asks.

"Yes, but I worked in New York for a year. I just moved back."

"I can tell you're from here; you appreciate the crafts-manship. I saw you admiring the details of that dress."

"Is that typically French?"

"European women have a greater appreciation for our designs. Most Americans tend to think of them as clothes, not works of art. I know—I see it every day."

A few minutes later, Rikash bursts into the salon with an armload of Dior bags and a big smile on his face. "You won't believe what I picked out," he exclaims, nearly knocking his giant sunglasses from the top of his head in his excitement. "I found the coolest *trompe l'oeil* jeans. They're designed to look as if your fly is permanently open."

"Not surprised you'd choose those," I say, sucking in my stomach as the sales assistant zips up my fancy dress.

"Ooh, gorgeous!" Rikash gushes.

"It looks lovely on you." The sales assistant and Rikash are both beaming as I stand in front of the tall mirrors.

"She could be the next Bond girl, given her new line of work." Rikash looks over his shoulder before continuing. "She's involved in anti-counterfeiting raids and deals with international criminals." He finishes in a whisper, as if I were a secret agent.

I really don't think we should be talking about this. I

give Rikash a look and raise my index finger to my lips as I step off the podium and slip out of the dress. I try to change the subject. "Okay. You can count on me to bring it back in mint condition. Would you mind wrapping it up? I want to make sure it doesn't get damaged in my suitcase."

"Is that all you're getting?" Rikash looks disappointed.

"Yes, why? I'm going home to pack after this." How much can I possibly need?

"No, you're not; there's no time for that. We have to go back to the office to pick up our travel visas, then get to the airport. We need to be there a few hours before our flight."

My heart sinks: this means I won't get to see Antoine before I go. My telephone screen is still blank—he hasn't called.

Rikash reads my mind. "Don't worry, sweetie. I'm sure he won't be upset. You've left the office for last-minute trips a gazillion times before."

I think back to the kind of business trips I took while working at Edwards & White. I was often called on to leave the office with no notice to jet off to dreary, far-flung industrial parks, carrying nothing more than the firm's emergency travel kit and cheap drugstore stockings. Considering the divine dress I've just tried on, it's obvious that my new mode of business travel is more civilized.

I pull myself together. "You're right. I've done it before, and so has he. I'm sure he won't mind." I turn to the sales assistant. "In that case, I need a few more items to take with me."

During a speedy tour of the ready-to-wear section, I pick out a navy blue pantsuit, the pink leather dress I spotted earlier, a nude sequined top, a funky nautical-style jacket, some jeans, and two pairs of shoes. The clerk slips a lipstick and matching nail polish into my bag.

I leave the boutique carrying thousands of dollars of couture but still feeling a bit disappointed that there's no time to stop at the apartment. I've never felt comfortable wearing head-to-toe designer garb. And not saying goodbye to Antoine feels wrong.

"What?" Rikash asks, seeing my conflicted expression.

"It feels awkward to be leaving for China without speaking to Antoine."

"What's the big deal? You two lived in different countries for months before you moved back to France, and now you're living together. A few days apart won't kill you."

"It's just that . . ." I look away. "We got into a bit of an argument over the weekend." I stare at the pavement.

"What about?"

"About me sending him Dior files or, more to the point, not sending him any."

"Oh." He raises his eyebrows and drops his bags on the sidewalk to hug me. "I'm sorry the subject has reared its ugly head."

"He brought it up during our weekend away, and I got upset. I guess it just shows his persistent nature. Generally, that's something I love about him."

"Don't worry about it, sweetie. Everything will be fine. God knows he's crazy about you."

"I know. It's just tough trying to please everyone. This new job means so much to me, and I don't want Sandrine to think I'm putting my interests first by lobbying for Antoine."

Rikash looks down at his watch and says, "Wait right here. Don't move." He dashes to the door of the Dior offices and hurries inside.

I wonder what he's up to now, but I wait patiently, keeping an eye on his bags, until he rushes back out and hands me an envelope. Looking inside, I see our visas. "How did the company manage to arrange these so fast?" I ask.

"Important connections. We're playing in the major leagues now, remember?" He looks around, then whistles for a taxi that's idling down the block.

It's nearly impossible to obtain international travel documents this quickly; everyone knows that bureaucracy moves at a snail's pace. Rikash is right: we *are* in the major leagues.

We wriggle into the cab, juggling our bags. "Sabbia Rosa on rue des Saints-Pères." Rikash gives the taxi driver a serious look. The driver responds with a grunt, clearly unaware that he's on his way to the city's mecca of women's lingerie.

"Well, you need something fabulous to wear under that dress," Rikash responds to my look of surprise.

"Do we have time for this?"

"Why do you think I ran all the way up to our office and back, dah-ling? New lingerie is guaranteed to make you feel better."

We make our way to a tiny side street, and Rikash asks the driver to stop in front of one of the most beautiful lingerie shops in the city. Sabbia Rosa is Italian for "pink sand." It's sort of fitting: my reluctance to shop here is disappearing as quickly as I would be if I were standing in quicksand.

"I've never actually been in here," I say, looking around. "It's divine."

"I told you, pussycat. Have I ever let you down?"

"Never. But I could have picked up something at the airport."

He shakes his head. "Oh dear, don't tell me you've developed that American habit of buying Hanes value packs at the drugstore. That is *not* sexy."

"Of course not, but I don't want us to miss our flight because of this."

"We have time." He points to a gorgeous white lace camisole and matching bottoms. "I read somewhere that French men prefer white and ivory undergarments because it makes women look pure and virginal." He moves down the aisle. "Not that I would know anything about that; virginal isn't my style."

The store is full of gorgeous lace slips displayed on silk hangers. I pick out a dusty pink ensemble made from the finest French lace, plus a few more practical items to carry me through our voyage. True luxury really is in the details.

At the airport, we learn that we're flying first class, and Rikash does a little dance near the check-in counter, endearing himself to the entire Air France staff. As we hand over our luggage, I mentally say *au revoir* to my expensive loot, hoping it will make it safely to Shanghai.

We pick up a few bottles of Perrier at the Air France lounge, and I'm relieved when my phone finally rings. But it's Chris, not Antoine. My heart drops, but Rikash's face brightens when he catches a glimpse of my call display.

"Ooh, it's Mr. Hottie. Pick up, quick."

"Hi, Chris. You got my message about meeting an investigator in Shanghai?" I turn toward the lounge windows for a bit of privacy, but I can feel Rikash breathing down my neck.

"Yes, no problem. I'll hook you up with one of my guys. He can take you to the right places. I'll have him call you tomorrow at your hotel. Just send me the details, okay?"

"That's fantastic. Will do, thank you."

"You have a great trip, okay? And give my regards to Rikash."

I hang up. It was nice to hear a friendly voice.

Rikash stares at me expectantly. "So?"

"I'm meeting one of his employees in Shanghai for a bit of espionage."

"Not about that." He points at himself.

"He says hello."

"Ah, I'm finally getting somewhere. I haven't given up on him. It just takes longer for some men to come around."

"Really? I didn't think you were the patient type." I think back to my recent trip to Aubervilliers with Chris and feel ridiculous for being attracted to a man Rikash is into.

"I'm not, but I have several side projects keeping me occupied. There's one waiting for me in Shanghai, in fact." He smiles naughtily.

"Oh? Who is it now?"

"A nightclub singer by the name of Zaza. He holds the keys to the city."

"Oh dear, should I be worried?" I'm subtly referring to one of his ex-lovers back in New York, a colourful character who stole Rikash's heart—and, later, his expensive camera too.

"No, mother."

"I'm just trying to keep you out of trouble."

My phone rings again, and this time, I sigh with relief. "Antoine, I've been trying to reach you for the last four hours. Where have you been?"

"I was in a partners' meeting." His tone is stone cold.

"It didn't go well, I presume?" I find myself pacing in front of the newspaper rack.

"No, it didn't. I was hoping we could discuss it at home tonight."

Guilt washes over me. For the past ten years I haven't thought twice about leaving on spur-of-the-moment trips when work demands it. But maybe now that I'm in a committed relationship, I shouldn't be taking off like this. I can't help but feel horrible about leaving Antoine behind.

"I'm sorry. I just couldn't say no. I was asked to take Sandrine's place at the company events."

"Mmm-hmm."

I need to try harder to sell this. "The really fascinating part will be visiting some of the markets where knock-offs are sold. It will make the trip totally worthwhile—professionally, I mean."

He's silent for a long moment. "I guess. When are you coming back?"

"In four days. I'll make it up to you, I promise."

Another awkward silence ensues. This cool conversation is making my heart hurt, and it only makes matters worse that I'm stuck in a noisy airport lounge, where it's impossible to really talk.

"I'll bake that soufflé you love," I whisper into the phone, trying to lighten the mood.

"I'll see you when you get back." His voice is flat, then the line goes dead.

As we're called for boarding, the knot in the pit of my stomach feels a bit tighter.

"Would you like another cappuccino, Mademoiselle Lambert?" The stewardess has asked three times in the last two hours. I've taken advantage of the lengthy flight to review the company's copyright protection policies. The collected documents are about as thick as the *Merriam-Webster's Dictionary.* I can't sleep anyway, between the upsetting conversation with Antoine and Jeffrey's trial looming. Rikash has been sleeping like a baby in his airline-furnished Balmain pyjamas.

"Dah-ling." Rikash removes his silk travel mask and gives me an exasperated look. "If you continue drinking caffeine at this pace, you'll be bouncing off the Great Wall."

"The Great Wall is in Beijing, not Shanghai."

"I know, that's my point."

"Sorry if I woke you. I'm using this quiet time to get a bit of work done."

"Can't it wait? You need to get some sleep or you'll be a wreck when we land and you'll look terrible at the show."

"I'll wear sunglasses. Nobody will know I'm there."

"Come on, sweetie, this is our big chance to mingle with the in-crowd at Dior. You want to show those fashionistas that you know what time it is, don't you?"

"I do know: I'm on borrowed time," I say, feeling anxious about everything that's going on.

"Oh, please. Enough with the drama."

I hesitate. I haven't yet told Rikash about Jeffrey's indictment. It's not that I don't trust him; I'm just a bit tired of rehashing everything that's been jumping around in my head.

He gazes at me with his deep brown eyes and, sensing my uncertainty, puts his hand on my shoulder so kindly that I can't help but spill it.

"Jeffrey's been indicted."

"Ooh, that's great news!" Then he frowns, seeing my uneasy face. "Why aren't you thrilled about this?"

"It means that my letter to the SEC will probably come out publicly, and I'll have to testify at the trial. You know I've been trying to put the whole thing behind me."

"Of course I do." He pats me on the knee. "But the

sooner he gets sent away, the sooner you can move on with your life."

I know Rikash is right, but I'd feel much better if I didn't have to get my hands dirty and testify in court. The initial heartbreak and embarrassment were bad enough; I really don't want to relive it all—publicly, no less.

The stewardess arrives with my cappuccino, served, of course, on a crisp white serviette next to a mango tartlet, and I give her a grateful nod.

I try to gather my thoughts. "You're right. I'm just exhausted by all my new responsibilities, including being a decent girlfriend, which I'm not succeeding at, apparently."

"Oh, come on. Don't be too hard on yourself. How many times has Antoine flown off on business at the last minute?" He shakes his head and takes a sip of my cappuccino. "It seems to me that he's acting a tad needy these days." He then proceeds to drink the entire cup.

"Excuse me? I believe that was my coffee."

"Not anymore, baby doll. We have to discuss your personal life." He puts away his travel mask and matching ear plugs. "And we have a solid ten hours to do so." He waves to the stewardess, signalling for her to bring us another round of coffees.

As he starts to turn his attention back to me, a young steward appears out of the blue, selling duty-free products. He's tall, with a chiselled jaw and a taut torso, toned upper arms peeking out of his short-sleeved uniform. Rikash is captivated and stops him mid-aisle. "Hello, handsome. What are you selling?"

"Whatever you ask for, you shall receive," the young man replies flirtatiously.

Oh boy, here we go again. I mentally say goodbye to the promised intimate conversation and pick up a copy of *Air France Madame* magazine.

"I'm looking for some moisturizer. Flying makes my skin flaky," Rikash offers eagerly. "What would you recommend?"

The steward pulls at least five boxes from his trolley and begins a comparative demonstration that would rival the work of the most talented Avon lady, dabbing samples onto his forearm and leaning over my head for Rikash's benefit. "They're all-natural: no parabens, no phthalates," he enthuses.

"And no shame," I mutter under my breath.

The steward provides Rikash with the prices, the product ingredients, and his phone number. The other cabin staff are forced to circumvent the grand beauty product demonstration with their dinner trolleys, creating a kerfuffle in the aisle and provoking a few dirty looks from the other passengers. I give Rikash an evil glare, pull out my D. Porthault travel pillow, plug in my earphones, and select a different kind of romantic comedy to watch on the touch screen in front of me. There's nothing quite like a Hollywood movie to make you forget your own romantic foibles.

# Chapter 16

"He's very ku." The young woman behind the reception desk at our hotel nods toward Rikash, who's decked out in a three-piece suit and a striking grey fedora. The look is *GQ* meets New Orleans jazzman.

He turns to me, clearly satisfied. "It's the Chinese slang for 'cool.'"

We're checking into the Okura Garden Hotel, located in Shanghai's French Concession, an area of the city once administered by the French consulate. It has since been reclaimed by the Chinese government but retains its Gallic charm, with tree-lined streets and quaint boutiques, art galleries, and stylish bars and restaurants. In the Second

World War era, Shanghai was known as the "Paris of the East"; now it's often called "China's New York."

On our way to the hotel, I was blown away by the city's spectacular skyline—dotted with landmarks such as the jewel-like Oriental Pearl Tower and the Lego-style Pudong skyscrapers—as well as the energy that emanates from the city streets. Peering out onto the busy sidewalks, I can understand why companies like Dior are investing heavily in new retail outlets and splashy events here: a new and lucrative generation of shoppers is emerging. I have read that, by 2014, the Chinese are likely to displace the Japanese as the world's predominant consumers of luxury goods. As we drive past Plaza 66 and the Bund, two of the city's exclusive shopping areas, it's clear to me why we're here this week.

"*Mais c'est pas possible!*" A tall man impeccably dressed in a newsboy cap, dark Wayfarer sunglasses, and a grey tweed suit calls out to Rikash from behind a cart of Louis Vuitton suitcases.

"*Ah, mon cher,* it is possible!" Rikash saunters to the man and leans in for an air kiss. "How are you? You look smashing, as always. I can't believe you're in Shanghai."

"I wouldn't miss it for the world. I'm a photographer—I

follow the beautiful crowd. The question is, what are *you* doing here?"

"*Moi?*" Rikash places his right hand on his slim waist. "I have a fabulous new job at Dior." He wiggles his hips proudly.

"*Ah bon!* Since when?" His friend takes a step back.

"It's only been a few weeks, but I've been so busy, it feels like years. And I've loved every minute of it." He waves me into the conversation.

"Edouard, I'd like you to meet Catherine, my charming boss."

"It's so lovely to meet you." He kisses my hand. All this gallantry makes me feel like we're in a movie set in La Belle Époque. I wish I was wearing a bustle skirt, and consider curtseying. "*Enchantée, Edouard.*"

"I met Edouard in New York at a party during Fashion Week," Rikash fills me in.

"I guess that means you're attending the show tomorrow?" Edouard says.

"*Absolument.* We're in the second row," Rikash whispers, his eyes wide.

"*Ah non!* I'm so jealous! I'm in the bullpen with the rest of the photographers."

One's seating at a runway show tells the world where you stand in the international fashion pecking order. Being a newcomer to this scene, I must admit that I'm quite proud of our second-row status.

"I'll see you there, *mon ami.*" Rikash air-kisses Edouard as we move on.

I look around the lobby. The crowd is uniformly lean, leggy, and clad in clothes that are black, tight, and expensive. I feel a surprising surge of adrenaline to be part of it all.

"So, dah-ling, are you up for cocktails with my friend Zaza tonight? We're heading to the Velvet Lounge with Laetitia, Xavier, and the rest of the PR team."

"Sorry, I'll be turning in early tonight. I'm exhausted from the flight, and I have an early conference call with Chris's local contact. Don't forget we have lots on the agenda for tomorrow."

Our stay in Shanghai was going to be a whirlwind four days. Within the next ninety-six hours, there would be a fashion show, the opening of a new store, and a celebrity-filled party to celebrate a Dior retrospective at a contemporary art museum.

"Suit yourself, sweetie, but Zaza has access to all the VIP

parties, so don't complain tomorrow when you find out you've missed all the fun."

"Don't worry, I won't. And don't stay out too late; we're representing Sandrine at all the events, so we need to be good. Promise me I won't smell anything suspicious on your breath in the morning."

"I promise." He turns around to show me the fingers crossed behind his back.

"The distribution channels have become less visible since the Xiangyang Road market shut down. It was a major sales area for fake merchandise," Frank Lee advises me on the phone early the next morning.

I woke up feeling rested after a quiet evening in my room munching on mini-bar snacks and enjoying the hotel's indecently-high-thread-count sheets. I'd resisted calling Antoine. Though I was still worried about his mood, I thought some space before we spoke again might be a good idea.

"Can you take me on a quick tour of one of the markets? I'd love to see how counterfeit merchandise is sold here."

"Yes, of course. The Nanjing Road market is known for its high-quality fakes. Why don't we go there?"

"How about tomorrow afternoon? I'm tied up most of today, but there's some room in my schedule then."

"Okay, Ms. Lambert. I'll pick you up at your hotel at one o'clock."

After I hang up, I fall back into the luxurious bed, thinking how lucky I am. During business trips for Edwards & White, I needed to be reachable at all hours of the day and night for conference calls, but today I feel free to manage my time as I please.

I'm grateful that I met Chris. His easygoing nature and helpful attitude are a breath of fresh air in the French business environment, which I have to admit has its own brand of rigidity.

I also reflect on my personal life and how far I've come in the last year. I've gone from having my heart mangled by a fraudster to finding Antoine, a loving and caring partner. Despite our petty squabbles, in my heart, I know that we're meant to be together. I guess it took me a while to finally understand the wise words of one of my all-time favourite television characters, Carrie Bradshaw, when she suggested that it's easier to spot a knock-off bag than a counterfeit love.

# Chapter 17

"Isn't this grand?" Rikash marvels as we take our seats at the day's first and most spectacular event: the runway show. We're seated in a twenty-thousand-square-foot tent on the Bund, along the Huangpu River. The space is luxuriously decorated with thousands of pink roses in honour of the company's new Rose bag. Hair stylists and makeup artists have been flown in from all over the globe to make this one of the glitziest fashion events of the year. International celebrities mingle with local models and actresses, most dressed in the season's collections and posing for the photographers and bloggers. It's obvious that the event has been orchestrated with military precision, and I take a moment to acknowledge Laetitia's organizational skills. I wink as Rikash fixes a pink flower to the lapel of my exquisite Dior pantsuit.

The fashion crowd reminds me of Yulia. "I forgot to tell you, I met with the model from the anti-aging cream ad before we left," I tell Rikash.

"Oh? What about?" Rikash turns my way while keeping his eyes on the A-list attendees taking their seats.

"Her name is Yulia. She asked me for legal advice; she's having immigration issues."

"Aw, that's sweet of you. I'm sure our marketing team will be grateful."

"That's not why I'm doing it. I just want to help out a girl who's a bit lost in the big city." As I say this, it occurs to me that I was pretty lost myself when I arrived in New York. Luckily, I had Rikash, Lisa, a decent amount of self-confidence, and some experience under my belt. It all makes me want to help Yulia even more.

We've been seated for twenty minutes when the crowd suddenly quiets and the mood intensifies. I assume this means that the show's about to start. But then the editor-in-chief of *Vogue Paris* and her assistant make a dramatic entrance and sit down just in front of us on the spindled gold chairs. The photographers go nuts, and I'm now officially blind.

"God just walked in," Rikash declares, gawking at our neighbours. "I could kiss the ground those two women walk on and breathe their second-hand smoke all day."

"Just don't forget that you have another day job."

"As Oscar Wilde put it, *Looking good and dressing well is a necessity. Having a purpose in life is not.*" He crosses his legs and fans his face with the invitation.

I look at the women sitting in front of us. It's obvious that the real stars of the show are not the supermodels but the editors. Top fashion editors have become celebrities in their own right. They receive perks like chauffeured limos, private jets, island vacations, and even invitations to the White House. More influential than models and bloggers, they can make or break a designer's career, and they have access to decision-makers in Washington and Hollywood alike.

A flock of young men begin to run around the tent, asking everyone in hushed voices to take their seats. Donna Summer's hypnotic "I Feel Love" blares out from overhead. Soon the models are sashaying down the catwalk in a rainbow of pastel shades and an avalanche of rich fabrics. Their makeup is dramatic: pale foundation punctuated by shiny red lips and dramatic eyebrows that remind me of the 1950s model Suzy Parker. I wonder if Yulia would have liked being in this show. I hope Lisa has found someone willing to help her out.

As the models slink by in their whirling skirts and swooshing dresses, Rikash leans in toward me to share a bit of context. "This collection is a tribute to some of Dior's earlier, classic collections: Corolle and Sirène."

The soundtrack alternates between disco and urban jazz, and concludes with French chanteuse Françoise Hardy's "Tous les garçons et les filles" for the evening gown finale. Emma Huan, a top local model, is wearing a dazzling layered red wedding dress, according to Chinese bridal tradition. Her beauty and the dreamy chiffon confection leave me breathless.

Rikash's hand reaches for mine as we take in this special moment. When the music stops, though, my appetite for beauty feels somehow unsatisfied. The fashion shows today are significantly briefer than they once were. We've been here for only twenty minutes. I read in the company archives that, back when Christian Dior presented the collections in his intimate salon, clients sometimes slipped out to get their hair done during the show, returning in plenty of time to catch the finale. Today, one couldn't dash out for an emergency toilet break without missing the entire show.

After Wolfgang takes a bow and salutes the roaring crowd, Laetitia asks us to keep the momentum going by moving on to the next event, a luncheon where Champagne will be flowing by the caseload and a trunk show will allow local guests to purchase the runway looks. As we leave the tent, I take a moment to congratulate Laetitia on a job well done.

She beams with pride. "*Merci!*" She pats me on the shoulder with the back of her silk glove, which matches the lace detail of her blush pink dress. She looks more relaxed than the last time I saw her, and I can understand why. For me, working in fashion is fun and loose compared to my job on Wall Street, but for others in my office, it's dead serious.

At the luncheon venue, a grand hotel atrium, I grab a Champagne flute from a passing tray. "That was sublime, wasn't it?" I enthuse to Rikash. "But it was too short; it left me wanting more."

"Yes, like most of my one-night stands."

"Speaking of which, how was the Velvet Lounge?" Rikash hasn't spilled on his big night out yet.

He replies by raising his eyebrows lasciviously.

"Okay, let's hear the details."

He looks around. "Well, it was a bit scandalous."

I brace myself for the worst. "Oh?"

"I dirty-danced with everyone and kissed Xavier *and* Zaza," he whispers. "And they almost got into a fight over me!" He shrugs his delicate shoulders. He knows he's irresistible. Clearly, neither of them could help themselves.

"Okay, so you caused a commotion on the dance floor. What else is new?"

"Laetitia had to intervene to break it up. She was a sweetheart."

I roll my eyes. "Whatever you do, don't put your job in jeopardy."

"Don't worry, sweetie, it was just an innocent flirtation fuelled by a few dirty martinis."

I shake my head, noting his suspect use of the words "innocent" and "flirtation" in the same breath. "Whatever."

We clink our glasses, giggling, as Edouard takes our picture for *Women's Wear Monthly*.

We spend the rest of the day schmoozing with the in-crowd, greeting local business figures, and rubbing elbows with senior management. Whatever my initial hesitations, the trip now feels completely worth the effort. I really feel part of the team. Even Laetitia has warmed up and has offered to take me on a tour of the fine jewellery atelier when we get back.

We end the day with a party at the spectacular Museum of Contemporary Art in People's Square. I'm over the moon as I slip into my rose chiffon Dior gown and Sabbia Rosa lace *dessous*. When we arrive at the museum, a thousand flashbulbs go off. Rikash smiles for the camera like a Hollywood actor hitting the red carpet on Oscar night. He slips my cashmere shawl off my shoulders, whispering, "Sophia Loren once said, *A woman's dress should be like a barbed-wire fence: serving its purpose without obstructing the view.*"

We're dizzy by the time we enter the museum.

"Dah-ling, you look absolutely ravishing." Rikash makes me twirl around in front of Richard Avedon's *Dovima with Elephants*, a photograph of a model dressed in a black Dior gown with a flowing white sash. She's stretching her arms out toward two enormous pachyderms. "This print was apparently bought by Dior for over a million dollars at Christie's last year," Rikash tells me.

We walk toward a giant oval video installation decorated with a wide white ribbon. We come across a digital "book" where one can peruse Dior's memorable words about beauty and fashion, then find a wall-sized star-shaped installation fitted with a tiny camera in its centre. Peering into it, I see a parade of Hollywood celebrities, including Grace Kelly and Elizabeth Taylor in footage from the golden age of movies, Nicole Kidman in her classic, close-fitting Galliano at the Oscars, and Natalie Portman in a dreamy emerald green gown.

Rikash's attention is drawn by something on the other side of the room. "If you'll excuse me, I have some unfinished business to take care of," he tells me, then makes a bee-line for the bar, heading straight for Xavier, who's dressed in a sharp black tuxedo and making sweet eyes at him.

I catch a glimpse of Charlize Theron chatting with some company executives. As I take another sip of Champagne, I find myself wishing Antoine were here to share this dazzling, over-the-top moment with me. I take a peek at my phone. *Génial!* I've received a text message from him: *Sorry for being in a sour mood. I really miss u. Can't wait to c u when u get back. Luv, A.*

We're in sync again. I'm so relieved. I text him back, letting him know that I can't wait to be back in his arms and adding, *Tu me manques*. The French version of "I miss you" literally means "You are missing from me." In my opinion, the expression really does justice to the ache you feel when you're longing to be with someone. That's how I feel right now.

I chat a little more with some of our senior managers. To my surprise, one of them praises my work on the raid in Aubervilliers. I silently raise my glass to the room before slipping out the back door and heading back to my hotel room for a luxurious soak in the tub.

# Chapter 18

"The most shocking thing I've seen during a raid? Well, once I walked in on a room full of tired, sick children who were all under the age of ten. They were making fake handbags and were actually shackled to the old sewing machines they were working on. It was awful."

Frank Lee and I are walking toward the market. As planned, he's filling me in on the lay of the land in the world of Shanghai counterfeiting.

"What happens to those poor kids afterward?" It's pretty horrifying.

"They probably get hired by someone else to do the same thing. These children are dirt poor, and what they earn manufacturing fakes probably feeds their entire families."

"Is anything being done to change this?"

"Chinese officials have been trying to crack down on child labour, but it's difficult to get them to prioritize the issue, since counterfeiting is such a lucrative industry. It employs thousands of people, conditions notwithstanding, so local governments are slow to act. But the good news is that there's now an international initiative under way to raise money for these children's education. It's a well-publicized non-profit organization that's gaining visibility."

I nod back. It's something.

When we reach the market, I'm surprised to see two big posters pasted outside the main door. They come from the Shanghai Administration of Commerce and Industry and are written in English, reminding commercial tenants that it's illegal to sell counterfeit goods on the premises. Those who contravene this rule will be investigated and prosecuted, apparently. The posters include a long list of the most frequently copied luxury brands and logos.

"I thought you said we would find fake merchandise here," I say.

"Don't worry, we will. They just put those posters there to cover their backs with international law enforcement. As you can see, the notices are written in English, not Chinese, so they're pretty meaningless." Frank lights up a cigarette as we walk along the aisles.

We wander further into the market, and I'm overwhelmed by the quantity of stuff for sale. This place makes Canal Street look like a village general store. There are even electronic gadgets, such as iPods and iPhones. I can't tell they aren't the real thing and am reminded of a recent news report claiming that Chinese counterfeiters have gone a step further, opening flawless fake Apple stores that even the employees believe to be real.

"After knocking off luxury products like expensive handbags for years, criminals are discovering there's money to be made in faking the more ordinary." Frank points to a stack of fake Angel Soft toilet paper.

"I guess counterfeiters are feeling the economic pinch like the rest of us. They're downgrading?"

"Absolutely. They follow economic trends."

We walk past a man dressed in a black T-shirt and jeans who's giving me a look that makes my skin crawl. As soon as I catch him staring, he runs off in the opposite direction. Should I be worried about my safety? At least I'm wearing my new underwear from Sabbia Rosa—it makes me feel like I'm ready for anything.

Frank picks up a poorly designed copy of an iPod and points to a feature that gives it away: a large on-off button added to the front of the device. "You see, the Chinese like to add their personal touch to American design," he adds, only half joking.

Sensing my uneasiness, he tries to lighten things up by sharing a bit of local gossip. "Did you hear that one of the big Italian luxury brands is suing a local salesman for selling fake merchandise to the Canadian singer Cecily Dutton?"

"No, why is that?"

"The store caught the media's eye when Cecily was pho-tographed by the *Shanghai Morning Post* picking up about fifty knock-off bags when she was here for a concert."

I'm appalled that a celebrity would bother with fakes. She can afford a private jet and multiple homes, so why buy counterfeit goods made of shoddy materials?

"I'm glad she got caught on film. Hopefully she won't do it again. The salesman, either."

Frank sees me looking around impatiently and reads my mind. "The vendors are more careful these days, so you won't see much Dior on display. You need to specifically ask for it."

He stops a stylish-looking young woman and asks her something in Chinese. She gives me a long, suspicious look, then points in the opposite direction. Before we can thank her, she has disappeared.

Frank signals for me to follow him. We meander past stalls filled with toys and home accessories and, eventually, women's apparel. Here we find row upon row of quilted bags in a rainbow of colours hanging from the ceiling, along with matching key chains and wallets. Frank stops at the first handbag stall to ask the vendor if he has any Dior. The vendor shoves a photocopied catalogue of last year's collection across the counter toward us while dialling his phone. I'm aghast that he has the gall to use an authentic catalogue to sell his fake stuff, but try to maintain my composure. I want to see how this plays out. Frank looks at me and I point to a picture of a black Lady Dior bag and a matching wallet. The young man nods and asks how many we want. I hold up the fingers of one hand for five.

As we wait for the loot to arrive, Frank fills me in further. "I'm not sure if you're aware of this, but genuine links have been established by Interpol between counterfeiting and known criminal organizations such as the Russian and Albanian mafias, the Japanese Yakuza, the Chinese triads, the Italian Camorra, and even the Turkish clans." He looks around to make sure no one can overhear us.

"Yes, so I understand. It's scary to think that these are the folks we're up against, *non?*"

Before Frank can answer, we see the vendor sprinting down the aisle with several large bags in hand, leaving a trail of torn catalogue pages in his wake. Two young Chinese women are close behind, trying to pick up discarded pages from the ground.

Frank gives me a perplexed look. "I wonder what gave us away." He walks around the counter and pulls a red curtain aside to reveal poster-size photos of Rikash and me with thick red lines across our faces. They're like No Smoking signs, but with our faces magnified for all to see. At the bottom are Chinese characters that Frank translates for me: *Be careful! They take your stuff!* Weak in the knees, I grab onto the counter with both hands while trying to catch my breath.

"I guess you and Cecily Dutton have something in common," Frank jokes, trying to calm me down. "A souvenir photo from the markets of Shanghai."

# Chapter 19

"The sooner you deal, the sooner you'll heal," Rikash advises me via Skype two days later.

I received an email from Frédéric in the middle of the night just after my traumatic market incident asking that I return to Paris early to attend a meeting with the eShop lawyers. I was wide awake and in a state of anxiety when the message came in, and was more than ready to jump on the next plane home. Within fifteen minutes, I'd rescheduled my flight and my bags were packed. Rikash stayed behind to help Laetitia with the last corporate event.

"It was traumatic, seeing my picture on a wanted poster. It made me feel like an outlaw cockroach. Aren't you even a bit concerned about having your face all over China? God knows where else our pictures are hanging."

"The American men's Olympic swim team locker room would be nice." He winks theatrically into the tiny camera.

"Stop it, this isn't funny," I chastise him. "I'm really upset about this. I've had nightmares since I arrived in Paris."

I twisted and turned in my seat the entire flight back, despite downing what felt like the plane's entire stock of red wine. Back home, I've barely managed to get any shut-eye.

"There's no need to worry, dah-ling. It's just a photo taken by a bunch of hoodlums. Your face will soon be replaced by another anti-counterfeiting agent or, who knows, maybe a nudie."

I'm comforted by Rikash's insouciance. He manages to soothe my nerves, even under the most nerve-racking circumstances.

"Have you been able to get anywhere with Xavier?" I ask.

"Nope." There's a long pause. "Not even a peck on the cheek." He makes a sad face into the camera. "But I'll try again tomorrow, I promise."

"Don't try too hard." I make a kissing gesture.

"Not to worry, dah-ling. I never have to work at it too

long." He brings his face right up to the camera and makes a loud smooching sound before sitting back. "I do have to tell you about my adventure at the museum party after you left. You'll be very proud of grand old me."

"I'm always proud of you, you know that. What happened?"

"On my way out, I noticed a tiny little shop behind the official museum store. There were handbags in the window. I pressed my nose to the glass, and what did I see? Fake Dior bags! I couldn't believe it. At our own party!" His eyes get wide with excitement. "I could see the shoddy stitching from ten feet away, so I went back to the party to let our president know."

Pretty bold. Rikash's no-nonsense and straightforward way of getting things done is both productive and endearing. With luck, this brave move will further prove what a great hire he is.

"That's amazing! How did he react?"

"You should have seen his face—it turned beet red. He had the museum officials unlock the shop and call the police. Within an hour, all the counterfeit merchandise was gone. He seemed very grateful, told me he'd take me out for lunch. And he's quite the looker for an older man, you know."

"Wow. I'm impressed, and I'm sure Sandrine will be too."

"Thanks, sweetie. I'm delighted you approve. How did it go with Antoine? Was he in a better mood when you got home?"

"He's fine. He's just going through a rough patch at work. He had a delicious home-cooked meal waiting for me when I got back."

"I hope he's not putting too much heat on himself. God knows, that firm isn't worth it."

I'm reminded of the offer I received from Harry Traum, Edwards & White's former managing partner, before leaving New York. He asked me to join the new boutique firm he was founding as a junior partner. I'm relieved once again that I refused. One person suffering from that kind of pressure in our relationship is enough.

"We're going out for dinner tonight. I'll make sure to convey the message." I smile.

"Please say hello for me. And good luck with the eShop meetings. I'll be ready to hit the ground running as soon as I'm back."

"Enjoy the festivities while you can," I say, turning my computer sideways so that he can see the files piled up on his desk.

"I will. In fact, I have a breakfast meeting tomorrow with a *Vogue Paris* editor. Should be fun." He grins mischievously. "See you in Paris, dah-ling."

Just as we sign off, my phone rings. It's Chris.

"I heard from Frank. Are you okay?" He sounds concerned.

"Let's just say that it wasn't exactly what I expected."

"It never is in this business. Don't take it too personally, though. You're not the first and won't be the last to have your picture posted in those markets."

It's hard not to take it personally, but I try to see his point. "Thanks for the support, Chris. I appreciate it."

"No problem. Take care, Catherine. We'll talk soon."

Despite myself, I feel butterflies in my stomach after we hang up. *Merde,* what does this mean?


It's a difficult pill to swallow, but the truth is, you can purchase a fake of pretty much anything these days from the comfort of your flannel pyjamas. Gone are the days when shopping for knock-offs involved shady deals in dark basements that looked like crack dens, or hiding in the back of dingy trucks shrouded by clouds of exhaust. Reports say that most counterfeiting transactions now take place in the digital marketplace, and a simple Internet connection gives you access to a world of fakes.

One consequence is that the customer relations departments at Dior and all the other luxury goods companies have been inundated with complaints from people claiming compensation after purchasing fake merchandise on websites like eShop. Initially, this seemed unreasonable to me, until I visited some of the fake sites, which had been designed to look just like the real deal. Relatively high-priced replicas were for sale, accompanied by photographs copied directly from our company website. Even the most sophisticated shoppers could be hoodwinked by the ruse.

Dior is about to launch a lawsuit that will likely have significant repercussions throughout the luxury industry. It's claiming that the world's largest electronic auction site allows vendors to sell knock-offs of its products without proper verification procedures. Sandrine, Frédéric, and I are preparing for the first meeting with opposing counsel, and I'm thrilled to be involved; this will be a landmark case. I understand why Antoine is interested in representing

Dior in this case, and it makes me sad to think that he won't work on it because of me.

Frédéric interrupts my musing by entering the board-room with several folders in hand. "Had a good time in Shanghai, I presume?" He takes a seat and places his reading glasses on the tip of his nose.

I wonder if I should tell him about the upsetting experience at the market with Frank Lee. Given that Chris works for Frédéric, the news is bound to get back to him sooner or later, so I figure I might as well spill the beans.

"It wasn't all fun and games." I catch myself nervously clutching my hands together.

"Come on, Catherine, don't tell me you actually worked between all that wining and dining?"

His sarcastic tone is a little irritating. I decide to put my cards on the table. "As a matter of fact, I did. I visited the Nanjing Road market with an investigator who works for Chris in Shanghai. I wanted to see first-hand what goes on in China."

He hesitates for a moment before speaking, his crystal blue eyes now looking right through me. He removes his glasses and twirls them in his fingers. "Catherine, I like your work ethic. Not many people would have skipped the martinis to do that."

This is better. It's good to know that I'm beginning to earn his trust. "Thank you. You know, I take my position here seriously. That's why I was pretty frightened when I saw big pictures of me and Rikash plastered on one of the market walls."

He looks at me sympathetically, then says, "I'm sorry to hear that, Catherine. But I'm afraid you'll need to develop a thick skin if you're going to succeed in this position." He takes a deep breath. "You and Rikash should wear bullet-proof vests going forward when you're out in the field. It's non-negotiable."

My heart sinks as I imagine myself dressed in five pounds of Kevlar. Never mind the look of it; the thought of someone shooting at me makes me feel nauseated.

He reads my mind. "I understand how you feel—we've all gone through it—but you don't need to worry. There haven't been any shootings in a very long time." He looks sincere and I believe him. "But you're dealing with criminals, so we can't afford to take any risks. Your safety comes first."

It seems insane that anyone would resort to violence in

connection with fake clothing and accessories, but then, these vendors are also involved in drugs and arms trafficking. We're not just playing cops and robbers here.

"We've all gone through what?" Sandrine asks, taking a seat at the head of the boardroom table. She slipped into the room during our conversation, Coralie following close behind. Sandrine is elegant in a camel-coloured jacket draped over a lilac shift dress with purple platform shoes. A delicate flower-shaped diamond brooch adds the finishing touch. She's the epitome of a French woman's style: exquisite restraint with a glorious touch of individuality.

I haven't seen much of Sandrine lately, and she never did give me any feedback on my counterfeit destruction initiative. It's obvious that I'm now reporting to Frédéric, which is a little disappointing. Sandrine is by far the best role model I've had in my career and is someone I'd like to learn more from. I try to push these feelings aside. She's busy, and I don't want to come across like a spoiled child asking her for more attention.

She tucks a flyaway strand of hair behind her ear, waiting for an answer. I'm frozen in my seat, visions flashing through my head of bullets whizzing by while Rikash and I run for cover.

"Catherine was just telling me that counterfeiters in Shanghai had posted pictures of her and Rikash in a market stall. I told her that, from now on, she should wear a bulletproof vest when she's on a raid," Frédéric said.

Sandrine looks shocked. "You were in the markets in Shanghai?" Her tone is cautious. "You must be careful, Catherine. These people are dangerous. We need to be aware of your whereabouts at all times." She purses her glossy lips.

I'm taken aback. Perhaps I've been taking this job too lightly. Am I putting my life in danger? I wonder what I've gotten myself into: this anti-counterfeiting mission makes swimming with corporate sharks at Edwards & White look like an afternoon at the wading pool.

"I'm sorry. I didn't fully grasp the security risks. I won't try that again without clear instructions." I try to sound unfazed, and decide not to mention Rikash's sting operation the night of the museum party. Neither Frédéric nor Sandrine looks to be in any mood to hear about it.

"*Très bien.*" She nods. "Now, to the business at hand. I understand the eShop lawyers want to try to settle with us today. Good luck with that!" She smiles coyly, a panther about to strike. She may be polished, but she's tough, too.

Coralie says, "I believe the lawyers are waiting outside."

"Show them in." Sandrine gives the room a focused look that sends shivers down my spine. I hope she doesn't turn out to be a control freak like Bonnie, my former boss.

A tall man in grey flannel and a pink Hermès tie walks in with a young female lawyer in a conservative black suit and matching pumps. Her attire reminds me of what I used to wear at Edwards & White. Looking down at my red Dior jacket and flared cream-coloured trousers, I realize how far I've come (at least in terms of dress code).

As introductions are made, Coralie bustles back in with a silver tray full of delicate pastries, which she places in the middle of the table. This is a welcome change from the heavy snacks common in New York meetings: unappealing deli sandwiches, bags of Doritos, and greasy muffins in tacky plastic wrappers. I reach for a chocolate éclair, but everyone stops talking and stares at me, so I set it down on a plate, surreptitiously licking my fingers. I guess at Dior, boardroom food is purely decorative.

"We're here at the request of our client, eShop," the male lawyer begins. "We have instructions to settle this matter before it goes to court. Our client wants to avoid further publicity and expenses. There's been enough media attention in the United States already, so the company's New York lawyers suggested we meet to resolve this."

"Which American firm is handling the case?" I ask, curious.

"We're not at liberty to reveal that at this time," the female attorney replies curtly.

"You're wasting your time," Sandrine declares. She places a manicured hand on her paperwork. "We have instructions from senior management to fight this tooth and nail. Does your client realize that hundreds of thousands of fakes are sold on their website every day? It's a major ongoing financial loss for our company. This has gone on for far too long, despite numerous cease and desist orders. We'll be asking for several hundred million euros. But if your client is willing to write a hefty cheque, by all means, be my guest."

The male attorney stares at Frédéric and me, looking as pale as a sheet. We remain silent as the tension builds palpably.

"Litigation is outrageously expensive," he says tentatively. "And we have an excellent chance of winning this case based on the recent U.S. decision."

"American precedents are irrelevant here," Sandrine insists. "And in any case, we have a large reserve fund set aside for this purpose. It's a priority."

Smoking is illegal in office buildings here, so I'm shocked when Sandrine lights up a cigarette. This is the irony of working with lawyers: they spend their days enforcing certain laws while disobeying the ones that displease them.

The male lawyer stands, picks up his briefcase, and says flatly, "Okay, Sandrine, I guess we're wasting our time here. Let's go." He beckons the female lawyer to follow him out of the room. The young woman's face is now the ash grey of the boardroom carpet. She politely nods to us in lieu of saying goodbye.

Sandrine nods back. "Now that we've taken care of *that*, we need to file the lawsuit with the commercial court right away. Which outside firm shall we retain?" She grabs a glass from the bar next to the boardroom table and taps her cigarette into it.

I want to stand on my chair and scream that Edwards & White has the best intellectual property team in the city, the most aggressive group of litigators, and by far the most talented, hard-working, and savvy lawyer that could ever handle this matter, but I hesitate, and Frédéric speaks up first.

"Let's go with Pineau Larochelle, the firm we normally retain for these matters," he says offhandedly. "Le Furet used them for intellectual property litigation for years, and we have a good relationship."

Sandrine is staring out the window, and I wonder what she's thinking. She turns to Frédéric, taking one last bizarre drag from her cigarette. "*D'accord*, it's settled. Pineau it is." With that, she's out of the room like a flash, Coralie running behind her, carrying the glass Sandrine used as an ashtray.

I'm frustrated and look down at my shoes. Clearly, Pierre Le Furet's influence is still felt in our department. It's official: Antoine won't get to work on this case. My heart sinks at the thought of telling him.

Frédéric notices the look on my face. "Don't worry, Catherine. She's just under tremendous pressure. She's been in meetings with senior management all day long these last few weeks." He pauses, then continues, "Sandrine thinks very highly of you." He stops in the boardroom doorway. "Oh, before I forget, I'll send you the catalogue for the security vests. It's not nearly as glamorous as our resort collection, but it's your life we're dealing with here, not a day at the beach." He winks.

A bulletproof vest might just be what I need to face Antoine later.

*J'adore Paris* 201

# Chapter 20

"How about grabbing an Obama burger at Coffee Parisien after work?" Antoine asks.

This is one of our favourite eating spots, located on rue Princesse, in the heart of Saint-Germain. It has just the right mix of Americana, comfort food, and people-watching. You can even brush up on your American history by reviewing the list of U.S. presidents on your placemat. It reminds me a bit of P.J. Clark's, a fun American pub near my former apartment on New York's Upper East Side.

Coffee Parisien's burgers are so popular that a rivalry has sprung up with Richard's, another trendy restaurant on boulevard Saint-Germain. Coffee Parisien's owner complained in a recent newspaper interview that Richard's outright copied their restaurant concept and menu. Clearly, no business is immune to the perils of plagiarism.

The French were once ashamed to be seen eating burgers, thinking they represented the worst of fast food: no taste, no sophistication. Now, following the lead of certain Michelin chefs, Coffee Parisien has joined the movement to make the burger more noble. It's just another part of the cross-Atlantic love-hate relationship between *les américains* and *les français.*

"That would be lovely," I answer quietly, knowing that our mealtime conversation won't be all that pleasant.

Antoine doesn't notice my tone. "I can be there for seven thirty. *À plus tard, ma chérie.* Can't wait to see you."

I wish Rikash was here to help me prepare for the difficult conversation. I decide to go for a walk along the Seine to clear my head. The right words tend to come to me when I'm strolling along the water. Before I can grab my coat and bag, my phone rings. The caller ID reads "anonymous," and I perk up, thinking it might be Rikash calling from China. But when I answer, I hear only a long pause, accompanied by some heavy breathing.

"Rikash? Is that you?"

The caller remains silent. Just as I'm about to hang up,

a deep, raspy male voice comes on the line. "Lady, lots of people are upset about what you've been doing lately. You need to start minding your own business."

I freeze in my office chair, petrified. There's no one around, and I'm on the receiving end of a threatening phone call. I inhale deeply, collect my thoughts, and try to regain my composure.

"Who is this? What do you want?" I muster my most controlled tone of voice, despite my racing pulse.

"You better leave us alone, or else."

Click, then a dial tone.

"Mmm. Delicious. Now this is what I call a real burger." Antoine takes another bite. "I wonder if Barack Obama is aware that a burger is named after him?" He cutely wipes ketchup off his chin, then takes a sip of his Diet Coke.

It's nice to be eating out with Antoine, but the anonymous caller keeps creeping back into my mind, and I feel beads of sweat forming on my brow. Plus, I need to give Antoine the bad news about the eShop case. While we're eating, though, I try to keep the mood light.

"You're supposed to have that burger with a root beer." I point to my half-empty glass. "That's the complete American burger experience."

"No thanks. You know I think it's disgusting: it smells like my grandmother's bathroom." He's not alone in feeling this way. Lots of people in France think root beer has the aroma of Canard WC, a popular brand of toilet-bowl cleaner.

"Speaking of the American experience, do you miss living in New York, Catou?" He reaches for my hand across the table.

Looking out the window and up at Paris's grey skies, it hits me that I do miss the sunny New York weather, as well as its upbeat, go-getter attitude. "I miss seeing the sun every day." I nod toward the window. "And I never thought I'd say it, but I miss the non-stop adrenaline rush."

"I know what you mean. I miss it too sometimes." He tries to cheer me up. "How about we go see some live music next weekend?"

"I'd love that. It would get my mind off work."

"I hear there are some great bands playing at Le Pompon."

Located in a former synagogue in the lively 10th arrondissement, in the east end of Paris, the quirky little venue is usually full of trendy local types.

"That sounds perfect. I just need to check my agenda and talk to my mother. We're planning another shopping expedition for Lisa's wedding, so she might be in town."

His smile fades. "Catherine, I know you're trying to help out your mother and Lisa, but . . . shouldn't our relationship be a priority? With all your travel and shopping, we hardly ever go out on weekends."

It's true that I've been swamped. Work has been intense, and I've been out at the shops on my mother's behalf in my free time. I can't deny that it's fun and interesting, though; the variety and activity feel as essential to my well-being as breathing. But I decide to avoid rocking the boat. He's going to be upset enough when he hears about the eShop case.

"You're right." I squeeze his fingers tenderly. "Pick a night and I'll be there."

He smiles. "I missed you while you were away in Shanghai. We haven't talked much about your trip. Was it worth it?"

"Absolutely. The runway show was divine, the opening at the museum was spectacular, and the visit to the markets was . . . well, umm . . . educational."

"How so?" He hands his empty plate to the waitress. I

had decided not to tell him about the photographs in the markets because I didn't want him to worry unnecessarily. But after the call today, perhaps my safety really is a concern. And since we have a policy of being honest with each other, it's probably best to share the details with him.

"I learned that Rikash and I are feared throughout Asia," I say jokingly. I want him to know, but I don't want to scare him.

"What do you mean?" He furrows his brow.

"We've been identified as threats to some Chinese counterfeiting operations." I try to downplay the matter, rolling my eyes to make it seem like nothing more than a nuisance. "It's no big deal, really."

He crosses his legs and looks out the window. "I don't like this, Catherine. You were in a country where you don't speak the language. What if you had been kidnapped?" He's imagining the worst.

"I was with a local investigator!" I protest.

"So? Both of you could have been taken away. These are dangerous people you're dealing with here." His voice is getting louder.

I look down at my unfinished Caesar salad. I have other things to tell him, but I don't know where to start.

He reads my mind. "What? Is there something else I should know about?" He nervously runs his fingers through his hair.

I take a deep breath. "I received an anonymous call today," I say without looking up.

"Oh?" I can tell he's taken aback. "What about?"

"I'm not sure. It was a man's voice, telling me to mind my own business. Clearly, someone's not happy about my work."

"A threatening call? *Merde,* Catherine! This is getting out of control! Have you told anyone at the office about this?"

"No, not yet. It happened right before I left." I meet his eyes.

"Chinese counterfeiting operations, threatening phone calls . . . what's next? Your body floating in the Canal Saint-Martin?" he asks, gesturing toward the river.

"I know what I'm doing, Antoine. I realize there are some risks, but I much prefer doing this to drafting prospectuses." I'm trying to appear in control of the situation.

"I know that corporate work isn't as exciting as going on raids, but Catherine, really. You need to tell your bosses about these threats immediately." He points to my phone on the table between us.

"Frédéric knows the risks," I counter. "He's asked me to wear a bulletproof vest from now on." I cringe in anticipation of his reaction.

"What?" Antoine howls, throwing his paper napkin on the table. "He thinks you might get shot? *Putain!*"

The people around us are staring now. Even the chef has stopped flipping burgers behind the grill to listen.

"Antoine, calm down. It's a remote possibility. We're just being overcautious," I whisper, clenching my teeth and beseeching him to lower his voice.

He crosses his arms. "Look, Catherine, I love you, and I think you're doing something very honourable here, but this whole business is run by crooks who wouldn't think twice about getting rid of you. You're dealing with people who have criminal backgrounds. I just don't think it's worth risking your life. There are other interesting jobs in fashion."

I know I'm involved in a dangerous game, but I don't want to give it up. I think long and hard before replying, not wanting to add oil to the fire. I fall back on my heritage: for centuries, French women have been getting what they want by subtly combining their intellectual, psychological, and sensual resources.

"I understand, Antoine. I know you're looking out for me, *mon amour*." I take his hand and slip my fingers gently into his. "But I'm being protected by senior management. That's why they want me to wear a vest. They just want to err on the side of caution." I lean in to kiss his tender lips. "Let's go. I'm in the mood for dessert." I grin mischievously. He stares back at me, then picks up my trench coat from the empty chair next to him. "Okay, you win. You always win." He kisses me on the side of the head as we stand to leave. "But I'm keeping a close eye on you, Mademoiselle Lambert."

The waitress nods goodbye as the chef shoots a loud "Be careful, kids!" in our direction.

Outside the restaurant, while we wait for the light to change so we can cross the street, I notice something unusual: in a car parked across the street, two people are in the back seat, wearing dark sunglasses. At night. Strange.

Once we've crossed, I casually look back and see that one of the two has gotten out of the car and is walking behind us. *Oh mon dieu,* am I being followed, on top of everything else? I get goosebumps. Is it the man who called me earlier? After a few long minutes, I look around again to see if the mystery man is still there, but he appears to have entered one of the cafés along the boulevard. I exhale with relief.

We reach our apartment at last, and it only then hits me that we haven't discussed the eShop lawsuit. I decide to drop it for now; talking about my anonymous caller and bulletproof vests was painful enough.

No sooner have I hung up my coat than Antoine embraces me from behind and begins to kiss me while we stumble toward the couch. He lifts my hair and kisses the back of my neck. As his fingers make their way to the small of my back to remove my Dior trousers, all thoughts about lawsuits and stalkers melt away.

# Chapter 21

"**B**onjour, *ma chérie*. I'm here in the city." My mother's cheery voice blasts through my office speakerphone. "Are you done work for the day? How about joining me for a few hours of shopping for Lisa's wedding? After all, you know your friend's taste better than I do."

Despite my heavy workload, a somewhat frazzled state of mind, and Antoine's protests about my packed schedule, I want to say yes. Our last shopping trip was fun, and accompanying my mother on one of her whirlwind excursions would be a welcome break, and inspiring, too.

"Where are you?"

"In the home decor department at Le Printemps."

"I'll meet you there in half an hour."

Thirty-five minutes later, I enter the famed department store on boulevard Haussmann in the 9th arrondissement. It's known for its breathtaking display windows and the legendary stained-glass cupola above its brasserie. Apparently, in 1939, to minimize the risk that it would be destroyed in bombing attacks, the cupola was dismantled and stored at Clichy, then later restored and registered as a historic monument. I'm in awe of its beauty and magnificence every time I set eyes on it.

I wend my way through the store's luxury offerings until I arrive at the home decor department. I'm blown away by the unique flower arrangements, eye-popping colours, and designer accessories.

I see my mother across the room. She's holding up a pair of vases, pensively peering through them as if looking into a crystal ball.

"Gazing into your future?" I ask, reaching her side.

"*Non, non.*" She shakes her head. "I want to see which one reflects the light in a more natural way. It's very important, you know."

I have to smile. My mother's as much of a perfectionist as I can be when it comes to work.

She puts down the vases and moves in for a hug. "I'm so

happy you could make it, *ma chérie.* I need feedback on my ideas for the wedding."

"Trust me, there's nothing else I'd rather be doing," I say, casually scanning the room for suspicious-looking characters from behind my oversized Dior cat-eye sunglasses, which somehow make me feel safe. "Besides, I needed the fresh air."

"I was thinking of a pastel theme for Lisa's wedding, with pink as the primary colour. It's fresh and feminine, just like your friend."

"That sounds perfect. I'm sure Lisa will be thrilled."

"Okay, so this is what I have in mind." She rolls out her grand plan. "Bouquets of pastel balloons suspended over each table." She lifts her arms over her head and stands on her toes. "Matching candles on candelabras at the centre of each table." She walks around, pointing out pink and blue candles. "We could hand out sparklers to light when the bride and groom arrive in the tent, and I was thinking mint green cashmere blankets to keep the guests warm. You know how chilly it gets in Provence after the sun goes down."

I'm amazed at her enthusiasm. I hope to have half her energy when I reach her age. "That sounds perfect, *maman.* Lisa will be over the moon."

She places her middle finger on the tip of her nose. "I'm not sure about the centrepieces. What do you think? Roses?"

"What about bouquets of lavender? They smell heavenly and would add a different colour accent." There are countless lavender bushes on my mother's property.

As I think about how beautiful it will be, another idea bubbles to the surface. "We could give out locally made French milled soaps as party favours."

My mother's eyes light up. "What a fantastic idea, Catou! Why didn't I think of that?" She flashes a grin.

Dior's newest home collection includes embroidered placemats and napkins with touches of violet and pink. They'd look divine against the white linen tablecloths my mother has chosen. Given that a prominent magazine photographer will be documenting the event, perhaps Dior will lend samples for free publicity. I decide to ask our marketing director.

Working on the wedding with my mother is a stimulating combination of business and creativity. I just hope Antoine will give me the breathing room to do it right.

Once we've scanned Le Printemps' entire home decor department, we leave the store feeling giddy.

"That was efficient! What a team we make!" my mother exclaims, balancing four packed shopping bags.

"You can't imagine how happy Lisa will be. Your home will look breathtaking in these pretty colours."

"That's what my business is about, *ma chérie*. Making homes look beautiful and welcoming."

"How does Christophe handle your busy schedule? Does he mind?" Maybe comparing notes will help me figure this out.

"Mind? Why would he mind? He loves that I'm successful and busy—he knows I wouldn't be happy otherwise." She studies my face, and I immediately regret asking the question. "Why do you ask?" she says suspiciously. She stops in the middle of the sidewalk in one of the city's busiest neighbourhoods and puts her bags down. A few pedestrians nearly trip over them. "I'm speaking from experience, *ma chérie*," she says, putting her hands on her hips. "Never let a man tell you how to spend your time or stand in the way of your aspirations."

"Don't worry. Everything is fine," I reassure her. "It's just that my schedule has been unpredictable lately, and it's taking Antoine some time to adjust. Things will get back to normal soon."

I leave out a few things—that I have moments when I question my relationship and even my move to Paris, and that my life now includes threatening calls and having unflattering pictures of me posted halfway across the globe. When it comes to my mother, some things are better left unsaid.

# Chapter 22

I t's been said that the two favourite pastimes of the French are eating and adultery. Since Rikash and I have no plans to engage in the latter, we're at Bistro Chez Georges to enjoy the former. Located behind the elegant Place des Victoires and its many chic boutiques, Chez Georges serves typical French comfort food: traditional delights such as duck breast with cèpe mushrooms, grilled steak with béarnaise sauce, cassoulet, chicken liver terrine, and endive salad with poached egg.

"I finally found an apartment," Rikash tells me as he takes a seat. "It's perfect—a tiny jewel just like *moi*." He places his serviette on his lap. "My real estate agent found it while I was away in Asia."

"That's great. Where is it?"

"Le Marais, of course. There are a few little changes I want to make, but overall I'm so pleased with it."

"I'm glad you managed to find a place that lives up to your high standards." When it comes to living spaces, Rikash expects nothing less than *Elle Decor*. In New York, his compact, rent-controlled apartment had nothing restrained about it. Vibrant paint colours, contemporary art, 1950s furniture, and artefacts from India made it look like the set of a Bollywood film.

"I like living in a space that reflects my personality." He winks.

"Let me guess: extravagant, bold, and beautiful." I scan the menus as the waiter approaches our table. "I'll have the pepper steak with fries," I say. "What are you having?"

"I'm in the mood for something traditionally French after all that Asian food. I'll have the andouillette AAAAA." He lowers his voice to ask me, "What does the 'AAAAA' stand for?" He shimmies on his chair to the popular Jamie Foxx tune "Blame It on the Alcohol."

"No, that's not it." I smile. "The acronym roughly translates as the 'Amicable Association of Lovers of Authentic Andouillette.'" Knowing how finicky Rikash can be about food, I can barely suppress a giggle.

"What's so funny?"

"Nothing. I'm just surprised you ordered *that*. I thought you were more of a fish and steamed vegetables kind of eater."

"I like experimenting; you know that." He raises his eyebrows to make sure I catch his double entendre.

"I know you do, but I'm not sure you understand what you've just ordered."

"I'm assuming it's some sort of sausage, right?"

"Yes. But not just any sausage. It's made with pork intestines and it can . . . well, you know . . . sometimes smell funny. That's why French chefs serve it with so much mustard sauce. I'm not sure you'll like it."

"Are you kidding me? First you tell me that it's good luck to step in the stuff, and now you're telling me that my food might smell of it! What's wrong with this country?" He waves his fingers in front of his face delicately as if dispelling a foul odour. "I'll tell you what that 'AAAAA' stands for: it means 'absolutely abominable and atrocious animal aberration.'" He makes a mock gagging gesture. "I'm changing my order *tout de suite*." He chases the waiter through the narrow aisles to make sure he isn't eating tripe for lunch. When he returns, he looks relieved. "Thank you for saving my virgin palate from something so ghastly."

"It's been part of French cuisine for centuries."

"Whatever. I miss my green juices." He takes a big gulp of water, presumably to purify his body before chowing down on our rich lunch.

"How was the rest of your trip? Did you track down any other fake goods?"

"I was too busy taking orders from Laetitia. When she found out you had left the country, she claimed me for herself. I had to get an ice sculpture in the form of a J'Adore perfume bottle to a restaurant halfway across the city for an event, and by the time I got there, part of the bottle's cap had begun to melt. I had to drag it into a freezer and wait for it to freeze again. Honey, it was like watching paint dry." He rolls his eyes. "Anyway, I did manage to sneak out for drinks with Edouard."

"And Xavier?"

He shakes his head. "That boy is so not for me. All he did was talk about politics and his views on religion. He is, shall we say, a tad B-O-R-I-N-G. We're just going to be friends, that's all."

"Oh, I'm sorry you weren't able to get anywhere with him." I wink.

"What do you mean, dah-ling? We had sex and it was

pretty hot. All that talking came afterward, and boy did it give me a migraine." He lounges back in his chair.

"Right." I take a sip of Perrier. "I'm glad to hear that you two are back where you started."

"How did the meeting on the website suit go?" he asks.

"Short and not so sweet. It's going to get nasty, I can feel it. The mudslinging has already begun. But that's not why I asked you to lunch. I have something more important to discuss, Rikash." I lower my voice to a whisper and take a quick look around the room. "I think I'm being followed."

He sits up straight. "Noooo, are you serious? Since when?"

"It started with an anonymous call yesterday afternoon. Then, when Antoine and I were on our way home after dinner, I saw two people sitting in the back of a car wearing dark sunglasses. As soon as we crossed the street, a man got out of the car and followed us. I was totally spooked."

"Oh dear. So what did the caller want?" Rikash asks from the edge of his seat.

"He told me that people were upset by my actions—he didn't say who—and to watch myself. It was definitely a threat, Rikash."

"Do you have any idea who it could be?"

"No, but I have a feeling that it might be linked to the vendors we came across on our first raid with Chris. Do you remember how angry they looked? Obviously, they're the ones who sent our pictures to Shanghai."

"Did the caller have an accent or give you any other clues?" Rikash's eyes are now as wide as saucers. He's clearly excited about this: it's an Agatha Christie mystery in the making.

"Not that I could tell, no. It was more American than European, I guess. I just can't figure it out."

"Don't forget that the networks cross continents. I guess accents aren't relevant. Have you told Sandrine or Frédéric about this?"

"Not yet. But they know about the pictures of us in the Chinese markets. Frédéric wants us to wear bulletproof vests from now on."

"Excuse me?" He nearly falls off his chair. "There's no way." He place his hands on his tiny waist.

"We need to take this seriously. I couldn't live with myself if something happened to you," I plead.

After a long pause, he capitulates. "All right. I'll wear that appalling garment, but on one condition: I'm in charge of monitoring all future correspondence with the stalker." He raises one eyebrow for effect, like Sean Connery in *Dr. No.* "You know how talented I am with recording equipment."

"Mmm-hmm." In New York, Rikash spent his free time making documentaries. His last work, about a famous Indian transsexual, was nominated for several prestigious awards.

"I want you to let me track all your incoming calls and emails. We'll nail this creepy dude."

I take a sip of water and gather my thoughts. The idea of having Rikash monitor my correspondence has me worried. "I'm not sure. You know I have complete confidence in your abilities, but this isn't a documentary we're making, and I don't want either of us to lose our job."

Unfazed, he moves in closer, a determined look on his face. "You think we can trust any of our colleagues to get to the bottom of this? We've been down this road before, Catherine, and it's just you and me looking out for each other, remember?"

He knows he's hit my weak spot. I've been stabbed in the back by colleagues in the past. Now I need to protect myself from being stabbed, period.

"I need to find out whether any of this is against company policy," I say, but I feel myself giving in.

He gives me an exasperated look. "We're not violating

any policy. Your life is being threatened, so you need to protect yourself. And I want to be in charge of that." His tone is so commanding, I don't dare refuse.

"Okay, but I don't want any funny stuff, understand?" I wag my finger, trying to show some semblance of authority. Deep down, I know it's completely futile.

After lunch, we stop by one of the few English-language bookstores in Paris, Librairie Galignani. It's on rue de Rivoli and houses an incredible selection of biographies, literature, and international magazines. I'm looking for a book on counterfeiting I read about in *The New York Times*, and Rikash is trying to hunt down *Wired, Wallpaper,* and *Gay Night Out.* We split up at the entrance.

The bookstore's dark wooden shelves hold a collection of nearly fifty thousand titles, and classical music plays softly in the background. The store is known for its fine arts section; even experts come here to shop. I make my way through to the fashion section and take in gorgeous books published by Assouline, Taschen, and Rizzoli, beautifully displayed on round antique tables.

A store clerk points me toward the right shelf, and I climb on a stepping stool to reach for my book. As I'm about to grab it, my cellphone rings. Thinking it's Rikash, I pick up, holding the phone between my ear and my right shoulder. "I just found it. I'll meet you at the cash in a few minutes."

A man's voice—not Rikash's—says, "Nice orange jacket, Miss Lambert. Makes it easy to spot you in a crowd." I freeze on top of the stool, and my hands begin to shake. I look at the screen: a blocked number. My first instinct is to scream out Rikash's name at the top of my lungs. Instead, I climb down and hunch behind a rack of greeting cards. I remind myself that I'm in a public space and need to remain calm.

"Who is this? What do you want?" I say, fingering a postcard of the Eiffel Tower.

"We've spoken before, Miss Lambert. It appears as though you are ignoring my warnings."

"What makes you say that?" I ask coolly.

"Your overzealous colleague is getting involved in matters that do not concern him, and we don't like it."

A thousand thoughts flash through my mind. Was this man in the restaurant? Did he overhear my conversation with Rikash? Is he in the bookstore now? I look around, hunting for anyone talking on a cellphone, but no one fits the bill. Annoyed with myself for being scared, I decide to play tough. "I don't really care what you think. You better stop threatening me or I'll have you arrested."

I hear a chuckle. "Good luck with that, Miss Lambert. You have no clue who you're up against. It would be better for both of you to stay out of our way. You have been warned." The line goes dead.

I stand there, shell-shocked, unable to move for a moment. Then I frantically search for Rikash, finding him near the entrance, flipping through a biography of Elizabeth Taylor.

"It's so sad that she's left us." He shakes his head. "She was beyond fabulous. And look at these jewels." He points to the famous Burton diamond. "Sixty-nine carats, can you believe it?"

I signal for him to drop the book.

"What is it, dah-ling? You're as pale as a ghost."

"I just got another call." I show him my call display.

"From?" He doesn't get it.

"My stalker," I whisper.

"What?" he says, looking around. "Do you think he's here?"

"He might be. He knew I was wearing an orange jacket—he told me so. That totally freaked me out."

"Damn. I wish I had installed the tracking device on your phone right away." He leans in closer. "And I'm convinced I saw someone staring at me from behind that bookshelf." He gestures toward the back of the room.

My stomach is in knots, but I try to calm down. Rikash might be dreaming this up to make it seem like he's landed a starring role in a suspense flick. "Are you sure?" I ask.

"Positive."

He sees that I'm panicked and tries to take control. "Here's the plan. I'm going to leave through the front entrance. You go back to where you were standing when the call came. I'll keep an eye out through the window. We'll see if I can spot him." He puts on his Ray-Bans and turns to walk out of the store.

I clutch my handbag, my eyes on the floor, and scurry back to the fashion section. Out of the corner of my eye, I can see Rikash peering through the store window. I pick up a copy of *American Dior,* feigning interest in the introduction.

I spend five minutes turning pages and looking at pictures before I'm tapped on the shoulder. I let out a shriek so loud everyone in the store turns my way, and spin around to come face to face with a drop-dead-gorgeous stranger who could be Jean Dujardin's twin brother.

"I'm so sorry, mademoiselle. I didn't mean to startle you. I was looking for the historical fiction section and thought you might know where to find it. My apologies." His face is a deep shade of red.

My mind races. This man is French, and the anonymous caller has more of an American accent. Besides, he looks nothing like the man who followed me outside the restaurant the other night. As a matter of fact, he looks like no man I've ever laid my eyes on before. He's sizzling. I'm so embarrassed I want to crawl behind a bookshelf.

"*Je suis vraiment désolée.* I don't know what got into me. I'm a bit jumpy today," I hurry to say. This is clearly not my day: not only am I being threatened by unsavoury characters, but I just made a fool of myself in front of one of the most handsome men in Paris. I put the book back on the display table and try to make up for my faux pas by extending my hand. "Catherine Lambert, lovely to meet you."

"The pleasure is mine. François D'Avignon." He smiles, revealing a friendly set of pearly whites. "I didn't realize I had such an effect on women."

I remember that Rikash is watching me. When I turn his way, I see that he's glued to the window, hands at the sides of his face to block out the sunlight. If I wasn't so far away, I swear I'd see drool at the corners of his mouth. Within moments, he's rushed to my side. So much for apprehending my stalker—now he's become one himself.

"This is my assistant, Rikash. We were on our way back to the office," I ramble on nervously.

"Lucky you to work with such a pretty woman." François shakes Rikash's hand. "Please watch out for her, though—she's a bit anxious." He winks, and I feel my cheeks redden. "Where do you work?" he asks.

"Dior. In the legal department." Rikash edges into the conversation.

"*C'est pas vrai?* I work for Pineau Larochelle. We've been representing Dior for years. I specialize in medical malpractice, but my colleague Robert is working on a few Dior matters at the moment. What a small world." He hands me a business card indicating that he's a partner.

"I look forward to seeing you both again soon. And I'm sorry to have startled you, Mademoiselle Lambert." He hesitates. "Well, maybe not." He bows politely before heading off toward the fiction section.

"Well, we haven't tracked down the evil caller, but we've found a masterpiece." Rikash pats me on the back as we watch François walk away. "With a tushy like that, he can engage in medical malpractice with me any time, if you know what I mean." He shakes his pelvis, humming Olivia Newton-John's "Physical."

"Rikash, this is no time to be joking around. We're being threatened, remember?"

His face falls. "What do you mean 'we'?"

"I didn't want to scare you earlier, but this time the caller mentioned you too. They're coming after both of us now." I decide to skip the shopping. "Let's get out of here. I'm spooked."

He straightens his jacket and fixes his cufflinks. "All righty then, let's go back to the office. I have some surveillance equipment to set up pronto." He puts on his sunglasses with the confident air of Agent 007, and we leave the bookstore empty-handed.

# Chapter 23

Simone de Beauvoir said, *If you live long enough, you'll see that every victory turns into a defeat.* As Rikash teaches me how to use tracking technology to protect myself, I realize that we may have won a few battles against counterfeiters on the streets of Paris, but I'm far from having won the war.

Rikash holds up two tiny devices. "Once attached to your phone, these babies will track your incoming calls. I'll also monitor your emails so that we can identify the sender's IP address. And if you sense someone following you, film them through this little camera. We're not going to let any rogue counterfeiters chase us out of town."

I smile as he plugs a cable into my computer. He's a miracle worker and, despite all the odds, makes me feel invincible.

"If the phone rings and it's your mystery caller, you press here." He indicates a button. "It will record the entire conversation. Now, if you're being followed or run into anything sketchy on the street, use this." He hands me a camera the size of a stamp. "You need to put it in a very safe place, like in your bra."

"Gee, thanks a lot. You may be surprised by some of the things you see." I wink.

"Oh, puh-lease." He raises a hand. "I hope you'll take it off when you get home at night. I'm so not interested in seeing any of *that*." He pauses. "Unless you're with Mr. D'Avignon."

"Not a chance. I'm happily attached, remember?"

"Whatever," he mutters. "Women in love suffer from severe memory loss—they forget that there are thousands of potential playmates available in the universe." He shakes his head, then turns to my computer to show me how the email tracking device works. "Can you open your inbox, please?"

I click on the mailbox icon, and messages from Frédéric, Antoine, and Chris appear. I spot an email from Lisa with

Yulia's name in the subject line. I click on it: finally some good news. After lengthy discussions with local immigration officials, Lisa's colleague in Paris has cleared Yulia's file of anything incriminating. She can stay in France so long as she finds a local sponsor.

I scroll down further and jump from my seat—there are dozens of emails from unknown sources, with subject lines like *You should get out of town, lady* and *We hate you, bitch!*

"It's more serious than I thought." I cover my mouth with my hand as I scan the other menacing messages. "Do you think there's one person behind this, or is the entire world ganging up on me? How could anyone send such hateful messages?"

Rikash takes control of my keyboard. "I had a feeling this was coming." He scratches his head. "They're from bogus Hotmail and Gmail accounts. They're probably from the same source, but it's too soon to tell."

"Can't your software track where they're from?"

"I'm afraid these messages were sent before I installed it, so we won't be able to find out just yet, but hopefully next time."

I guess we can expect more threats. What kind of cat and mouse game are we in for?

I meet Yulia at the Galeries Lafayette food court. Helping out with her immigration dossier feels like a breath of fresh air. I've decided to act as her visa sponsor. Although we're only acquaintances, offering her guidance makes me feel good.

Yulia's asked me to come with her to a photo shoot for the cover of an Italian teen magazine. The assignment is an important stepping stone in her career, and I am more than happy for the change of pace.

I find my new friend at a sushi restaurant. She's wearing skinny red jeans, a crisp white shirt, and a navy blazer. Her hair is up in a high ponytail, giving her a polished and professional look. I wave and smile.

"I have some great news," I tell her.

Her face lights up like a Times Square billboard.

"We've found a solution to your visa issue."

"Really? How did you manage that?"

"A colleague of a friend of mine works here in Paris and has connections with local immigration officials."

"Will this be expensive? I'm not sure I can afford a lawyer."

Her face becomes serious, and I remind myself that I'm discussing legal fees with a fifteen-year-old.

"No need to worry. My friend is doing this as a favour."

"Really? That's amazing, Catherine!" She reaches across the table and gives me a warm hug. I wish all my clients and colleagues were this grateful. "What a good friend you have."

"Yes, well, I'm helping her organize her wedding, and it's no small task. Besides, that's what friends are for, *non?*"

"Oh, I love weddings!" she gushes. "Especially the flower arrangements. I can't wait for my own big day," she says, a dreamy expression in her eyes.

"You have plenty of time to worry about that, *ma chérie*. There's no rush." Oddly, I've caught myself blurting out something my mother would say. I look at my watch. "Speaking of time, I think we should order; otherwise, we'll be late."

"I'm so excited about this magazine cover; apparently the photographer is a rising star in the industry." She smiles broadly, revealing her sweet dimples.

"I'm happy for you, Yulia. It seems like things are looking up."

"Catherine, you are one cool lady. I like you a *lot.*"

Her comment warms my heart and makes me feel as though I'm helping the younger sister I never had. "The feeling is mutual, Yulia. So what are we having for lunch? I'm starving."

After taking the metro to the 15th arrondissement and walking along boulevard du Montparnasse, we wind up at a large warehouse. We trek up to the third floor and enter a spare, dusty room. There's just a single photo umbrella, a far cry from the Dior photo shoot with Jean-Michel. There are no platters of fresh fruit, no miniature bottles of Perrier, no battery of assistants or stylists on hand. A scrawny man with tattoos, dishevelled hair, hipster glasses, and baggy jeans is fiddling with a camera lens while a bored-looking hairstylist in a tight black top sucks on a cigarette.

"*Bonjour.* I'm here for the cover shoot," Yulia says, attempting to hand over her portfolio.

The photographer barely looks at her and seems uninterested in taking it. "Just sit over there with the others and wait your turn, okay, sweetie pie?"

"The others?" I mutter. Perhaps it's a group photo, I tell myself.

I see two girls sitting in the dank hallway. One has dark hair and heavily glossed red lips, and is wearing a white tube top that leaves little to the imagination. The other, a petite blonde with high cheekbones, looks like a young Diane Kruger. When I say hello, they respond by smacking their gum and staring at their nails.

Yulia joins them on the row of chairs in silence and nods my way, hinting that I should do the same.

The type A in me decides to figure out what's going on. I approach the photographer. "Excuse me. Why do we have to wait in line? Isn't Yulia on the cover of the magazine?"

"Who are you? Her mother?" He looks me up and down condescendingly, like I have as much right to be on the set of a photo shoot as Lindsey Lohan does designing a Paris couture collection.

"If you *must* know," he says, grimacing, "there are three candidates for the cover of *Italiana*. It hasn't officially been decided yet."

I walk back to the hallway and pull Yulia aside as discreetly as I can. "I don't like this guy, and I don't have a good feeling about this. I think we should leave."

She stares at me incredulously. "You can't be serious. Catherine, I need this cover for my portfolio. And I still owe my agency money; they would never forgive me if I walked out on a job. Please stay. I need your support."

I'm a sucker for puppy dog eyes. I give in. Who am I to come between Yulia and her dreams?

The photographer calls out the first model's name. "Okay, Athina, *mon bébé*, you're up. Show me what you've got." His tone and the lecherous look in his eyes give me the creeps.

The dark-haired girl disappears behind a thin white curtain and reappears moments later in a leopard-print bra with neon pink straps and matching panties. The hairstylist teases her dark mane and adds bronzing powder to her face and cleavage. I want to hide under my chair as Athina begins to gyrate her tiny hips and pout for the camera. She rolls on the floor and poses suggestively. So much for teen magazines, I think. In my day, the covers featured Matt Dillon and Duran Duran in pastel shirts.

I'm embarrassed watching this spectacle, and I cringe at the thought of Yulia going through a similar degrading exercise. Sensing my discomfort, she reaches for my hand, pressing her palm tenderly against mine. She's soothing me when it should be the other way around, and I'm reminded that the fashion world isn't just about handcrafted gowns and photo shoots at Versailles. There is a darker side to this shiny world, and I'm witnessing it first-hand.

When I look back, the photographer has removed his shirt and is kneeling on the floor. Athina is sucking her thumb and placing her other hand down her panties. This makes me want to take two showers and bolt out of here, even if I have to carry Yulia away kicking and screaming.

Once the creepy guy is done with Athina, he slaps her on one butt cheek, then calls for Yulia and the blonde girl. I flinch in my chair. Will he be taking lewd pictures of them together? I imagine the worst and try to calm myself by checking my messages. Being threatened by counterfeiters all of a sudden seems easier to deal with than watching the creation of borderline child pornography.

After a few moments, I hear a shriek from behind the curtain and recognize Yulia's voice.

"*Espèce de connard!*" She throws a red two-piece bikini at the photographer and runs toward the exit with flushed cheeks.

"*Vas te faire foutre!*" he yells. "And take your mother with you!"

I waste no time reciprocating. "*Salaud!*" I shout back,

giving him the middle finger. If I learned one thing in New York, it's how to use it.

"Yulia, please wait for me!" I try to catch up with her, tottering in my four-inch heels.

Once we're outside, she finally speaks. "What a jerk! I'm so ashamed." She places her face in her hands and begins to sob.

"What did he do?"

She stares at the sidewalk. "He waited for us to undress, then told tell us that Athina was getting the cover. He said something about blow jobs . . ."

*Merde!* I want to sue this jerk for sexual harassment and file a criminal complaint with the police. I try to cool down and think this through: I'm disgusted by his actions but relieved the peep show is over. The legal world is competitive, with its back-stabbing and politics, but the modelling world makes it look like a day at the beach. At least lawyers have a steady income and the means to defend themselves, unlike fifteen-year-old girls.

"You deserve better than this," I tell Yulia.

She closes her eyes.

I imagine scores of underage girls keep this kind of exploitation to themselves for fear of the consequences. I decide I'd better tell our marketing team, as well as Yulia's agency, about this so-called prominent photographer/predator/pervert.

"I'm proud of you for telling him off. Not many girls would have the courage to stand up to him like that," I say.

"I'll probably get blacklisted for it." She shrugs.

"So what? You don't want to work with him. It's degrading." I wonder how long Yulia will put up with this kind of treatment. I know full well that for every top model, there are thousands of girls who get burned by the industry. Of course, it's easy for me to say—I have a law degree on my side. I try to be positive. "There'll be other covers, Yulia," I chirp reassuringly, but it's hard given what we've just seen. "Your career is only beginning."

"You just don't understand." She starts to walk toward the metro, tears filling the corners of her eyes.

My heart sinks seeing her so dejected, and I search for comforting words. "Fashion Week is coming up. I'll speak to our PR director about the casting for the show."

She shrugs her slender shoulders and places one hand in her jeans pocket, like she's given up.

I guess she's right: there are certain things I just don't understand.

# Chapter 24

"We've ordered the vests," Frédéric says the next day, when I walk into his office. "You should be receiving yours shortly so you can get back to the streets."

"Can't wait," I lie, knowing that whoever sent me those vicious emails, posted the pictures in Shanghai, and has been following me around town will be tickled pink. I might as well paint a bull's eye on my back.

"In the meantime, you can sink your teeth into the eShop lawsuit. It will be a precedent-setting case. Did you know that a pair of shoes is sold every eight seconds on that site?" he asks conspiratorially. "I'd be curious to know what percentage of those shoes are fake."

I do my best to appear interested, but I'm stressed about

my stalker and sad about the outcome of Yulia's photo shoot. I try to focus. "What are our chances of success, do you think? The American courts have ruled that eShop does enough to track down fakes on its site through its verification program. Are we not wasting time and energy?" Clearly, I'm a little punchy.

A broad smile appears on his face. He looks amused. "Mademoiselle Lambert, have you forgotten how important the luxury industry is to France? Perhaps you've spent too much time in New York?" He laughs good-naturedly. "As you know, the French courts are very diligent in protecting this industry's intellectual property rights. It's critical to the national economy. I think we have a strong case and excellent representation."

I'm reminded of my bookshop encounter. "Speaking of outside counsel, I ran into someone from Pineau Larochelle the other day: François D'Avignon. He's a partner, and said he specializes in medical malpractice." I refrain from telling him that I almost scared the poor man to death, and also leave out that he's got some impressive credentials in the hotness department. "It's a great firm. I see why Dior retains their services," I hear myself say. Why can't I start bragging about Edwards & White instead?

"We'll find out soon enough if they're still as good," says Frédéric. "The court documents were filed against eShop this morning."

*Merde.* That means Antoine probably knows about the filing and is fuming that I didn't give him a chance to work on the case. I want to call him, but Frédéric pulls out some more documents.

"I'll need your help to prepare for the information requests we're likely to receive from eShop's lawyers." He hands me a large manila folder. "This is the information we've gathered so far about the supposed Dior products for sale on the site. Perhaps you could spend some time going over it?"

"Yes, of course." I prepare to return to my office, but Frédéric signals for me to sit back down.

"Catherine, I know we never got back to you about your suggestion to publically destroy the fakes stored in the warehouse. I want to explain. Sandrine is under lots of pressure these days with this lawsuit. She's asked me to tell you that she thinks it's a great idea, but the timing is just off."

Oh well. It's too bad, really. In New York, this type of initiative would likely have been applauded. In the land of opportunity, talent and boldness are both revered and rewarded. I feel the more conservative French business attitude is holding me back a bit. But really, I've got enough going on.

"I understand. I have lots on my plate, anyway. Is that all?" I'm eager to call Antoine.

"Yes, and good luck with everything." He gives me a grave look, as though he senses what's ahead for me.

# Chapter 25

Dorothy Parker said, *It's not the tragedies that kill us, it's the messes.* After I listen to the messages from Antoine waiting in my voice mail, I'm convinced that she's right.

"What the hell happened?" he says when we finally speak. "You didn't even give me a chance to put our firm forward for the case. We have way more experience than Pineau does." His voice is harsh. "Have you forgotten that Edwards & White paid your bills for close to seven years? Have you no sense of loyalty?"

He hangs up and I sit in my office chair, dejected. My insides feel like they're filled with broken glass. Rikash is on the phone. When he finally turns my way, I can't help getting emotional.

"Antoine wants to tear my head off because of the case," I say pathetically.

"Oh, sweetie, I'm so sorry." He comes over and kisses me on the side of the head. "Antoine loves you. I'm sure it will soon be forgotten. It's just work, for god's sake."

But I can't help but feel bad. This is the most important case yet to pit the French luxury industry against the websites. And Antoine was the one who introduced me to Dior in the first place.

"I feel awful. I just couldn't bring myself to push for Antoine and my former bosses so soon after starting here. And now that Pineau has been retained, Antoine is livid. What kind of a girlfriend am I?" A tear runs down my cheek.

"Here, blow your nose." He hands me a tissue. "He'll get over it. It's not the only case being tried in France, after all."

"I'm not sure I can go home and face him. A shouting match is the last thing I need right now."

"So he didn't get the lawsuit. La-di-frickin-da. You should tell him off for being so self-centred. I mean, what's more important: some lawsuit or your career?" He puts one hand on his hip and waves the other around theatrically, like Tyra Banks does when she's ticked off.

"Come on, Rikash. I know Antoine cares about me, it's just . . . the pressure, you know?"

"Whatever you say, pumpkin. Just take a moment to exhale all of your negative energy." He circles his hands in front of his chest like a yogi.

I follow his instructions and immediately feel better, until I realize I haven't told him about what happened with Yulia. "I also saw something awful yesterday. A perverted photographer was trying to take advantage of Yulia and some other really young models. It disgusted me."

Rikash shakes his head. "Dah-ling, unless you've had your head in the sand for the last twenty years, it's a pretty well-known fact that some unscrupulous photographers take advantage of models."

"Okay, but that doesn't make sexual harassment acceptable. It's revolting."

"Speaking of which . . . you know I've been receiving copies of all your emails, right?" He returns to his computer with a look I haven't seen before.

"Mmm-hmm. What did I receive now? A bomb threat?"

He crosses his legs and places his hands on his knees like a social worker. Now I know I'm in trouble. "You've received a half-dozen messages from a special dating website."

I furrow my brow. "What do you mean?"

"Well . . ." He pauses for a moment, at a rare loss for words. "It's called S&M Wonderlove."

"How would sadomasochists get my email address, and why would they be writing to me?" I ask him, bemused.

He hesitates, then opens a new window on his computer. "I think you'd better check this out for yourself." He jumps from his chair, as though running for cover.

I bend at the waist and squint at the screen. There's a picture of me under the words "New Member Profile." My name and professional contact information are there, along with a description: *Dominatrix lawyer looking for some accomplices to tie up and get it on in hard-core style.*

Other pictures of me, ones I've posted on my social network profiles, have been modified to make me look as if I'm half-naked and holding a whip. I want to crawl under my desk and never come out again. So much for trying to save Yulia from the soft porn industry. I've just found myself in the middle of it.

"Don't worry, I'll take care of having your profile deleted," Rikash is quick to reassure me. "I know someone who works for this site."

"What are you waiting for? Do it now!" I gasp, mortified. "Who could have done this?"

"I'm sure it's the same outfit that's been calling and emailing you. It's just another form of intimidation."

"They're really coming after me full force, aren't they?" Their scare tactics are working. This last stunt has put me over the edge. It's one thing to make threatening phone calls and send silly emails, but messing with my reputation is crossing the line. I haven't worked hard all these years to have my name dragged through the mud by a bunch of hoodlums. I'm on the verge of tears, ready to raise the white flag and call it quits.

"I know how you must be feeling, but don't you dare give up. That's exactly what these counterfeiters want. But you can't let them win," Rikash insists, his hands on my shoulders in support. "Besides, you've been intimidated before, and you never backed down." It's true: Jeffrey attempted to keep me from speaking out about his financial fraud back in New York, but I stuck it out.

"I'm just really tired right now. It's been a rough week." Today's roller coaster has me feeling burnt out. I wish I could escape to a winery in Bordeaux and lie low, gorging on red wine and foie gras until the storm passes. But Rikash is right. I need to face life's challenges like an adult.

I force a smile. "So . . . what's next?"

Rikash goes back to his computer and clicks on a message that turns out to be from François D'Avignon.

> *Mademoiselle Lambert,*
> *It was truly a pleasure meeting you and your charming assistant the other day at the Galignani bookstore.*

Rikash interrupts his reading to repeat the word "charming" twice.

> *I would be delighted if you would accompany me to Melody Gardot's concert at the Olympia two weeks from now. Perhaps followed by a dinner at La Closerie des Lilas?*
> *I hope to enjoy the pleasure of your company,*
>
> > *Yours very truly,*
> > *François D'Avignon*

"Did you hear how he finishes his message? You know what that means, sweetie? He's yours for the taking."

"Thanks, Rikash, but I don't want him. I have a man waiting for me at home. At least, I think I do."

"Okay, suit yourself. But if Antoine acts like a toad tonight, at least you have a backup plan with a solid backside." He winks.

"Come on, I want to make my relationship work, not play childish games."

"I know, honey: love is the answer," he allows, purring like Eartha Kitt. "But remember that carnal pleasures are equally satisfying."

"Thanks for the reminder." I put on my jacket and grab my handbag, ready to head home. "Don't forget to remove my profile from that dating service."

"Yes, of course. And don't worry about the messages you've received from members wanting to hook up. I'll gladly take care of those myself," he tells me with a grin.

"How could you do this to me, Catou? You know how much I wanted this case." Antoine is sitting on our living room sofa with his head in his hands, rubbing his temples. His Charvet shirt collar is unbuttoned and his silk tie loosened.

His hair is dishevelled like he's run his fingers through it a thousand times. I close the door, put my briefcase down, and silently take a seat next to him. I place a hand on his knee and tears roll down my face. I try to speak but can't. I don't know where to start.

"I'm sorry." I begin with the obvious.

"Sometimes sorry just isn't good enough." He stands up, glaring at me with a fierce look I've never seen before. He places a hand on the mantle and looks away. "You know that developing our client base is one of my main responsibilities. Or maybe you've forgotten that now that you've joined the jet set," he adds, a touch bitterly. "How quickly you've left us little people behind."

Now I'm angry. Is one lawsuit so important? But I try to remain calm. "We've gone over this before, Antoine. It's important to me that my personal and professional lives remain separate."

"I know, but this will be a precedent-setting case, and you let Sandrine hand it to Pineau Larochelle without even giving me a chance to fight for it. Is that how you show your love? Did you even mention our firm to her?"

I look down at my stilettos. Antoine waits for my reply, but I can't speak.

"In that case, your so-called two lives are not the only things about to be kept separate." He storms out of the apartment and slams the door before I can say a word.

You knew this was going to happen, says a voice in my head. You could have avoided this awful scene. I berate myself for not having told him sooner.

After a few minutes of silence, I manage to get up from the sofa and walk past the fireplace. I catch my reflection in the starburst mirror above the mantle: a miserable-looking woman dressed to the nines in this season's most fashionable styles stares back at me, and I begin to cry. I've landed both a dream job and the perfect man, but right now, my life feels like a nightmare.

As I head for the kitchen for a glass of water, the doorbell rings. Hoping against hope that it's Antoine with an apology and sweet kisses, I rush to open it.

A skinny man in an ill-fitting suit stands in front of me. I could be facing my stalker! I realize I should run back inside to activate Rikash's tiny camera, but before I have the chance, the man shoves an envelope toward me.

"Mademoiselle Catherine Lambert?" he asks in a bored voice.

"*Oui,*" I say as my heart drops and my expression hardens. What is this about?

"Thierry Lebel, bailiff." He points to the letter. "You've been served with a subpoena by the New York District Court."

My hands trembling, I tear open the envelope and scan the document:

> You are hereby commanded to report in person to the clerk of the U.S. District Court to testify in the matter involving The Government of the United States vs. Jeffrey Richardson. Failure to attend this court hearing can result in contempt of court, a criminal offense. Govern yourself accordingly.

The trial is set for next week.

The bailiff vanishes, leaving me alone with this dreaded piece of paper. Just when I thought I'd reached an all-time low, this is the final nail in the coffin. I knew I couldn't wash my hands of the Jeffrey situation forever, but the timing couldn't be worse: I'm being threatened by sadomasochistic, counterfeiting thugs, Yulia is depressed, and Antoine has just walked out on me.

I shut the door and find myself gravitating toward a bottle of red wine. I pour a glass and gulp it down in ten seconds flat, then repeat this self-preserving gesture several times.

Some say if life hands you lemons, make lemonade. I say if you're dealing with sour grapes, drink lots of wine.

# Chapter 26

I wake up the next morning on our living room floor, hugging my vintage Madeline doll and feeling the effects of a deadly hangover, my shirt covered with purple stains. *Dieu merci*, it's Saturday, the only silver lining to the dark clouds hovering over my day.

There's no sign of Antoine, and the subpoena is lying at my feet, staring at me like some scary hallucination. I get up, grab the damned piece of paper, and fling it across the room.

My mind whirls at the thought of seeing Jeffrey again. Not only has he hurt and humiliated me, he came close to ruining my career. I go to the washroom for some cold compresses to soothe my throbbing head, wondering how

I'll explain this unexpected trip to New York to my colleagues—and to Antoine, if he ever decides to speak to me again.

Just then, my phone beeps with a text message from Antoine: *Please read your emails. Thx. A.*

Not very warm. I turn on my laptop, dreading what's to come, while holding a wet facecloth to my forehead. In addition to a dozen new anonymous messages calling me a "mean cow" and a "nasty whore," there's something from Antoine sent at 11:56 last night:

> *Catherine,*
>
> *I'm staying at my friend Jacques' apartment in Neuilly. I need some time to figure things out. I took a long walk tonight and it occurred to me that in everything we choose to do or not do in life, there's an intention. By not giving me a chance to represent Dior in the eShop lawsuit, you clearly stated yours: your career takes precedence over our relationship.*
>
> *And although it's admirable that you want to help out your mother and Yulia, it feels like they are taking up most of your free time.*
>
> *Perhaps I'm taking all of this too personally, but*

*after everything we've gone through, I have to say it's*
*disappointing. You know how much you mean to me,*
*Catherine. Right now, it doesn't feel reciprocal.*

*I've decided to stay here for a few days. I think it's*
*best if we both take some time to cool down.*

*Antoine*

I close my computer, wipe the tears from my cheeks, and force myself to take a freezing shower, hoping for some reinvigoration and some help making sense of it all.

As cold water pours over my body, I realize that throughout my life I've tended to shut myself off emotionally when times get tough. I have vague memories of my mother falling into a depression after my father passed away, and I've vowed to never let that happen to me. But perhaps I've taken it too far. Antoine is better than I am at expressing his feelings. I need to learn how to communicate my needs too.

The truth is that my career is satisfying, and helping my mother and Yulia has given me great joy and reconnected me with my creative spirit. But I love Antoine, too. How can I reconcile all the different passions pulling at my heartstrings? And do I want to be in a relationship where I constantly have to justify myself?

I don't have a clear answer. For now, I'll try to placate Antoine by recommending him as co-counsel on the case. Now that I've started to prove myself at Dior, it should be okay. And it's true that Antoine's knowledge of the company's operations and his background in intellectual property might increase our chances of success.

I slip into a silk Princesse Tam.Tam robe, turn on the Nespresso machine, and dial Rikash.

"What now? Did someone break into your apartment?" He's sarcastic.

"I guess you could say that."

"What? Oh my god!" Now he's shouting. "Things are getting out of control. You need to call the police!"

"Calm down. I was being facetious. But last night I got served with a subpoena. A bailiff showed up on my doorstep."

"What's this about?"

"Take a guess: I have to testify against Jeffrey."

"Oh boy, here it is, coming back to you like a boomerang. Well, we knew this would happen sooner or later. What will you do, sweetie?"

I take a sip of coffee. "I could go to jail if I don't show up, so I have to go to New York. Can you believe that the trial is next week?"

"You should be pleased the bastard is probably heading behind bars. It serves him right after what he did to you. Lucky for him, stripes are all the rage at the moment."

"I'm not sure how to tell Sandrine and Frédéric that I need the time off."

"I wouldn't worry," he says soothingly. "You're complying with a court order. Dior can't fault you for that. " He's quiet for a moment, and I imagine the mental wheels in his head turning. "What I'm concerned about is your security. What if the stalker follows you to New York? It would be best if I came along."

I briefly wonder if he wants to tag along for the sheer pleasure of seeing Jeffrey try to defend himself, but I know better. Rikash always has my best interests at heart.

"Will they let us both go? We're swamped with work."

"Hmm. Good point. Well, we can tell Frédéric and Sandrine that I worked on the case too, and that you need me for evidentiary purposes."

Is this a good idea? We've already kept things from our bosses. "I know you don't want to hear this, Rikash, but I think we should come clean about the threatening calls and emails, in case something serious happens to either of us over there."

"Do you really want to get them involved now?" He sounds almost offended. "We're doing well so far. I even have a lead or two on the emails. We'll bring them into the loop when we have something more solid. Hey, if we bust this counterfeit operation wide open, our next stop will be the executive suite."

He's all confidence, but I'm worried we're in over our heads. "You may be right, Rikash. I just need to mull it over. I'm afraid I'm not thinking that clearly at the moment." I pause before confessing, "I got into a big argument with Antoine last night, and he walked out on me."

"Oh dear, I'm sorry. Same issue, I presume? He needs to sign up for anger management classes."

"I should have put him forward as outside counsel on the eShop case. He didn't come home last night."

"Don't worry, dah-ling. His lawyerly ego has been bruised, that's all. It happens all the time with attorneys. The two of you will be just fine."

"Thanks." He's speaking half in jest—I know he has respect for Antoine.

"I'm thinking of asking Frédéric to add Edwards & White as co-counsel on the eShop suit. Do you think he'd go for it?"

"Sounds reasonable. Do you have a persuasive argument?"

"Besides the expertise and knowledge they'd bring, I think it would be efficient: lawyers keeping other lawyers in check."

"Not bad, counsellor. You may need to tweak your sales pitch a bit, but you're off to a good start. I'm sure you'll find a way to bring Antoine into the fold. Do you at least know where he is?"

"Yes," I say, finishing my coffee. "He's staying with his friend Jacques in Neuilly. He needs time to think, he said."

The knot in my stomach tightens. Taking time out from a relationship is never a good sign.

"Is that so? Well, if you're in the mood for a distraction, don't forget that Mr. D'Avignon is willing and able to help out in that department," he says with mischief in his voice. "Have you at least replied to his invitation?"

"I've been a little preoccupied." I place the empty cup and saucer on the counter.

"It's impolite to ignore such a generous offer. Tsk tsk."

"I'll just tell him my agenda is fully booked for the next fifty years."

"Oh, puh-lease. Don't do anything you might regret later. Go! Do it for *moi*."

"Thank you, your highness, prince of etiquette. Your tips are much appreciated."

"My pleasure. And just for the record, I'm not a prince, I'm a queen."

When I hang up, my phone indicates that I've missed a call from a number with a blocked ID. I shake my head—probably my stalker again. As I stare at the crumpled subpoena at my feet, it occurs to me that Jeffrey could be paying someone to scare me off. I wouldn't put it past his crooked mind. I run to the door and turn the deadbolt, then draw the living room curtains. If it's Jeffrey, I'll know soon enough. He doesn't scare me anymore. Not really.

I open a box of Pierre Hermé *macarons* and reach for a salted caramel treat. Overindulging in exquisite *macarons* is the French woman's equivalent of drowning your sorrows in a tub of Ben & Jerry's. The creamy ganache creates such an overwhelming sensation of *bien être* that you forget all your troubles after one bite. Today, I'm liable to finish the box.

I pull out a comfy cashmere blanket and turn on the television to watch the season finale of *Gossip Girl*. Watching Serena and Blair gallivant about in their fabulous frocks helps me forget my troubles for a little while, and I take comfort in the fact that there's usually a happy ending on these shows.

I just hope there's one in store for me.

# Chapter 27

"These threats remind me of my first gig," Frédéric says as I take a seat in his office. "I worked for a small litigation firm in the 7th arrondissement and was sent to Le Grand Hotel on rue Scribe with a police officer to confiscate counterfeit textiles."

After a good night's sleep, I decided to tell Frédéric about the stalking. Rikash's feelings notwithstanding, I want there to be no more secrets. If I can't trust the person I report to, what good is it to pour my heart and soul into my job? To keep my promise to Rikash, I'll keep quiet about his tracking activities. For now.

"How long ago was this?"

"A very long time ago," he says warmly. "Probably before you were born."

"Ah, yes, that was a long time ago," I joke.

"We were representing textile manufacturers whose designs had been copied illegally. I arrived at the hotel, where the copies were being sold, wearing a suit, with a single gendarme. After I'd knocked on a few doors with my warrant, some hulky guys tried to hit me with a crowbar and chased me down the fire escape. I was so scared, my legs nearly gave out."

"*Oh mon dieu!* Did you get away safely?" I try to picture it: Frédéric, refined and professorial-looking in his tweed jacket and tie, against a pack of thugs.

"Yes, luckily the policeman had called for reinforcements. We managed to seize four million euros worth of textiles, and the group we arrested was forced to pay five million in fines. Although it scared the living daylights out of me, it created a big splash in the media and was a great start to my career."

"I would have loved to see you in action," I say.

"The clients were so happy, they took me to the Moulin Rouge to celebrate." He smiles at the memory.

"I guess the moral of the story is that I need to toughen up."

He nods.

"It's all new to me: the threats, being followed. I've been subjected to some vile behaviour in the past—in New York—but it was mostly done behind my back."

"I'm sure you were expecting assignments that were a bit more glamorous when you joined Dior, but I'm afraid our work is far from it most of the time. But at least we don't have to deal with the divas upstairs in the atelier," he says, rolling his eyes.

I think of Wolfgang and his entourage; it must be exhausting to spend your days catering to the demands of a crew like that. Of course, I've sometimes fantasized about working in a more creative department at Dior, but I keep that to myself. "You can say that again." I want him to know that we're on the same page. "I hope you know that I really enjoy working here."

"Yes, and it shows. I'm sorry about the threats, but unfortunately, that comes with the territory. Keep in mind that there might be even more intimidation as you press forward." He adjusts his reading glasses. "But that's good news: it means you're getting the job done and getting under people's skin. I know it's easier said than done, but don't let it get to you."

"I'll try," I say, reassured. Speaking to him has lifted a weight from me. "There's something else I need to tell you," I continue tentatively. "I've been served with a subpoena to testify at a trial in New York."

"Oh?" He's surprised.

"Yes, and it's set for next week." I cringe.

"That's short notice." He frowns.

"I realize that the timing isn't great. It's regarding a matter I was involved in last year at Edwards & White."

"I see." He takes a sip of water. "Could this trial bring negative publicity to Dior? You must know by now that senior management frowns upon anything that could tarnish our reputation."

Testifying about the financial misdeeds of a CFO with whom I had a romantic liaison isn't exactly synonymous with refinement and luxury, but I refrain from sharing any details. I just hope the trial will receive minimal media coverage.

"Not to worry. It's about an IPO that went sour," I say, going for nonchalance.

"Ah, one of those." He sounds relieved. "I bet you encountered a few in your days at Edwards & White."

I nod, trying to keep the conversation short. "Rikash

needs to accompany me to New York. He was involved with the matter too."

"Well, if you've been subpoenaed, then what can I say? I'll ask someone else to cover the eShop paper chase while you two are away."

I figure that, while I'm on a roll, I might as well keep going. "One last thing. Speaking of eShop, have you considered retaining another firm as co-counsel? It's a major lawsuit, and sometimes it's better to have two firms on board. The added expertise is a bonus, and it tends to keep both firms honest."

"That hadn't occurred to me, but we've budgeted for only one firm and, frankly, I have my hands full trying to manage it."

He clearly feels I've overstepped my bounds. *Merde.* I try to backpedal. "It was just a suggestion. Of course, I understand your position."

Just then, Sandrine sashays into the room in ivory palazzo pants, a royal blue silk blouse, and a collection of enamel Hermès bangles. She looks as though she's just come from the salon.

"Catherine needs to run off to New York next week," Frédéric says. "She's been subpoenaed to testify at a trial."

"Really?" Sandrine smiles. "It's always exciting to go back to New York, isn't it? While you're there, you must try this new restaurant I heard about in the East Village; apparently, they make the best truffle risotto."

I'm surprised. I expected her to be annoyed about this sudden leave of absence, but instead she's sharing restaurant recommendations?

Frédéric looks puzzled also. He crosses his arms. "Rikash needs to go too, it seems."

She's unperturbed. "Actually, this timing is perfect. If the two of you are going to be in New York anyway, I'd like you to attend an anti-counterfeiting conference on my behalf. It's being hosted by one of the magazines. Also, I'd appreciate it if you could meet with the American firm representing eShop. It might help us in our negotiations." She leans against Frédéric's desk, nearly knocking off his eyeglasses with her elbow.

"We'd be happy to attend the conference and meet with eShop's lawyers," I say, relieved that I'll be able to do something productive for Dior while I'm in New York.

"*Fantastique!* I'll have Coralie arrange a meeting as soon as your plans are confirmed. I think you'll enjoy the conference. Diane von Lucas is the master of ceremonies."

I gasp. "She's one my favourite designers."

Frédéric rolls his eyes and bites his lower lip. I'm guessing these types of job perks don't come his way very often.

"Now that I think of it," Sandrine continues, "you may know eShop's lawyers. They're using Harry Traum's new firm, Traum and Associates. Wasn't he a partner at your firm in New York?"

When Harry Traum, the former managing partner of Edwards & White, decided to branch out on his own, he had offered me a junior partner position. But I'd run far and fast upon finding out that Bonnie Clark, his lover and my former boss, would be part of the new outfit. The thought of seeing them nearly makes me keel over.

"Catherine?" Sandrine asks. "Are you okay?"

Her voice snaps me out of my trance. "Yes, sorry. I do know him. We worked together on a few matters at Edwards."

Testifying against my ex-boyfriend in a criminal court might be a breeze compared to coming face to face with Harry and Bonnie again. This trip promises to be anything but dull.

I turn to Frédéric. "Where did you say I could find those bulletproof vests you ordered? I may need to take one along in my suitcase."

# Chapter 28

"What the fuck are you doing? Can't you see this is a drop-off zone?" A limo driver is shouting at our cabby and spitting toward our car with such force that I can almost feel the saliva hitting my hair.

"Jesus Christ, what does it look like I'm doing?" our driver screams. "We're coming from the airport."

"What's taking so long, a-hole?"

"Whoa, calm down, children!" Rikash calls out from the back seat. "Let's play nice and no name-calling, okay? It's offensive to my virgin ears." He covers the sides of his head while I pull out my wallet.

*Welcome back to New York.*

The Gramercy Park Hotel brings back some of my best

New York memories. I spent hours gossiping with Lisa at the Rose Bar, sipping their killer fig and ginger martinis. As we walk through the door, a bellboy takes my bags with a welcoming smile. It's clear that we're not in Paris anymore, the cab melee notwithstanding. I've actually heard the words "How can I help you?"; "My pleasure"; "No problem"; and "Yes, ma'am."

Cheery American optimism is scarce in France. Even after-work drinks have an upbeat name here: "happy hour." The French equivalent is the unimaginative "5 à 7." (Why be so restrictive?)

It's also refreshing to see ordinary people dressed boldly and with individuality, something rarely seen in Paris these days. A tall blonde woman sitting at the bar in a periwinkle blue top and brightly coloured paisley pants, a fuchsia scarf around her neck, is a case in point.

After checking in, we rush to our hotel room to change. We'll just make it to the conference on time. I slip into a light grey chiffon cocktail dress and matching dove grey satin pumps, courtesy of la Maison Dior. A touch of hot pink lip gloss gives me a bit of colour after the long trans-Atlantic flight.

Waiting for Rikash in the hotel lobby, I text Antoine

to let him know I've arrived safely. We spoke only briefly before I left Paris. Despite my pleas for us to meet and resolve our differences, he wanted to wait until my return. I also text Laetitia about casting Yulia in future Dior shows—not really my area, but can it hurt?

Rikash struts into the lobby, as ebullient as a soufflé, looking dashing in a striped grey and navy suit, a pair of stylish leather brogues, and his Ray-Bans.

"Ready when you are, dah-ling. We don't want to keep Lady Diane waiting."

Just as we hop in a cab, my cellphone rings. A blocked number. I pass the phone over to Rikash. "This one's all yours, Mr. Bond."

"Hello, this is Rikash." He activates the speaker feature so that I can hear.

"I see the two of you have made it safely to New York."

My eyes widen. How does this guy know our where-abouts? Did he follow us here?

"Yes, we have, and I must say the weather is simply spec-tacular on this side of the pond." Rikash is nonchalant, crossing his legs as if talking to a friend.

I frown, wondering why he isn't being more aggressive, but he waves me off with the back of his hand.

"I must commend you on your choice of hotel. It's one of the best in the city." Now it's our stalker who sounds casual.

Okay, now I'm really starting to panic. This maniac knows where we're staying, and I'm not wearing my bulletproof vest. I'm under enough stress as it is with Jeffrey's trial; I don't need this added anxiety.

"Well, I have simple taste—I'm only satisfied with the best." Rikash likes to paraphrase Oscar Wilde.

I give him an exasperated look and nudge him in the ribs. This is no time to make small talk.

"So, what gives us the pleasure of your call, scumbag?" To my relief, he finally kicks it up a notch.

"Just making sure neither of you gets into any trouble while you're here. You've shown way too much initiative in the recent past, and we strongly recommend that you keep a lid on it."

Rikash's face turns purple, but I can see he's trying to stay composed. He signals for me to talk while he fishes for a gadget in his suit pocket.

"We wouldn't dare do anything out of the ordinary. That's not the purpose of our trip." I try to play along.

Rikash plugs a wire into my phone and gives me the okay signal.

"That's what we like to hear, Miss Lambert. But we'll be keeping an eye on you two, just in case." The line goes dead, just when we were getting somewhere.

"Should we head back to the hotel?" I'm a little panicky. "What if he's following us to the conference?"

"Not so fast, sweetie." Rikash grabs my arm as I'm about to instruct our driver to do a U-turn. "Don't do that. He's probably bluffing to scare us off. For now, just put on a smile for the cameras."

I take a deep breath and put my phone back into my Lady Dior bag. We arrive at Hearst Tower, on Eighth Avenue. There's a scene outside: Cecily Dutton, the pop singer, is stepping out of her limo. Cecily caused a minor scandal by buying fake purses in Shanghai, I remember.

"How quickly the world forgets," Rikash murmurs, clearing a path through the crowd.

Inside, we're ushered into a ballroom, where scores of counterfeit bags, sunglasses, and perfume bottles are lined up on a long table next to signs identifying them as fake.

"Nothing we haven't seen a hundred times," Rikash declares. But when an attractive waiter cruises by offering Champagne, he perks up. "Okay, now we're talking. Here's something I haven't come across before." He watches the man walk away.

We make small talk with lawyers from a number of New York luxury goods companies and compare notes about recent raids.

"One guy hit me with a giant garbage bag filled with fake handbags," says a lanky man.

"Oh, that's nothing," a woman in her early forties, wearing a red suit, chimes in. "While I was on a raid, someone pushed me out of a second-storey window. I broke my arm!"

"Once, I was held up at gunpoint," a man in a sharp pinstriped suit says. "I thought I was going to get killed right there in the middle of Canal Street."

I raise my eyebrows and glance over at Rikash. Having our pictures taken and being threatened over the phone seems pretty tame in comparison. I just hope we don't have any experiences like theirs.

"Thank you for being here today." Diane von Lucas stands at the front of the room, ravishing in one of her signature silk dresses. "I'm not sure if you're aware of this, but it's been reported that the Madrid train bombings of 2004 were financed in part by the sale of counterfeit DVDs." You can hear a pin drop. "It's a major epidemic that we need to fight together." She clears her throat. "But there's an added complexity to the fight against counterfeiting today: eighty percent of fakes are sold online."

Rikash is scribbling on a napkin. Good idea: I should take notes in case Sandrine wants a report.

Once the panel discussion is over and dessert arrives, my shoulders loosen and I turn to Rikash, only to catch him passing his napkin to the handsome waiter.

"What was that about?" I ask him.

"I have a date tonight."

"What? You can't leave me alone the night before Jeffrey's trial! I'll be a nervous wreck. Besides, I need your help going over some of the practice questions the prosecutor sent me."

"Don't worry, dah-ling. It's a very late rendezvous. You'll be sound asleep by the time I slip out."

"Okay," I sigh. "Let's say our goodbyes and get out of here. We need to pay a visit to our old friend Harry."

# Chapter 29

B onnie Parker and Clyde Barrow notoriously became both lovers and partners in crime. This is what comes to mind when I step into the white marble lobby of Traum and Associates. Not that Harry and Bonnie have engaged in illegal activities, that I know of; rather, they shared the most titillating secret of all—illicit sex. Bonnie was Harry's mistress and the cause of his divorce.

"Well, well, well, if it isn't the French B team back to play in the major leagues." Harry Traum's voice bursts down the hallway. He reaches for my hand, and I remember that unmistakable iron grip. "So nice to see you again, Catherine." He turns to Rikash and asks, "What's your name again, son?" He moves in for a handshake, and I fear for my assistant's delicate fingers.

Rikash answers but looks insulted.

"Ah yes, now I remember," Harry says. "I knew it started with an R."

"As long as you don't call me 'Reject,' we'll be fine." Rikash says, using his fingers as quotation marks.

Harry lets out a loud belly laugh, causing the receptionist to jump in her seat. "God almighty, I forgot how funny you two can be!" He slaps his beige Dockers while holding on to one of his suspender straps, then wipes his face with a handkerchief and shows us the way to the boardroom. "Have a seat, kids. I'll fetch my files and be right back."

As soon as he walks out the door, Rikash lets it rip. "Can you believe that big toad doesn't remember my name?" he whispers loudly. "After all those personal errands I ran for him. That's outrageous." He shakes his head. "He once made me go across town in the middle of rush hour to pick up some wines for his cellar." He crosses his arms and pouts.

"Don't take it personally. That's just the way he is: rude. We should be out of here in less than an hour. I don't want to be here any more than you do."

"Hello, Catherine."

I freeze in my seat. That voice is like nails on a chalkboard. I look up, and there she is in all her glory: Bonnie Clark, fresh as a rose in a suede Oscar de la Renta safari jacket with a low-cut camisole, a close-fitting black skirt, and killer metallic Louboutin heels. She approaches the boardroom table, and we're greeted by a wave of her Joy de Patou.

I grit my teeth. "Hello, Bonnie, nice to see you again."

"Yes, it is." She nods. "Hello, Rikash. How are you?" She closes in on him with her arms open, obviously looking for a hug. He takes a step back and pats her shoulder awkwardly instead.

"You have beautiful offices," Rikash says, looking around the spare, modernist boardroom. "They're very you." I know he's only being polite—white, chrome, and shag carpet isn't his style.

She accepts the compliment graciously. "Thank you, Rikash. That's very sweet of you. I worked hard to make it look good. I'm glad you like it." She flips her hair back as she takes a seat. "It's great to have you both here, even if you're not on our side. Which is too bad for Dior."

I realize we might well have an uphill battle ahead of us. Bonnie and Harry are heavyweights. Bonnie wasn't easy to work for, but she's one hell of a corporate lawyer, and Harry, a former military man, is a formidable litigator with a take-no-prisoners attitude: he aims to win every time.

"Yes, it was quite a surprise for us to find out that you're on the other side. It'll be quite a challenge," I say with my best poker face.

"May the best client win," Harry adds, re-entering the room with a stack of manila folders in one hand and a cup of coffee in the other. He's already spilled a few drops onto his shirt. Bonnie shakes her head in disgust. "Okey-dokey," he continues. "Let's get down to brass tacks. Your company is taking a very aggressive approach in this lawsuit, Ms. Lambert. You're well aware that this case would never fly in front of an American court. The damages claimed by Dior are astronomical, and the basis for your demands is pretty shaky. However, we know that the French *tribunal de commerce* will likely side with a homegrown company like yours." He takes a sip of coffee. "Not to mention that the luxury market represents a big chunk of France's exports, so chances are you'll try to take us to the cleaners." He looks over at Bonnie, who's silent but watching like a hawk. "But, just as with everything in life, there has to be a quid pro quo."

I nod, waiting for him to go on, but there's just silence.

"What do you mean?" I finally ask.

"Listen, kiddo, eShop isn't going anywhere. It's the largest online auctioneer in the world. We all know this is an intimidation gesture by your company to gain greater control of the distribution channels, at the expense of consumer choice and law-abiding sellers. I don't believe it's in either side's interest to let this lawsuit get out of control." He finishes his coffee in one giant swig.

I take in what he's just said. Despite his rough exterior and less than refined manners, Harry is one smart cookie, and he's clearly trying to get me to convince Sandrine to settle. But based on what I've heard from her, there's no way that's going to happen.

"I understand your position, Mr. Traum," I say slowly, "but Dior isn't backing down on this one. We can't allow counterfeit sellers to continue to flood the market with fakes. We're not going to resolve this out of court unless your client is willing to write a big cheque."

Bonnie smirks, then kicks Harry's leg under the table, and Rikash looks my way with an expression that tells me he thinks we're a step closer to success. I must confess to feeling some satisfaction; for the first time in our professional relationship, I have the upper hand.

"Okay, suit yourself, but don't come crying to old Harry when we appeal the decision of the French magistrate and it costs you guys an arm and a leg in legal fees."

While I listen to his spiel, I imagine pulling on one of his suspenders and letting it snap off his large belly. I'll admit this isn't the first time the thought has crossed my mind. "We won't. This isn't grade school, Mr. Traum; we don't cry over spilt milk." I stand decisively to indicate that the conversation is over. I've seen Bonnie use this negotiation tactic many times before. Rikash follows my lead and rises from his swivel chair. Bonnie raises her eyebrows when she sees us head for the door. "We'll be in touch through our outside counsel, Pineau Larochelle," I say, feigning confidence I'm not sure I feel. "We probably shouldn't speak directly from now on. This was a courtesy call."

"Not so fast, Lambert." Harry's voice stops me in my tracks. "There's something we haven't discussed."

"Oh?" I reply coolly.

"You may want to sit down."

I sigh and return to my seat. What could this be about?

Harry looks over at Bonnie. She nods, encouraging him like a parent reassuring a child about to recite his alphabet.

"We found out about Jeffrey Richardson." He pauses, pulling on his suspenders. "All of it."

I blush, and Rikash jumps in to save me. "I don't see how this is relevant to the eShop case."

"Stay out of it, Deepak," Harry answers bluntly. That's enough for Rikash, who storms out the door, muttering, "I don't have to put up with this crap."

Trembling a bit and expecting the worst, I muster the courage to say, "What's your point?"

"My point is that what you did was impressive. Taking matters into your own hands and turning Jeffrey in took a lot of guts."

"The trouble is," Bonnie says, "at the end of the day, you didn't have the authority to do what you did. Things could get tricky if the Bar Association were to find out." She's examining her cherry red nails, and I picture a tigress sharpening her claws.

Are these two for real? Am I really being blackmailed by my former colleagues? Forget suspenders; my fantasies have moved on to ice picks and chainsaws. I stand corrected: they are outlaws, after all. I want to follow Rikash right out the door, but I know I need to be smart here. My reputation is at stake. If these two clowns disparage my professional ethics,

I could lose my law licence, and even my job. I realize it was bold what I did back then—I took the shares Jeffrey wanted to misappropriate and transferred them to Browser's support staff—but I assumed that my colleagues would support me in my attempt to right a wrong. What a mistake.

"Are you blackmailing me? Do you think that will make Dior back down on the eShop case?" I'm fuming now. "Because the Bar Association would probably not appreciate *that*."

"Of course not," Bonnie smiles, looking weirdly like Jack Nicholson in *The Shining*. "We would never do such a thing."

"Really? It sounds to me like you're using this to further your client's interests." I try to stay calm, imagining myself as an Eastern warrior about to attack. I gather all my inner strength and go for the kill. "And I'm not sure that's such a good idea. I have some compromising information of my own that could be *very* damaging."

Bonnie laughs, tilting her head back as though she's untouchable.

Harry looks less sure of himself. "Is that so? What would that be?" he says.

"I won't beat around the bush. I caught you two having

sex on Bonnie's office floor when I worked at Edwards & White." They stare at each other with blank expressions. "I just happened to activate my camera phone as I walked by." Now I'm lying, but maybe I can match their callousness. "I'm sure your soon-to-be-ex-wife would love to see the results, now that you're finalizing your divorce, Mr. Traum. I hear things are a bit tense in that department."

He goes as white as a sheet and gives me a wary look. I know I've hit him where it hurts. He shoots Bonnie a sideways glance and reluctantly responds, "I guess we'll see you in court, then, Ms. Lambert."

Rikash and I do a little victory dance in the back seat of our cab on the way back to the hotel. In my room, I deadbolt the door and collapse on my bed with a stack of the trashy celebrity mags I've so dearly missed. I have messages from my mother and from Chris, who asks when I'll be back so we can go on another raid together, but nothing from Antoine. The message from Chris makes me feel good: it's kind of nice that he misses my company on the raids. If only Antoine missed me too.

I suddenly feel a little less triumphant.

# Chapter 30

J effrey is in a downward spiral of self-destruction, I think as I watch him enter the district court at Foley Square. His hair is longer than when I last saw him, he has bags under his eyes, and he looks as pale as a ghost. He's the image of a man who has lost it all. He's wearing handcuffs instead of cufflinks, an untidy white shirt, and a black suit. He looks nothing like the man I was once attracted to.

He walks slowly to his seat, flanked by a pair of police officers. His eyes meet mine, and his stare is glacial. I once gave my heart to him, and now I can't maintain eye contact. Why did he choose me to be his accomplice? Do I come off as accommodating and weak? Would another woman have played his game, falling prey to his empty promises? I thought I might break down or even shed a few tears when I saw him again, but I feel nothing at all.

There are journalists from *The Wall Street Journal* and the *Financial Times* in the room. One more financial scandal in the making, and I'm caught in the middle of it. I wish Antoine was at my side, bolstering me through this gruelling exercise. I miss him. I take comfort in the fact that Rikash is sitting not far behind me.

When the judge calls the court to order, the prosecutor presents his case against Jeffrey. He's accused of securities fraud, conspiracy, and obstruction of justice. Before long, I'm called to the stand. I'm convinced that Jeffrey's lawyer will try to discredit me. After the meeting with Bonnie and Harry yesterday, I know what to expect.

I walk to the witness box in my light grey Stella McCartney pantsuit and my grandmother's triple-strand pearl necklace, which I put on for good luck. Rikash discreetly gives me a thumbs-up. Next to him is another former colleague, Scott, who smiles warmly. At least somebody from my old firm is on my side.

The attorney begins with standard questions about my background and my involvement in the Browser IPO before getting down to the nitty-gritty. "Ms. Lambert, what exactly did Mr. Richardson ask you to do before Browser's public offering?"

I take a deep breath. "He asked that I transfer shares that were meant to be distributed to business partners and employees to a personal offshore account instead."

"When did he ask you to do this?"

"A few weeks before the Browser IPO."

"How many shares did this represent?"

"Several thousand."

"Do you have evidence of this?"

"Yes. I taped his request."

The prosecutor introduces the tape into evidence. Jeffrey's lawyer objects but to my relief is overruled. As my tape is played for the jury, I get chills. I can feel Jeffrey's eyes boring holes into me, but I can't allow him to get to me.

The tape is a recording of the last conversation we had before things got ugly. I asked him to repeat the details of his illegal scheme while speaking to him from my office phone. I hope that this piece of evidence will be the nail in the coffin.

When it's the defence's turn, Jeffrey's lawyer, a scrawny, nervous type, jumps from his seat and, as I expected, attempts to reduce me to a bobble-head doll, nodding "yes" to each of his leading questions.

"Your name is Catherine Lambert?"

"Yes."

"You represented Browser as counsel in its IPO last year, right?"

"Yes."

"Part of your mandate was to handle a directed share program, correct?"

"Yes, that's correct."

"And as part of this program, you gave instructions to the investment bank handling the public offering to distribute shares of Browser to its support staff, didn't you?"

There it is, the question that could discredit my testimony. I look in Scott and Rikash's direction for moral support, and they both nod with tight smiles.

"Yes."

"Did you have the authority to do so, Ms. Lambert?"

"Not exactly," I mutter. I decide to take a chance. "No one at Browser seemed to mind."

"Stick to answering the questions, Ms. Lambert. Is it true that you and Mr. Richardson had a romantic liaison while you were representing his company?"

I feel myself getting as red as a tomato, and I want to hide under the judge's robe. Why did I ever get involved with this *connard?* The prosecutor tries to object, but the judge overrules and directs me to answer the question.

"Yes, but it ended immediately after Mr. Richardson's request—his *illegal* request."

"Stick to answering the questions, Ms. Lambert," he repeats impatiently. "Isn't it against Bar Association rules to have a romantic involvement with your client?"

"Not unless you're a matrimonial lawyer," I answer confidently, having long ago done my homework on this key issue. "Which I am not."

"Were you upset when the relationship ended?"

"Yes, of course."

"If that's so, Ms. Lambert, isn't it possible that you overstretched the boundaries of your mandate as Browser's counsel to get back at Mr. Richardson?"

I hold back tears. After everything I've gone through to nail this jerk, now he's claiming that I acted out of revenge, like a jilted lover. I imagine throttling him with my pearl necklace. After all, that's why they call it a choker, *non?* I quickly dismiss the thought—my grandmother wouldn't approve.

"Objection!" The prosecutor intervenes.

"Sustained. You're out of line, counsellor," the judge adds, looking miffed.

"No further questions." Jeffrey's attorney returns to his seat, looking pleased with himself. Jeffrey smirks at him, seeming equally satisfied. I want to scream at both of them for humiliating me in public.

I leave the stand drained, as if I'd completed four triathlons. I hope to god I haven't jeopardized the government's case.

Dodging reporters on my way out of the courtroom, I make the only sensible observation under the circumstances. "I need a drink."

"How did it go?" Lisa asks when she joins me and Rikash at Pastis, one of our old haunts in the Meatpacking District. Rikash invited her along for dinner to help calm my jittery nerves. I'm in the mood for familiar comforts: a continuous flow of Ricard in the company of good friends. After two glasses of the anise-flavoured liqueur, I've begun to unwind, but I still make a face in response to her question.

"Well, the good news is that you've done your part. Now all you can do is sit back and wait for the verdict," Lisa says.

"Easier said than done," I have to counter. "You're not the

one who was made to look like a sleazy whore. I just hope not too much of it makes it into the papers tomorrow."

Rikash pats me on the shoulder. "Don't worry, the press have other things to talk about. The president of Mutual Bank was caught in a bordello yesterday, the stock market tanked again this morning, and Lady Gaga is playing at Madison Square Garden tonight."

My friends are trying to cheer me up, but I can't help but feel defeated, vulnerable, and angry. Jeffrey's lawyer made me look like the wrongdoer in this whole bloody mess.

"I hope you're right," I reply meekly. I place my head in my hands and sigh. "I just want this to be over so that I can go back to a normal day of receiving threatening phone calls and nasty emails."

Lisa, ever the optimist, keeps trying to make me smile. "Rikash told me that you guys kicked butt in Bonnie and Harry's office yesterday. Way to go, sister! You rock!" She tries to give me a high-five, but I can't muster the energy.

"I wish I could say the same about my court performance today. Let's talk about your wedding plans. It's way more fun," I say, pouring myself another glass of Ricard. Our ceramic jug is running suspiciously low.

Rikash's eyes light up. "Girl, what you need is a bachelorette party. How about holding it at the Crazy Horse in Paris?" He's aglow with excitement.

"Sure, why not? I'm game," Lisa says.

I would give anything to have Antoine by my side right now. I'm about to text him when I feel Rikash poking me. "Look who just walked in: Mr. Hot Buttocks."

François D'Avignon is standing next to the bar, looking laid-back in light blue jeans, a checked shirt, and designer running shoes. He doesn't see us until Rikash stands up and waves flamboyantly.

"*Bonjour!*" François addresses me first. "Now I see why I haven't heard from you, Mademoiselle Lambert. You've been hiding on a different continent."

I blush with embarrassment. Rikash looks at me with an expression that clearly says, "I told you so."

"I apologize for not getting back to you, François," I say, still flushed. "My schedule seems to be frantic at the moment." Oh-la-la, I'm beginning to slur.

"I understand. What brings you to New York?"

I really need to get my act together. "A conference and a few meetings." I keep it vague. I really don't want to talk about the trial or the eShop lawsuit. "François, you've met Rikash. And this is my friend Lisa."

"*Enchanté, mademoiselle.*" Lisa's cheeks redden as he reaches for her hand in that gentlemanly European way.

"Lovely to meet you too." She's a touch flirtatious herself now. "Would you like to join us?" She points to an empty chair.

François looks at me, waiting for my approval. The last thing I want to do right now is chit-chat with another lawyer and pretend I'm in good spirits, but I don't want to be rude, and I feel Rikash and Lisa begging me with their eyes. I give them a look to say Jeffrey's trial is off limits.

"Yes, please join us." I nod at the seat next to Rikash. "We're talking about Lisa's wedding. It's going to be in France."

"Ah, lovely." He smiles. "May I ask where it's being held?"

As the conversation goes on, it dawns on me that François speaks English fluently, and without any accent. Hmm. That's interesting, I think to myself, but I quickly dismiss my suspicions. It's been a long day. I'm just exhausted.

"Catherine, your mother's home sounds wonderful. My parents also own a house in the south, near Saint-Tropez," François says.

Rikash chimes in, ever the enthusiast. "I just adore Saint-Trop," he says, using the local lingo. "The clubs are amazing, especially La Voile Rouge."

I have visions of Rikash attending private soirées organized by the likes of Paris Hilton and her entourage, spraying Champagne onto yacht-bound revellers until the wee hours, and I crack a smile.

François grins, looking a lot like George Clooney, and winks at me. "Yes, well, I'm afraid I don't go there anymore. I'm a bit too old for that." His wink, on top of the alcohol and my fatigue, makes me a little giddy.

"Would you like some Ricard?" I ask, reaching for the ceramic carafe and knocking a third of its contents onto the table.

Tone it down, Catherine, I tell myself. You're going to get yourself into some major trouble.

Rikash and Lisa realize that I've reached my alcohol limit and try to take control of the situation.

"Perhaps François would prefer something more sophisticated, like a whiskey?" Lisa muses, removing the carafe from my hands.

"Actually, I'll have a beer." How American. His down-to-earth manner and easy smile please me; he's not an uptight French bourgeois, after all. I feel a sudden, shocking rush of attraction, and decide I'd better watch what I say.

"When are you heading back to Paris?" François asks.

"Tomorrow, in the late afternoon," Rikash replies. "We have lots of work waiting for us in Paris."

"Ah yes, the famous eShop lawsuit. My colleagues are looking forward to working with you on that file."

"Likewise." I find myself leaning across the table and making sweet eyes at François. Rikash pulls me back. I cover my mouth with a hand and try to control the slurring. "We attended this great conference on counterfeiting, and it really got us primed up for the fight."

"Good to hear. I had a feeling you were hot-tempered," François say, lingering a bit on the word "hot."

This is ridiculous. I'm flirting with François in front of my two best friends while someone is waiting for me back home. And honestly, François is way too slick for me.

I peer down at my phone. There are still no messages from Antoine. Couldn't he at least have texted me after the trial? Maybe I don't have someone waiting for me, after all.

"Shall we order food?" I ask, feeling deflated. "I need to eat."

"Dah-ling, I think that's a grand idea." Rikash shoves a menu in front of me. "Will you be joining us for dinner, François?"

"Thank you, but I'm here to meet some friends. It was

great seeing you again, Catherine." François leans over to kiss my cheek. "Please let me know if you're up for the concert in Paris."

My eyes follow him to the door, where he has a word with the maître d'. Then he steps out the front door and into a cab. That's strange—didn't he say he was meeting friends? Perhaps they didn't show, I tell myself. There are enough mysteries in my life, and more important matters to attend to right now, first and foremost the steak and fries I've just ordered.

# Chapter 31

Greenacre Park, on East 51st Street between Second and Third Avenues, is one of the loveliest public spaces in Manhattan. It's richly decorated with honey locust trees, whose branches dangle over the outdoor tables and chairs, as well as lush plantings of pink and blue hydrangeas. There are three levels of seating, the lowest one dominated by a breathtaking waterfall. I discovered it once during a lunch break and found it a wonderful place to meditate and relax. The city beyond vanishes.

I'm sitting at one of the tables on the second tier, relishing some quiet time before heading back to Paris. I texted Rikash early this morning, letting him know I needed some time alone before our flight, then packed my bag, leaving it in the hotel's luggage room, picked up a cup of green tea at a local café, and headed to the park.

As I listen to the waterfall, the trial replays in my mind like a bad horror movie. The cross-examination and the allusions to my lack of judgment were painful. I just hope Jeffrey isn't set free because of me. How could I forgive myself? I think back to the IPO fiasco. The strategy I came up with now seems like a reckless plan scribbled too quickly on the back of a paper napkin.

I take a comforting sip of tea and try to find a Zen state, but my mind wanders to last night's dinner at Pastis. How could I have behaved like such a lush? Although I enjoyed François's attention, it was just a passing fancy fuelled by too many glasses of Ricard. Antoine's silence is creating a distance between us. I hope things get back to normal when I get home.

A hummingbird hovers nearby, then lands on one of the bright pink hydrangeas at my feet. It puts a smile on my face; all is not dark in the world.

I stroll across town toward Rockefeller Center and make a pit stop at J.Crew, where I pick up boxer shorts with a nautical pattern for Antoine. It's a reminder of our trip to Normandy, which feels like ages ago now. At

Henri Bendel, I select a chocolate and ginger cologne for Rikash; he deserves it for putting up with me. I then buy a gorgeous silk scarf with Bendel's signature brown stripes *pour moi*, since I've come to realize that the best gifts are those we give ourselves. Or so I tell myself.

Just outside the front door, I come face to face with a pair of street vendors hawking counterfeit handbags and sunglasses on the corner. As I stare at them, one of them looks away and begins to pace nervously. He signals to his partner to throw the loot in a black plastic bag. Here we go again: it seems I've been recognized.

I check my watch and see that I still have plenty of time before I'm due at the airport. I decide to take a quick trip down to Canal Street, one of the world's largest counterfeit emporiums. It would be a shame to be here in New York and not even give it a look. As I walk toward the nearest metro station at a brisk pace, it occurs to me that I should probably let Sandrine, or at least Rikash, know what I'm doing, but I don't plan on actually carrying out a raid. I just want to have a look around, and I'll be extra-careful. Surely my stalker can't possibly know where I am at this point, after all my meandering this morning. I run to the nearest subway, hop on the 6 train, and head south.

I step out of the subway station and into chaos, with vendors selling everything from satellite radios and Chinese beer to barbecued duck and fake Rolex watches. I walk past one selling bottles of Chanel and Dior perfumes that are clearly counterfeit. Thinking about their disgusting ingredients still makes me want to throw up. I wrap my new scarf around my head to remain incognito.

One vendor sees me lingering on the sidewalk and grabs my arm. "Lady, you want a bag? You want some Louis Vuitton?" I nod and he signals for me to follow him up a dingy staircase. I hesitate; should I be doing this alone, without any police backup or my bulletproof vest? What if I'm recognized? My heart in my chest, I decide to follow him—I've made it this far; I can't back down now.

At the top of the stairs, three men in baggy jeans and black T-shirts are leaning against rusty radiators, talking to customers ranging from young Eastern European tourists to middle-aged women who sound like they're from New Jersey. I'm reminded of something Chris told me during our last raid: occasionally, when sellers sense police activity nearby, they lock their doors and turn off the lights. Shoppers can be detained for hours. I suddenly become worried for these people's safety. But then I decide I'm being ridiculous. Nothing's going to happen so long as I keep acting like a regular customer.

I scan the room and see fakes of everything from the latest Gucci bags and Prada wallets to Burberry raincoats and UGG boots. Surprised not to see any counterfeit Dior on display, I ask one of the vendors for Lady Dior bags. He nods and I follow him to an adjoining room. Here, the cream of the crop of fakes is on offer: Hermès Birkins, Chanel 2.55s, and Lady Diors in every colour I can imagine. I wonder if these vendors could be connected to the group I've encountered in both Paris and Shanghai.

As I take stock of the merchandise, my eyes are caught by some official-looking papers littering the floor. I squint and try to decipher what's written there.

The vendor approaches, interrupting my snooping. "What colour?" he asks. My mind races. Will I actually have to go through with a purchase? I indicate that I need a few more minutes. He lights a cigarette while I try to decide what to do. I notice that some of the documents have been haphazardly shoved underneath a red Lady Dior bag, so I move toward it. I remove my sunglasses and pick up the bag, pretending to admire its stitching. Looking down, I can finally make out what's on the crumpled paper. It looks like a list of points of sale around town.

I risk a glance behind me at the vendor. He has turned away to talk to another customer, so I pull out my phone and quickly take a few pictures of the document. The path between me and the door is clear: time to go.

As I try to slip past the vendor and his new customer, the scarf slips from my head. The man looks at me and makes the connection. He yells something in a language I don't understand. I panic, rushing toward the exit, pushing vendors out of my way with my shopping bags. Luckily, three women are in the front room, paying for purchases, and this buys me time to run to the stairs. "Please, ladies, get out now!" I scream.

I've made it halfway down the rickety stairs when a pair of hands pushes at the small of my back with such force that I tumble down, landing in the street with scraped knees and bruised elbows, but my limbs otherwise in working order. I'm seeing stars, though, and feeling a bit stunned.

"We know who you are, bitch!" one of the men spits down at me. "Come here again and we'll kill you!"

I wobble out onto the street, and the women from the shop rush after me.

"Are you okay, dear?" one of them asks.

Another says, "Sweetie, are you trying to stop these boys from doing business? They're just selling a few bags."

I brush the dirt and specks of blood from my hands and skirt. "I'm sorry to break the news to you, ladies," I say, "but it's worse than that." I put my sunglasses and scarf back on and begin to walk briskly away, calling back, "Much, much worse!"

Back at our hotel, Rikash zeros in on my knees. "Are those carpet burns, sweetie? Did I miss something?"

"No, of course not. I was pushed down a flight of stairs by some thugs on Canal Street."

"What?" he says, gaping. "You went there alone? Are you insane?" His raised voice is attracting looks from the hotel staff.

"I know it wasn't the smartest move," I admit. "But I did come across what looked like important information in a seller's backroom." I pull out my phone and show him the photographs.

"What is that?"

"I think it's a list of addresses where fakes are sold in New York."

He gasps, covering his mouth. "Oh! What a thing to find!"

"As I was leaving, though, they recognized me. I think these guys are connected to the group in Paris and Shanghai."

"Wow." He seems to register the seriousness of this. "We'd better get out of here before they show up with a gun."

We collect our luggage, and the hotel's doorman hails a taxi for us. We're on the Triborough Bridge when my phone rings. The blocked caller again. I let it go to voice mail. A few moments later, Rikash and I huddle together to listen to the message: "Miss Lambert, I understand you've been snooping around in our neck of the woods today. Not the smartest move. You're in way over your head. Next time, we won't be so nice."

I spend most of the overnight flight back to Paris giving some serious thought to my job. Is it worth risking my relationship and maybe even my life for? The excitement I felt upon arriving at Dior is starting to wear off. But I don't want to let Rikash down.

I can't keep the Canal Street incident under wraps—it could have far-reaching implications. I decide that Chris is the best person to share the sensitive information with. I call him as soon as we land at Charles de Gaulle, whispering into his voice mail and concluding, "I assume you'll want to take a look at the pictures. Call me and let me know the best way to send them to you."

Rikash silently nods behind his Ray-Bans. I can only hope neither of us is the target of any further retaliation.

*Chapter 32*

*I* *f it has tires or testicles, you're going to have trouble with* *it.* I once saw this scribbled on a bathroom stall in an American airport, and I think of it when I enter our apartment and find no one home. I drop my heavy suitcase in the foyer and look for a note from Antoine—he knows I'm getting back from New York today—but aside from some scattered credit card and utility bills, there isn't a trace of him. I sigh in disappointment, longing to feel his warm embrace again, especially after the incident on Canal Street. Maybe he's gone out to pick up a bottle of wine? I try calling him, but it goes straight to voice mail.

I decide to unpack my bag and take a bath. I'm dragging my suitcase into the bedroom when I see a piece of paper placed on top of our bed. It's a clipping from *The Wall Street Journal* with the headline "Former Browser CFO Stands Trial for Securities Fraud—Talk of Foul Play Involving Law Firm Sweetie." There's even a picture of me leaving the courthouse. My knees go weak and my heart skips a beat. I speed-read through the article, taking some comfort in the fact that at least the account is accurate. The only really awful details relate to my romantic involvement with Jeffrey.

But still, now I expect the worst: I fear Antoine will want to call it quits after this. He knows all about my history with Jeffrey, but perhaps seeing it in print has pushed him over the edge. And god knows who else has read the piece.

I pace back and forth in our living room, then try calling Antoine again, with the same result. Should I go look for him? Surely our relationship is worth salvaging. If I were him, where would I be right now? Maybe he's at his favourite local bistro, Le Pré aux Clercs, on the corner of rue Bonaparte and rue Jacob. I rush outside, determined to find him and resolve our issues once and for all.

As I race down the street, teetering a bit in my heels, I nearly knock over a few pedestrians exiting the local Monoprix. I leave them in my dust and arrive at the restaurant out of breath. I peer through the bistro's large open windows. At first glance, it looks like Antoine isn't here, but then I spot him at a table in a back corner. He's seated alone, with his back to the door, reading the menu. Maybe he wanted me to find him this way so we could talk about things over a bottle of white. Just as I resolve to join him, a young woman with a jet black bob, dark jeans, and a crisp white linen jacket strides to his table. He stands to greet her, and they kiss each other on both cheeks, then sit down across from each other. She places her handbag on the cozy banquette and elegantly sips water from a glass, looking very comfortable indeed. I want to scream.

I crouch down to avoid being seen. It feels like a knife is slowly slicing through my heart. A young boy seated near the window spots me, and stares as though I'm an alien. "*Qu'est-ce qu'elle est bizarre, cette dame,*" he tells his mother, pointing in my direction.

I've just been sized up by a child of six. He's right: I'm a total basket case.

# Chapter 33

I n France, we say, "*Un malheur n'arrive jamais seul.*" It's the equivalent of "When it rains, it pours."

I was definitely not prepared to see Antoine dining with another woman, not after a journey of five thousand kilometres, a gruelling cross-examination, and a nasty run-in with a mob of angry counterfeiters. I think about the newspaper clipping in my pocket. Could this be the end of our relationship? The lyrics of "Ne me quitte pas" by Jacques Brel drift into my mind. The singer begs his lover not to leave him, in a voice dripping with emotion, promising her everything under the sun. Do I need to do something equally dramatic?

Dejected, I walk down the street with my head hung

low, unable to shake the woman's face from my mind. They greeted each other so affectionately, and it sends jealous shivers through me. All of a sudden, everything is clear: Antoine means the world to me. I don't want to lose him.

I reach for my phone, hoping for a bit of reassurance from Rikash. Perhaps the gorgeous brunette is a colleague and I'm jumping to conclusions. I need to fight through the exhaustion that's fogging my head.

"What is it, love? The stalker again?"

"No, it's much worse." I get choked up in the middle of the sidewalk. "Antoine is sitting in one of our favourite restaurants with another woman."

"Oh, honey, that *is* urgent. Sounds like we need to debrief. I'll meet you at Les Philosophes in thirty minutes."

I cross over to the Right Bank and make my way down the narrow streets and past the thrift shops where I like to browse on Saturday afternoons. Right now, my heart isn't in it.

Les Philosophes, on rue Vieille du Temple, is one of the most popular cafés in Le Marais, and is mere steps away from Rikash's bachelor pad. I've been here before for the mouth-watering coffee cake and people-watching. Musings such as: *I doubt* and *What am I allowed to hope for?* are painted on the restroom walls. Today, they seem fitting.

I take a seat on the terrace and order a glass of red wine. Artistic types walk by with their cameras, canvases, and laptops. They appear lighthearted and happy.

Rikash arrives, looking squeaky clean in a pair of trendy Energie jeans, a fresh T-shirt, and a pair of white Converse sneakers. I look down at the pathetic ensemble I've been wearing for the last twenty-four hours. It's covered in dust and dots of blood. I realize that I look the way I feel: horrible. I want to crawl under the table and sob into my linen serviette.

"I'll have whatever she's having," Rikash says gaily to the waiter.

"I'm having a really bad day. Are you sure that's what you want?"

He just reaches for my hand and gives me a compassionate smile. I pull the *Journal* article from my jacket pocket and hand it over. He scans it quickly and slides it back to me, neatly folded. "That's old news, dah-ling. There's nothing to worry about."

"You should tell Antoine. He left it lying on our bed and then went out on a date with some hot stranger."

"Don't worry, sweetheart. The two of you are just going through a rough patch, that's all. You're in an adjustment period."

I take a gulp of wine. "Adjusting to what? My self-destructive behaviour? I'll end up an old maid. I know it." I let my face fall into my hands.

"Come on. Antoine knew the Jeffrey story from day one. He was jealous, remember? I told you how he used to come over to my cubicle at Edwards & White and pretend to shoot the breeze when all he really wanted to do was talk about how much he hated seeing you with that snake."

"I guess that explains why he's shut off his phone and is having lunch with a Marion Cotillard lookalike," I say, anger and despair having it out inside me. I've been careless about our relationship.

"Listen, sweetie, you're reacting out of fear. Spell it out: False Evidence Appearing Real. You don't know who this woman is, so stop being paranoid," he says.

I sit back in my chair and try to pull myself together. "You're right. But why won't he talk to me so we can resolve our issues?"

"That I don't know." Rikash shakes his head. "I'm not the best judge of a heterosexual man's mind."

My phone rings. I can't look, so Rikash peers at it. "If I'm not mistaken, it's Chris," he says, handing it over.

I've almost forgotten I called him from the airport. "Hi, Chris, you got my message?"

"Yes. Where are you, Catherine?"

"I'm with Rikash at Les Philosophes in Le Marais."

"I'll be right there."

"All right, we'll wait for you." I reach for my wineglass. "At least one man is concerned about my well-being."

"And what a man he is." Rikash bats his eyelashes.

Twenty minutes later, Chris walks in wearing a charcoal grey blazer, dark jeans, and a sharp white shirt, and carrying a vintage leather laptop bag. He causes a few Parisians' heads to swivel as he approaches. He shakes Rikash's hand and kisses me on the cheek. Pathetically, I feel a bit flustered. It must be the jet lag.

"I was intrigued by your message," Chris says. "What were you doing in New York?"

"Oh, we attended a conference in Sandrine's place and met with lawyers there about a case we have coming up," I say offhandedly. I don't want to go anywhere near Jeffrey's trial.

"Okay, and the visit to Canal Street?" He sounds concerned. "What was that about?"

Rikash and I exchange glances. I'm cornered now.

"I thought it would be a good idea to visit the area and see what goes on now that my perspective is different." I remember Sandrine scolding me about visiting the Shanghai markets without any notice and realize I could be in hot water again.

"You went there alone? Is that where you got those?" Chris points to the bruises on my elbows.

I stare at the ground sheepishly. "I'm afraid so."

"You're on international counterfeiters' watch lists, Catherine. You should know that by now. Something terrible could have happened to you," he says gravely. His protectiveness tugs at my heart strings. He's right, and he doesn't even know half the story.

Rikash seems unsure of what to do next. Sensing that I'd like to speak to Chris privately, he rises from his seat and places his sunglasses on top of his head. "Okay, *mes adorés*, I'm off to meet friends at Le Silencio for cocktails. I'll let you take over the work discussion, Chris; I've had enough for one day." He winks in my direction and disappears into the night.

I know that I have to come up with an explanation for my erratic behaviour. I decide to tell Chris everything. "We've been receiving anonymous threats," I finally say.

"Emails, phone calls, you name it. And someone has been following us, too."

"Since when?"

"For a couple of weeks now."

He stares at me in disbelief. "Why didn't you call me? I'm here to help you. And I have lots of experience in this area." He's disappointed in me, and my heart sinks. I talked to Frédéric about the threats, so why not Chris?

He reaches for my hand, and my heart begins to race. I wonder how rational my thinking has been when it comes to him. Have I been keeping my distance on purpose, trying to squelch an attraction? He senses my unease and pulls away. "Sorry."

I must remain all business. Now that Antoine and I are on shaky ground, it's important. But it takes all of my resolve to ignore his hand next to mine. Part of me wants to grab on to it and hold on tight.

"I guess it wasn't the smartest move not to tell you. I just thought Rikash and I could get to the bottom of things on our own. Anyway, there's one good result, at least: I found this on Canal Street, in a vendor's backroom." I show him the photos.

He takes my phone and zooms in on the document.

"Please email these to my work address," he says, after examining the pictures. "I'll send them to my New York investigators. Keep this up and you'll be taking Sandrine's job in no time." He smiles.

"Unlikely. This is France, not New York. Protocol rules here—hierarchy and seniority come before everything."

"You'll get there." He winks. "Besides, New York is such a rat race. It excites everybody because success is ephemeral." He slings his bag over his shoulder and again kisses me on the cheek. "Please watch out for yourself, Catherine, and call me if you need anything. In the meantime, I'll make sure this information is put to good use." He heads to the door, looking back at me one last time.

I can't deny it anymore: I am attracted to Chris. He's smart, friendly, and ambitious, and he makes me feel good. But despite all this, it was Antoine I missed when travelling, and Antoine I wanted by my side when I was in trouble. I love him, and I know now that I want to make things work.

There are certain things a woman keeps locked away in the secret garden of her heart. My attraction to Chris will be one of them.

# Chapter 34

"Hi," Antoine says casually when he walks in the door an hour or so after me. I've unpacked, taken a bath, and put on some jazz to unwind. Dinah Washington's "Is You Is or Is You Ain't My Baby" is playing in the background.

I've decided to follow Rikash's advice and calmly try to get to the bottom of things. Instead of placing blame, I'll focus on our future.

He walks over to the sofa tentatively, kissing me softly on the top of the head, and then on the lips. I'm surprised, and his kiss feels forced to me, but I let it go. He sees my bruised elbows. "What happened to you?"

"Nothing serious. I fell down a flight of stairs," I say

vaguely. I don't want to start another fight, so I'll wait until later to share the details of my Canal Street encounter.

"Really? That's terrible, Catou." He gently rubs my knee. "I'm sorry I wasn't here when you arrived. I had a meeting."

*Yes, I saw your meeting partner, and she had perfect hair and makeup.*

"No problem." I try to sound nonchalant. "I took a bath; it was an exhausting trip."

"Hmm." He removes his tie and places it on the arm of the sofa. "I read about the trial in the *Journal.* It sounds like they really put you through the wringer."

"Yes, they certainly did. The good news is that the prosecutor was permitted to play my tape in court. Jeffrey is probably heading to jail." I sound surprisingly calm, but I can't keep all my feelings inside. "Antoine, I think we should put the trial aside for a minute." I pat the seat next to me, inviting him closer. "You've been distant lately and I don't want it to be like that."

He sighs, then slumps into the sofa resignedly. "I'm having trouble with your new job, I can't deny it," he says. "The threats, the stalkers, the bulletproof vests; it's not exactly what I had in mind when we moved in together. And all the time you spend helping out Yulia and your mother . . . I'm just feeling left out."

"I understand," I say, placing a hand on his shoulder. I do.

"And you know I've been having a hard time getting over missing out on the eShop lawsuit."

"I feel terrible about that. But there's still a chance you could be retained as co-counsel. Dior might need the additional bench strength."

He shakes his head. "Don't worry about it. I'm going to be working on a class action suit for a big toy manufacturer. I just got the go-ahead at lunch today, actually, over at Le Pré aux Clercs," he says, his expression brightening.

"Oh," I sigh with relief. I guess the woman I saw was a business contact, after all. "I'm so sorry about everything." My shoulders drop and I let myself fall into his lap. "I don't want to lose you." Tears roll down my cheeks as he strokes my hair. "Please tell me we can work things out," I plead.

"I'll give it everything I've got," he whispers, cupping my face into his hands, "if you do too, Catou." He kisses me tenderly and I let myself melt into his embrace.

We fall asleep on the sofa in each other's arms. I awaken a few hours later, feeling the warmth of his breath on my neck. For the first time in a long time, I feel at peace again.

# Chapter 35

On Sunday afternoon, I'm in an upbeat mood as I head to meet Yulia at one of the city's trendy spots: Hotel Murano, located in the northern Marais. I found her work visa waiting for me at the apartment when I finally got around to opening my mail. I haven't seen her since the disastrous magazine shoot and have been a bit worried about her. I hope she's managing to navigate the murky waters of modelling and hasn't been subjected to anything else awful.

I enter the beautiful, modern lobby and feel like I'm back in New York. Sleek white leather couches hold court in the atrium, flanked by sleek glass tables. Pink accessories and pastel lighting accent the room. Glass sculptures, chandeliers, and mirrors are showcased throughout the space, and relaxing lounge music is playing in the background.

I find Yulia at the hotel bar, curled up on a white banquette with a bottle of water in her hand. Her eyes are swollen, her complexion is haggard, her hair is messy, and she reeks of nicotine. She looks nothing like the luminous beauty I first met at Angelina's. I kiss her on both cheeks and notice her collarbones jutting out under her T-shirt. I fear she's lost weight.

"*Bonjour,* Yulia. I've got your immigration papers to sign. I'm officially your sponsor, so it looks like you're stuck with me for a while." My attempt to make her smile falls flat, so I ask, "What's wrong, *ma chérie*?"

She just shrugs and stares at her water bottle.

"Did something happen while I was in New York? You can tell me anything, Yulia. I won't judge you." I pray it's nothing serious.

"I've been getting the cold shoulder from my agency ever since I told off that photographer. It'll be a while before they forgive me for *that*."

"They'll get over it. Have you been working? Anything glamorous?" I try to be positive.

She shakes her head. "A few pictures for *La Redoute*'s fall catalogue, but nothing major."

"I asked my contact at Dior to call your agency about the upcoming show. Have you heard anything?"

"Yes. I'll be at the casting. Thanks for arranging that, Catherine." But there's no enthusiasm in her voice. Before I can say another word, she breaks down. "I can't take this anymore!" she cries, looking lost and desperate.

I stroke her back gently. Right now my job is to listen.

"I'm so depressed," she sniffles, pushing a loose strand of hair behind her ear. "I'm not earning enough to cover my expenses, and I don't know what to do."

"Aren't you getting paid for your work? What about that ad for the Dior cream?"

"I was paid for it, but I'm still reimbursing the agency, and then rent . . ."

She's on a slippery slope. Some girls in the industry get sidelined into shady territory in an effort to make ends meet. My motherly instincts kick into high gear.

"It's a cutthroat business and it's really tough out there. Are you sure this is what you want to do?" I venture. I may work in fashion, but this is her life we're talking about. "Have you thought of going to school instead?"

She nods, nervously scratching her hand. "Yes, but I can't afford it."

I lean back into the banquette, trying to figure this out. It's not easy for a fifteen-year-old to find work that will allow her to pay her way through school. And if she quits modelling, she might be forced to leave the country. I resolve to find a solution somehow.

I catch a glimpse of a book peeking out of her Vanessa Bruno tote bag; she's told me it was a gift from the designer. Hoping to distract her from her troubles, I ask, "What are you reading?"

"Oh, it's nothing. Books keep my mind occupied while I'm on the metro."

"You're lucky. I don't have much time to read these days. Can I see?"

I'm expecting vampires and witches, so I'm caught off guard when she pulls out a book by the famed French decorator Jacques Grange.

"You're into design?" I ask, unable to hide my surprise.

Her face brightens. "Yes. I love seeing how people decorate their homes—it's inspiring."

I'm taken aback. Aren't most fifteen-year-old girls into boy bands, Coachella, and neon nail polish? I dig a little deeper. "Is this something you would be interested in studying?"

"Oh yes." Her tone is unequivocal. "I'd love to be a designer. That would be my dream job."

She pulls a camera from her bag and leans closer to show me some pictures. "This is my room at the agency apartment. I decorated it myself and hardly spent any money at all." She's proud, and rightfully so. I peer at the camera's display and see a tableau straight out of the movie *Marie Antoinette:* billowy curtains frame the room's small windows and antique furniture lines the wall opposite her bed. A lavender bedspread and flowery pink cushions add a feminine touch. "I found some of it in the trash and just repainted it. I made that bedspread from fabric scraps. There's a Bulgarian seamstress in my neighbourhood who lets me use her sewing machine at night."

"It's beautiful," I say. "I don't know many girls your age who are as resourceful as you, or as creative." I think back to my one teenage attempt to sew myself a pair of shorts. I gave up after an hour of mangling the expensive fabric I'd ambitiously bought.

Ideas are whirling through my mind. I'm stretched to the limit at work, and helping out my mother has been taking up a fair bit of my free time. A competent assistant might come in handy. "Have you looked into taking design classes in Paris?" I ask.

"Yes. Once I've paid off my debts, I could probably afford it part time."

It's a long shot, but if my mother agrees to hire Yulia, maybe she could take classes at night. That would allow her to remain in France on a student visa. It could be a win-win, helping both of them. But I figure I should ask my mother before promising anything, so I keep the idea to myself for now.

"I hear Dior pays its runway models well." I wink conspiratorially. "If you're in the next show, maybe you'll earn enough money to start."

"I guess." She finally grins, and it lights up the whole room.

I signal for the waiter to take our order. "I've heard that this place makes the best chocolate chip soufflé in all of Paris. Shall we?"

"*Absolument.* Thanks, Catherine." She leans her pretty head on my shoulder, and it makes my day.

# Chapter 36

"Antoine and I have made up. All is good," I tell Rikash when I get to the office on Monday morning.

"I'm so happy." He comes over to hug me.

"You were right: I worried for nothing. The woman I saw him with was a work contact."

"I knew it. Antoine isn't the bad boy type."

"But he did make me promise I would do something about the stalker and the threats," I say, trying to send a not-so-subtle message. Since returning to Paris, I've received a dozen more nasty emails. "This nonsense has to stop, Rikash. I hope to god you've made progress in tracking down our *cher ami.*"

"As a matter of fact, I have." He rubs his palms together.

"I've identified the caller's address. He's from the 1st arrondissement, near Les Halles. I'm going to stop by there tonight after work to scope it out."

I'm frightened to death by the thought of Rikash going sleuthing without any backup, especially after what happened to me in New York. "Are you sure? I don't like the idea of you going there alone. What if you get caught? Maybe we should contact Chris or Sergeant Larivière."

"Please don't worry, dah-ling. I know how to be very discreet. I'm just going to check it out and see what there is to see. Once I've identified who's calling you, we can devise a plan."

"All right, but please wear your vest." I point to the as-yet-unworn piece of Kevlar lying under his desk. "And promise me that you'll send me a text message when you get home so I know you're safe."

"Okay, okay, I promise." His snippy tone makes me feel like the mother of a rebel teenager, but I'm genuinely worried. Is this espionage mission a good idea?

"How did things go in Manhattan?" Sandrine asks, gliding into our office late that afternoon. She's wearing a silk blouse with blue-and-white stripes and wide masculine cuffs, matching blue palazzos, and nude platform heels. The look is sexy sailor meets serious business woman. She picks up a Haribo candy from a glass tray on Rikash's desk.

I decide to be direct. "The conference was fantastic; the meeting with eShop's U.S. counsel not so much. As for the trial, I'll just have to wait for the jury's decision."

"My husband showed me the article in *The Wall Street Journal.* I'm so sorry you've been dragged into it like this."

Frédéric cautioned me about protecting Dior's reputation. I tense up.

"You should be proud of yourself for standing up for what's right and making an example out of that man," she continues. "You're a brave young woman."

She's caught me off guard, and my shoulders relax. Given how unpredictable Sandrine has been lately, I wasn't expecting such an enthusiastic show of support.

"When will the verdict be announced?"

"I'm not sure yet." I'll hear from the prosecutor when the verdict is rendered. In the meantime, I've decided to stop reading about it in the press. I can't wait for it to be behind me; the trial feels like a dark cloud hovering over a sunny Saturday afternoon.

"I hope everything works out for you," she says. "Now, tell me about our friend Harry Traum. How's he doing?"

"He's not our friend, believe me."

"*Ah bon?* What happened?" She reaches for another candy.

"He and his partner tried to intimidate us, but it didn't work. The bottom line: don't expect a settlement cheque to come out of his client's pocket anytime soon."

Sandrine tilts her head back and laughs. It's been a long time since I've seen her so relaxed. It's a refreshing sight.

"I wasn't looking for a cheque; at least, not yet. I want them to sweat it out first." She smirks.

"Harry thrives on the theatrics of the courtroom. He's like an actor on stage," I say. I've seen it. "He's not going to back down from a chance to prove us wrong."

She discards the candy wrapper and becomes serious. "It's going to be a very costly battle for them. Harry should know that they're going down on this one." She looks down at her perfectly manicured nails. "We're not settling."

While she's discussing strategy, I figure I might as well ask about getting Antoine's foot in the door. I realize that it will look to Frédéric like I went over his head, but I'll risk him being angry at me. Antoine is worth it. "Have you considered retaining another firm to act as co-counsel with Pineau? It appears to be eShop's way of doing things. Is it an option?"

She looks up. "Who do you have in mind, Catherine?"

"The best person I know to get the job done: Antoine Brisson, a junior partner at Edwards & White."

Sandrine gives me a look that tells me she's aware of our relationship. She walks over to the window and looks out before speaking. "Are you looking out for the company's interests or your own, Mademoiselle Lambert?" Her tone is colder now. But what did I expect?

"Both," I reply coolly. "I'm looking out for Dior's interests by recommending one of the best lawyers in the city, and for Antoine's interests by offering him a chance to work on a precedent-setting case. That's what I call a win-win situation."

She remains planted at the window, with her arms crossed. I continue, "He's experienced in this area: ask around. And he's worked on several Dior cases in the past. He understands our business."

She turns to face me. "In that case, perhaps I should get to know him better over dinner at my home this weekend." She walks toward me. "It would be a chance for us to finally meet, and I'm sure that my husband would love to meet you and share war stories about Wall Street."

This invitation comes as a total surprise, but I jump at the chance to help Antoine get more work. "We would be delighted."

"How about Friday at eight? We live in the 16th arrondissement."

After she leaves, I shake my head in disbelief. Things are really starting to look up: Jeffrey's trial is behind me now, Antoine and I have reconciled, I have a great idea about how to help both Yulia and my mother, and Sandrine has invited Antoine and me over for dinner. But my smile fades when I think of Rikash heading out to stalk our stalker. I tuck my cellphone into my jacket pocket and head home to wait for his text.

# Chapter 37

Winston Churchill said, *Success is going from failure to failure without losing enthusiasm.* I must admit that mine is starting to wane. Antoine and I are waiting for Rikash at Willi's Wine Bar on rue des Petits Champs. We're seated at the front oak bar, pretending to enjoy the red wine the bartender recommended while anxiously keeping an eye out for the man of the hour.

I received a text from Rikash two hours after I left the office asking me to meet him somewhere in the 1st arrondissement. His message was cryptic and involved the words "urgent" and "top secret," so I coaxed Antoine into coming with me. I've come to realize that it's foolish for Rikash and me to keep trying to handle things on our own. After tonight, I'm calling it quits on our undercover mission.

"Do you think Rikash has managed to get anywhere with this, or has it all been a colossal waste of time?" Antoine asks. "I've told you, I don't want you fooling around with these guys, whoever they are. Your lives could be in danger, Catou." He reaches for my hand, and I'm comforted.

"You're right. But Rikash is sure he's on the right track," I say, reaching for an olive from a platter on the bar.

"I want these threats to stop. It's gotten out of hand, don't you think?" He absent-mindedly picks up his glass of wine and swirls it before continuing. "A fake profile of you on an S&M website? Imagine what else they can do to intimidate you. It's only going to get worse."

I stare pensively out the window. As long as I'm director of intellectual property at Dior, dealing with counterfeiters will come with the territory. But I do need to draw the line at my reputation.

Rikash is out of breath when he finally arrives, and looks as though he's seen a ghost. I ask the waiter to bring him a glass of water, and he drinks it in one gulp, then pats his forehead with his silk pocket square.

"I don't know where to start," he says.

Antoine attempts to calm him down by patting him on the back. "The beginning would be a good place."

"I'm feeling dizzy. I need to eat." Rikash looks around for a menu. Antoine shoots me a quizzical glance, but I shake my head. I have no clue why Rikash is in such a state, but for once I don't think he's just being dramatic.

We head to the dining room, where we are approached by a young waiter who resembles Prince Harry. He makes sweet eyes at Rikash but is completely ignored. That makes me nervous. Whatever Rikash has uncovered must be *very* serious.

After Rikash has devoured an entire bread basket— another shocker, since he shuns carbs—he finally manages to tell us what happened.

"I tracked down the caller's number via Catherine's cellphone and was able to link it to an address. Once I got there, I didn't want to look like I was lurking about, so I sat in the courtyard next door, pretending to read a book, and waited." He gulps another glass of water. "I'd been there for about forty minutes when I saw a man come out onto the balcony. He was young, with a black leather jacket and slicked-back hair. He was talking loudly on the phone and had an American accent, so I was sure it was our man. He left the apartment just a few minutes after I saw him."

Antoine and I nod, like two young children riveted by a ghost tale by the campfire.

"I sat out in the courtyard for another twenty minutes, and then another man appeared. He lit a cigarette and looked in my general direction, so I pulled out my phone and took some pictures—discreetly, of course. After a few minutes, he went back inside." Rikash pulls his phone from his jacket pocket. "If I'm not mistaken, this is a familiar face."

He turns the screen toward us and Antoine gasps. My hands fly up to my mouth. "*Oh mon dieu, it can't be!*" Rikash and I have seen this man in pictures in the company archives. It's Pierre Le Furet, my predecessor at Dior. My mouth is agape, my heart is beating fast, and my enthusiasm for this mission just came roaring back.

# Chapter 38

"*Allez*, a toast to our guests!" Sandrine raises her Champagne flute. Antoine and I are seated on an antique sofa in her elegantly appointed living room, getting better acquainted with her husband, Arnaud.

Antoine and I have had a hard time sleeping since Rikash's big discovery four days ago. Although we were shocked by the news—Antoine most of all, since he worked with Le Furet—we are both high on the thrill of the chase. It makes sense now: Le Furet is collaborating with counterfeiters! Maybe that's why he left Dior; perhaps the retirement story was just a cover. Sandrine seems to react oddly every time his name is mentioned. Maybe that's because she was forced to fire him after his unlawful activities were uncovered.

Rikash and I are nearly ready to share our findings with Sandrine and Frédéric. We expect that a formal investigation will ensue, charges will be pressed, and we'll be able to continue on with our work without these threats—or at least fewer of them. But Rikash has insisted that we wait just a few more days, to give him a chance to gather more evidence. His plan is to stake out Le Furet's apartment over the weekend and try to catch him on film. The covert investigation feels a bit over the top, but it's giving me a feeling of excitement I've never experienced before. I'm starting to agree with Katherine Hepburn, who said, *If you obey all the rules, you miss all the fun.*

Arnaud is seated across from us in an opulent wing chair. He's friendly, if a little distant. He's dressed in a Prince of Wales sports coat, grey flannel pants with a light blue shirt, and a Patek Philippe watch. He's tall, tanned, and debonair, and has the look of a former tennis champion, just as I imagined him.

Sandrine's home could be featured in *Architectural Digest*: cream leather couches are tastefully mixed with both modern and antique pieces. A large Cy Twombly painting hangs over the fireplace, and family portraits line the impressive hallway.

Sandrine is friendly tonight. "Antoine, Catherine tells me you're one of the brightest legal minds in Paris. I understand you worked on a few matters for us."

"Yes, Pierre Le Furet asked me to do some research on U.S. anti-counterfeiting laws for your company's internal policies and procedures."

"I see." She lights up a cigarette. "He never mentioned your work. Did you handle other files for him?" Her gaze zeros in on him, and I wonder if she thinks Antoine could have been in cahoots with Le Furet. There's a lot of subtext going on here.

He nods. "I sent out cease and desist letters to copyright infringers in the United States."

"Edwards & White breeds lots of talent," she allows, turning toward me. "Catherine's done a fantastic job so far, out on raids and in the courts, but I do prefer having her by my side in the office."

I hope to get back out on the streets with Chris and the gendarmes, but she's complimenting my work, so I decide to keep quiet. "Thank you, Sandrine. I'm really enjoying it so far."

"You're about to get an eyeful," she says, taking an elegant drag from her cigarette, her wrist delicately bent skyward as she exhales. "Fashion Week begins tomorrow and it's one big *fête.*"

"So I understand." I look toward Antoine and try to bring him back into the conversation. "Antoine also assisted Pierre in lobbying for changes in U.S. copyright laws."

"*C'est vrai?*" She reaches for a goat cheese canapé and suddenly looks interested. I sigh with relief.

"It was fascinating to discuss the future of copyright with the big players on Seventh Avenue," Antoine says with enthusiasm. "It would be great if the United States finally enacted laws to protect fashion designs."

I peer at Sandrine's husband out of the corner of my eye. He's pouring himself another whiskey, looking a little bored by our conversation. It hits me that Sandrine and Arnaud haven't made eye contact with each other since we've arrived. Clearly, all is not well in the 16th arrondissement.

I try to find a way to include him. It's a breach of French etiquette to ask Arnaud personal questions so soon after meeting him, but surely Antoine and I can charm him.

"What about you, Arnaud. What kind of work do you do?"

He holds his glass of whiskey awkwardly in mid-air for a moment. "Not much these days, I'm afraid," he finally says, a bit tensely. "I was let go a few months ago from my position as a managing director at an investment bank." He looks at me and laughs. "My racquetball game has greatly improved, though."

Sandrine, now uncomfortable, squashes her cigarette into an expensive-looking porcelain ashtray and crosses her legs, glaring at her husband.

Antoine tries to smooth things over. "I'm sorry to hear that, Arnaud. I have several clients who are going through the same thing. I can sympathize."

I squeeze Antoine's hand tenderly, relieved that he's covering for my faux pas.

"Thanks, Antoine. I appreciate that." Arnaud takes another sip of his drink. "It's refreshing to hear some words of support." He glowers in Sandrine's direction, and she responds with a glacial stare. "Lucky for me, Sandrine is always here to save the day."

Sandrine ignores him and stands up. "Shall we?" she says, gesturing toward the dining room. As soon as I'm on my feet, Arnaud puts his arm in mine. "I'm dying to hear about that trial in New York, Mademoiselle Lambert," he says, seeming more relaxed now. "I read about it in the *Journal*, and I admire your *savoir faire*."

I walk with Arnaud down the narrow hallway, shooting Antoine a look that says, *Please save me now*. He winks and continues making conversation with Sandrine. I'm comforted that he has my back. We walk past a vintage black-and-white photo of a surfer, and I blurt out, "Antoine loves to surf."

"*Non! C'est pas vrai?*" Sandrine flashes him a dazzling smile.

"Yes, I took lessons in Sydney on college break once, many years ago."

"I've been dying to learn! I hear Elle Macpherson is amazing at it. Perhaps you can teach me?" Sandrine puts a hand on Antoine's shoulder, a little flirtatiously it seems to me.

I decide to ignore her. She's probably just getting back at her husband for sharing details about their private life. It's the oldest trick in the book. Despite her veneer of wealth and glamour, maybe she's genuinely unhappy. I feel a little bit bad for her. But just a little.

"Whoa, have you ever met a couple less in sync than those two?" Antoine says once we've settled into his car for the drive home.

"I'm so sorry to have put you through that. I was just trying to get you in on the eShop lawsuit."

"I appreciate it, but I don't really care about that anymore, Catou. I just want us to be happy—unlike those two."

"Her husband looked miserable, didn't he?"

"He's with her for the money, I think," Antoine says, turning toward the Champs Élysées. "It must come from her family."

"It's a sad reason to stay in a relationship. No wonder they don't seem close."

"No kidding. I wouldn't want to live in that place, no matter how beautiful it is."

"I wonder what Arnaud meant when he said Sandrine always saves the day." I open the window to get some fresh air. It's a welcome treat after the claustrophobic evening.

"Maybe she spent some time on the old *promotion canapé*. Is it possible she got where she is by sleeping her way up?"

"Noooo . . . you think?"

"It could be."

I look out wistfully at the shimmering Eiffel Tower, feeling a little saddened by the evening's turn of events. Sandrine's mood swings are making me wonder about the wisdom of Rikash's plan. Who knows how she'll react when she discovers we've been following a former Dior employee behind her back. My train of thought is interrupted when I realize that Antoine has missed our turn.

"You just passed the bridge," I say. He stays quiet. "Unless . . . we aren't going home?"

He smiles naughtily. "You're correct about that."

"*Ah bon,* and why not?"

"There's somewhere we need to check into instead."

"Check into? You mean a hotel?" I ask, pleasantly surprised.

I get a nod and a grin in return.

"How fabulous! Which one?"

He's determined to surprise me. We zoom through the city until we get to rue de Navarin, in the 9th arrondissement near Pigalle. He stops the car in front of Hôtel Amour, a happening boutique hotel, and I grin like a Cheshire cat. We check in and climb the tiny staircase, taking in the erotic art on the walls and giggling. When we reach our room, Antoine opens the door to black lacquered walls, sexy vintage magazines, and a very large bed. He throws my handbag to the floor and begins to kiss me while unzipping my dress.

I interrupt his ardour. "You always manage to save the day, don't you, *mon chéri*?"

He laughs as we fall to the black satin sheets and turn out the light.

*Vive la différence.*

# Chapter 39

"Where are you?" I ask Rikash over the phone as I'm browsing at Ragtime, one of my favourite vintage shops on rue de l'Echaudé. I adore its selection of little dresses by Cardin and Saint Laurent, and have become friends with the owner. The dainty vintage dresses and skirts have become my uniform, and I've been accessorizing them with modern costume jewellery and Dior heels.

"In hot pursuit." He's walking fast, I can tell, because he's huffing into his phone.

"What do you mean?" I have visions of Rikash trailing Pierre Le Furet around Paris like Eliot Ness in purple cashmere.

"We're dealing with something major. I've seen cash being exchanged, and I've recognized some faces from our raids with Chris. You need to meet me as soon as possible. I need backup." His voice is uncharacteristically tense.

"Okay, where?" I drop two vintage dresses onto the counter in my haste.

"I've overheard conversations. Something big is going down in the Jardin des Tuileries later this afternoon. Can we meet near there?"

I think fast. "Let's try to be inconspicuous and go somewhere you'd naturally be on a Saturday afternoon."

"Colette's water bar. See you there in thirty minutes."

Colette is Paris's hottest concept store. It's a pioneering retailer that offers an eclectic selection of *objets d'art*, fashion accessories, CDs, and books to a savvy international clientele.

Rikash is sitting downstairs at the water bar, sporting a sideways baseball cap, giant sunglasses, a T-shirt bearing an illustration of Bernadette Chirac, ripped jeans, and bright green sneakers.

"If you're trying to go incognito, it isn't working," I joke, but he doesn't bite. Instead, he yanks his cap further down and lifts a newspaper in front of his face.

"Have a seat, dah-ling. But please remain discreet in case we're being watched."

"Okay, got it." I smile exaggeratedly and pretend to read a magazine someone's left behind on the table. "What's going on?" I ask.

He scans the room from behind his shades before responding. "Something B-I-G." He slides his glasses to the tip of his nose and looks straight into my eyes. "I caught Le Furet on film with a man we saw on our first raid—the one who took our picture."

"Oh!" I have flashbacks to the angry vendor spitting on the ground and telling his accomplice to take pictures of us. He's right, this is major.

"The good news is, I managed to plant a tiny microphone in his leather jacket. It was hanging on the back of a chair in a bistro, and I had an opportunity when he went to the bar for a drink."

I'm blown away by Rikash's fearlessness. "Okay, so now what?" Call me crazy, but I'm convinced he has this sting operation under control, so I'll let him call the shots.

"I overheard them arranging another meeting in the Tuileries at four. This might break the case wide open." He adjusts his cap and looks at his watch. "We have thirty minutes to get there, sweetie. Let's hit the road."

We take the stairs up to the main floor, where a DJ is spinning trance music and a crowd of young hipsters is shopping for designer tchotchkes. There are gold balloons at the entrance in honour of Fashion Week. As we approach the door, Rikash pushes me behind a tall rack of sneakers. "Oh my god, Le Furet just walked by! Let's wait a moment. Then we can follow him."

We exit onto rue Saint-Honoré. Le Furet is walking briskly and carrying a black leather suitcase. Rikash signals for me to keep up, but it's a little tough in my Miu Miu platform heels. I feel like Diane Keaton in Woody Allen's *Manhattan Murder Mystery.*

When Le Furet suddenly turns around, Rikash grabs my arm and pulls me into Manoush, a French boutique best described as the Gypsy Kings meet Bollywood. To keep us from being spotted through the window, he holds a bright fuchsia dress adorned with oversized feathers up in front of us. The feathers tickle my nose, and I can't suppress a sneeze. An employee gives us an evil stare and suggests with her eyes that we leave the premises if we're going to mess with the merchandise.

"That bitch nearly blew our cover," Rikash says, panting, when we're out on the street again. "Remind me not to shop there anymore."

"'Anymore?' You mean you've actually bought clothes there?"

"Well, sure. Boas and sparkly jackets, for gay pride, you know. I love their collection, but not her."

"I think we lost him," I say, looking down the street for Le Furet.

"It doesn't matter. I know where he's headed. Let's go."

During Fashion Week, the Jardin des Tuileries is jammed with fashionistas, editors, models, bloggers, and various varieties of hangers-on. A giant tent is installed at one end of the park for the shows themselves. Before anyone actually hits the runway, young women strut about in the garden in pieces from the season's most recent collections. An impressive number of street-style photographers take their photos while the magazine editors and celebrities make their way to their seats. The street-stylers have become celebrities in their own right, and their mini photo shoots are a giant spectacle that impedes everyone's entrance to the shows.

Arriving at the garden out of breath, we hide behind a gelato stand near the fountain while Rikash prepares his surveillance equipment.

"I hope we aren't recognized by anyone from Dior," I worry. "That could blow our cover."

"This is no time to worry, dearest. Just cover my back while I set things up."

I take off my khaki Marc Jacobs jacket and hold it open, making a screen while Rikash works his magic.

"I still have trouble believing that Le Furet is collaborating with an international counterfeit ring," I say quietly. "It's preposterous."

"He's not the first person in the corporate world to have gone bad. We know a few," Rikash says, playing with some wires.

"You're right, but it creeps me out that he had my job at Dior. I wonder if he's threatened anyone else. We need to nail this guy fast."

"I hear you." He looks at his watch. "It's five to four. They should be here any minute." He plugs a wire into his phone, then pulls his video camera out of his leather saddle bag. He pulls off the cap, adjusts the lens, and pretends to film me.

"Please, no close-ups. I'm getting too old for that."

"Come on, sweetie, talk some more. I need to make sure this baby works before the gang shows up."

"You're going to delete this, right?"

"Of course, it's just a test. Say whatever's on your mind."

"Antoine and I had dinner at Sandrine's apartment last night. Let's just say that it wasn't exactly a rollicking old time."

"Right, I forgot to ask you about that," he says, peering into the camera lens while adjusting some buttons. "Go on."

"It was so strange. She invited us over so she could get better acquainted with Antoine, but she and her husband ended up airing their dirty laundry in front of us instead."

"She does tend to be rather unpredictable," Rikash murmurs, still looking down at his camera.

"She looks at her husband with such disdain, it's disheartening."

"Not surprised—she seems like the domineering type."

"It got me thinking. She might not be too happy that we're spying on a former Dior employee behind her back. I really think we should come clean soon."

"That seems like a very unlikely scenario at this point," Rikash says, having turned his camera toward the fountain, "given that she's just showed up with three policemen to arrest Le Furet."

I whirl around to see Sandrine near the fountain in dark sunglasses, a beige trench coat, and towering nude heels. Sergeant Larivière and two other gendarmes are close behind her. She points to Le Furet, who is in the midst of handing over a suitcase to one of the vendors we saw on our first raid. One of the men who pushed me down the stairs in New York is there too. The policemen close in on them, carrying handcuffs and holding guns close to their chests. In the commotion, a man I've never seen before manages to break away, escaping arrest.

What's happening? I'm running through all the possibilities in my head, but only one makes sense: somehow Sandrine has found out what we were doing and is trying to take credit for our work. Given her heavy workload and managerial responsibilities these days, it's nearly impossible that she could have figured things out without listening in on our conversations and having us followed. Rikash and I kept our sleuthing to ourselves.

"This can't be happening." My voice is weak.

"Oh my god!" Rikash exclaims. "I just recognized the man running away." He adjusts the focus on his camera while turning it to follow the man as he runs out onto rue de Rivoli.

"Who is it? Tell me!"

His face goes white as a sheet. "One of the most notorious criminals in the Indian underworld."

"What?" I can hardly wrap my mind around it. How far do these networks reach?

"He's feared all over India, especially in Mumbai. They call him the Godfather of Mumbai, and he's at the top of India's most-wanted list. He just ran into the Saint James & Albany Hotel." He puts down his camera and turns to me, his eyes nearly bursting out of their sockets.

"It looks like he's on the run again," I note.

"No kidding." He shakes his head, disappointed.

"So, should we do something about—"

"Shh, I'm trying to hear what Sandrine is saying." He holds the phone between us so we can follow the conversation.

"*Merci beaucoup, Pierre.*" Sandrine's voice transmits clearly through the tiny device. "You've led us right to the counterfeiting ring we've been trying to catch. Too bad you weren't more careful." I look across the park and see her place her hands on her hips with a superior air. "I knew you couldn't be trusted—that's why I fired you. I just wish I'd done it sooner."

That's a little ironic, since it seems she can't be trusted either.

Larivière secures the handcuffs on Le Furet's wrists.

"Shame on you for collaborating with them," Sandrine continues, her face just a few inches from his. "You've undermined everything I've worked so hard to achieve."

I turn toward Rikash and see that he's just as flabbergasted as I am. We've played a part in this too. What about our contributions?

"No, thank *you*, Sandrine," Le Furet retorts. "Working for you gave me all the inside information we needed." He spits on her Louboutins before Larivière pushes him toward a police truck that's waiting on rue de Rivoli. Sandrine seems unfazed.

"Do you think she saw us?" I wonder aloud.

"Maybe. I can't believe she did this. What a selfish cow!" Rikash's voice is shrill.

Blindsided, I pace a little, trying to put the pieces together. Sandrine had no contact with the counterfeiters on the street and acted aloof when Le Furet's name came up. And then there was her husband's cryptic comment about how she always saves the day. I have no doubt Sandrine is using the fruits of our labour to get ahead at Dior. It's unthinkable! I've been subject to threats, blackmail, embarrassment, and harassment. And for what? So that Sandrine can get the credit in front of the company's board of directors? She's been manipulating me just like Jeffrey did.

"I'm kind of speechless," I say, watching Sandrine get into the police truck.

"Not for long, I hope. We can't let her get away with this."

I know Rikash is right—he's worked so hard to get us here—but I'm too angry to think. "I'm not sure who we should talk to. Who we *can* talk to, even."

"Well, let's scoot out of here before anyone sees us."

"Where to?"

"We need to devise a strategy . . ." He perks up, pointing toward Place de la Concorde. "I know! Let's go to the Vogue Bar at Hôtel de Crillon.

Inside the luxurious hotel, we walk through the grand marbled lobby and past Les Ambassadeurs, the hotel's restaurant. We wander down the hall and stop at the bar, settling onto one of its comfortable sofas. During Fashion Week, it's renamed the Vogue Bar, so that fashionistas know where to go between shows. The cocktail menus feature pictures from recent fashion editorials, and magazine covers hang on the walls. I recognize British fashion icon Alexa Chung giving an interview to *Vogue Nippon.*

Just then, Rikash's photographer friend Edouard appears.

"Ah, *mon cher ami,* I knew I'd find you here during Fashion Week, he says, air-kissing Rikash. "Were you at the Valentino show? It was sublime!" Edouard kisses his thumb and index finger. "The princess dresses were to die for."

"It's lovely to see you again, Edouard," I say, smiling, then signal to Rikash to cut the conversation short. After the two of them air-kiss for about five minutes more, Edouard disappears and we begin our official debriefing session.

"I can't believe what I captured on film—it's unreal," Rikash whispers as a posse of models and editors strut in. "I could be killed for it." He's referring to the footage of the Indian mafia king. His face is sombre.

I nod, his words slowly sinking in. "And we need to be extra-careful about how we manage this. If we go over Sandrine's head, we could lose our jobs." I'm gun-shy about grand disclosures since Jeffrey's arrest. How can we keep this low-profile but still stand up for ourselves? "Perhaps I should talk to Frédéric about it?" I offer.

"I'm not sure we can trust him," Rikash says, taking a sip of his juice. "What if he's in on it with Sandrine? It's hard to tell."

"I trust him. He can be . . . difficult sometimes, but he's reliable, and I think he would want us to get the recognition we deserve."

"I want to find a way to get Sandrine to admit what she's done." He smirks. "And I just had an idea."

"Oh boy, here we go." I gently poke him in the ribs. "I hope it's nothing too crazy. Remember, the key word here is 'subtlety.' Our jobs are at stake."

"Trust me: I know what I'm doing. Besides, for me it's more than just my job that's in danger. I don't want my body to end up floating in the Ganges."

*Mon dieu!* "I assume that whatever you have up your sleeve will take care of both Sandrine and your friend from Mumbai?"

He grimaces. "I sure hope so."

At that moment, every head in the room turns toward the bar's entrance. I look too, and see our very own chief designer, Wolfgang de Vrees, wearing dark sunglasses and a fitted suit, and surrounded by an entourage of assistants, models, and journalists trying to catch him on film. He struts in at top speed, waving away the bloggers and photographers. His eyes meet mine and, to my surprise, he stops right in front of us. His entourage is forced to a halt as well, creating a giant pileup in the middle of the bar.

"Well, well, what do we have here, hmm? It looks like the legal department is out on the town." Is he implying that we ought to be at home ironing our shirts for work on Monday morning?

"We were invited to lunch by some journalists after the Valentino show," Rikash lies, not wanting to appear uncool, I guess.

"*Ah bon.*" Wolfgang points to the hallway. "Please do stop by the Salon Marie-Antoinette. We're showing the new, ultra-secret, *ultra-luxe, ultra-spéciale,* limited-edition resort collection. You're part of the family now, *après tout.*" He signals for the group to proceed, the assistants tottering on their stilettos while managing mountains of bags and hangers. They parade away like a circus act in motion. A few of the photographers snap our picture, assuming that we must be pretty important if we've stopped such an impressive cavalcade.

Rikash looks at me with raised eyebrows. "I suppose we should drop by, since the great man himself invited us."

I shrug. "Okay, but I want to be out of there in less than ten minutes. My head is spinning."

"That makes two of us."

At the salon, we're greeted by two young women decked out in tight black Dior dresses and layers of pearl necklaces. They're reaching for the guest list when Wolfgang appears.

"*Non, non,* there's no need for that. They're from Dior. You've probably never met them, though—they work in the legal department." He laughs, once more acting as though we're the scum of the earth. "Please do have some Champagne." He snaps his fingers, and a waiter in black tie magically appears with a silver tray filled with bubbly. Boy, this guy runs hot and cold.

I'd much rather have a tall glass of water and a couple of Aspirins, but I grab a flute, then look around the majestic room. My jaw literally drops: a crystal chandelier hangs from the high ceiling, a gorgeous tapestry inspired by a

Boucher painting is displayed on one wall, and tall doors open onto a terrace overlooking Place de la Concorde. Wolfgang joins me.

"Beautiful, *non*? It is said that Marie Antoinette took music lessons here." He points to a rack of clothing at the far end of the room and leads us toward it. "Please come see my darlings." He spins the rack around, then nods to an assistant. I guess the show's about to begin.

A woman in a silver sequined mini dress begins to strut around the room. Wolfgang places a finger on his chin, clearly satisfied with his creation. Rikash and I can't help but nod in approval.

"This is a line we've created for a younger, very fashionable client: the socialite who jet-sets across Europe and spends her time on the Riviera."

"My kind of client," Rikash pipes up.

"They've become an important target group, you know—the ultra-wealthy." Wolfgang sprints over to the model to remove a loose thread, and I imagine a stunning European royal dancing the night away in Ibiza or on a yacht.

But Rikash and I have less superficial concerns to attend to. It's time for a quiet exit. I'm about to tap Rikash on the shoulder when my eyes are caught by a pair of models walking half-naked around the room. One is bare-breasted and wearing only a nude-coloured feathered skirt and sky-high heels; the other is in barely there panties that emphasize her buttocks. It's one thing to see sexually provocative ads in glossy magazines, but I'm disarmed by the sight of virtually undressed women in broad daylight in the name of fashion.

Wolfgang catches me frowning. "You are displeased with my work, Mademoiselle Lambert?" His tone is a touch accusing.

I've had more than my share of drama for today; nevertheless, I decide to be upfront with him. "It's not that I find your work unpleasant. I just feel sorry for those poor girls. They're walking around almost naked, and they look miserable."

He gives me a withering look. "It's important for me to create sexy clothes that your boyfriend will want to tear off you. Are you a prude, *ma chérie*?" His expression changes to amusement.

"No, I just appreciate it when people are treated with respect. And, by the way, those girls look younger than sixteen." The few sips of Champagne seem to have rid me of my usual reserve.

"Is that a reproach or some unsolicited legal advice?" Now he looks annoyed.

I put my glass down next to the collection catalogues. "Consider it both."

I signal to Rikash that I'm ready to leave. If Mr. de Vrees wants my head on a platter, so be it. He'll have to wait in line on Monday morning.

Rikash and I part company in the Crillon's lobby. I need to get out of this crazy scene. Antoine agrees to meet me in front of Le Bon Marché, the venerable department store in the 7th arrondissement, on rue de Sèvres. The cosmetics, shoe, and handbag departments are enough to make any woman squeal with delight, but today, I've had enough of fashion. I step instead into the food hall, La Grande Épicerie, where I find a mind-boggling array of delicacies such as exotic mustards, dried mushrooms, and jams made of rose petals, raspberries, and violets. There are imported products here too: the American section contains M&Ms, Twizzlers, and Ocean Spray cranberry juice—not exactly fine foods stateside, but exotic to the French, I suppose.

I walk through the aisles like a puppy that's lost her master. I can't believe I've been bamboozled again. I trusted Sandrine and have tried to do good work for her. And this is the second mess I've gotten myself into in less than two years. Have I turned into a major *caca* magnet? The singer Lena Horne once said, *Always be smarter than the people who hire you.* My advice would be somewhat different: Always run a background check on the people who hire you.

I make my way to the café and order a green tea and a *crème brûlée à la framboise* to calm my nerves. This situation with Sandrine is bound to affect my professional future: no one in the fashion world will take me seriously if I'm fired for complaining that my boss took credit for my work. It'll make me look like *une enfant gâtée.* But I can't help but be resentful.

Antoine appears in shorts and a T-shirt, having just been for a run along the Seine. He can tell by the look on my face that something's wrong. "What is it, Catou? You look like someone just died."

I finish my tea. "Well, that's not too far off."

"What do you mean?" He sits down and wipes the sweat off his face with his T-shirt.

"It's Sandrine. We caught her apprehending Pierre Le Furet and some other counterfeiters in the Tuileries Garden today. She somehow got access to our information and beat us to it."

Looking stunned, he shakes his head and reaches for my hand. "Here we go again."

# Chapter 40

I show up for work on Monday morning unsure what to expect. Antoine suggested I send the video from the gardens to the police and plead my case with senior management to protect my security.

I'm waiting for Rikash to show up so we can put our heads together when I hear voices in the hallway. Sandrine is outside her office, wearing new gold jewellery and a look of satisfaction, while the president of Dior and two senior executives shower her with praise. I'm at a loss.

Rikash saunters into our office looking like the cat who's just swallowed the canary. "I think I've managed to execute my plan flawlessly. You'll be proud." He sounds very sure of himself.

"Oh, really? What did you do?" I try to downplay my doubts.

He turns on his computer and brings up a video entitled "Sandrine in the Tuileries Garden." Whatever this is, it certainly doesn't look like it will be drama-free.

"And now, the *pièce de résistance.*" He logs onto Facebook and shows me that he's just loaded the video onto the site. "They say privacy is dead and that social networking holds the smoking gun. So there you have it."

He presses Play. First we see Le Furet shaking hands with the street vendors; then shots of us in the Tuileries, setting up the electronic devices; then Sandrine showing up to arrest the group; then the Indian criminal running away on rue de Rivoli. The words "Sandrine Cordier drops the ball in major Dior investigation" appear in bright red letters at the end of the clip.

*Merde!* I want to jump out the window onto avenue Montaigne.

"Rikash, what have you done?" My voice rises. "You've put our safety and our jobs at risk." I break out into a cold sweat and clutch at my office chair, gasping for air.

"Chill out, sunshine. I sent the video to her privately, so

there's no need to worry. Besides, it won't be on there for long—you just watch." His tone is still confident.

As my mind is cycling through the possible catastrophic consequences of what Rikash has done, Sandrine storms into our office, her face as red as a sauna bather's bottom and a look of terror in her eyes. She slams the door, then locks it. "Are you mad? How dare you?" she sneers, fixing her glare on Rikash. "Your video is very amateurish. Who do you think you are?"

"A very capable filmmaker, in fact. It was in my resumé. Don't you remember?" Somehow, he musters a sly grin, though I can barely move.

It's time for me to speak up. "How dare you leave us out of Le Furet's arrest? We did all the work, and even put our lives at risk for it. I can't believe your gall!"

Sandrine sees that we're not backing down. She bites her lower lip and switches tacks. "In case you two have forgotten, I'm the boss here. Whatever work you do for Dior is to the credit of the entire department." Her voice is low, but she looks a bit like a wild cat that's been captured by hunters. "What do you want from me?" she continues defensively.

"We want you to tell management the truth: that we're the ones who laid the groundwork for apprehending the counterfeiters, not you. Simple as that, really." Rikash sounds a lot calmer than I feel.

"Ha! You think I'm going to take orders from you because of this little video?"

Rikash points to his computer. "You're underestimating us, my dear. In case you missed it, one of the counterfeiters—the most dangerous one—got away from your ambush. It wasn't exactly a seamless operation. From my perspective, you botched it, and I think the media would agree with me. It's all in the presentation, isn't it?" He finishes with arms folded.

Sandrine's eyes narrow. She darts forward, trying to snatch Rikash's laptop away. "Give that to me!" she cries hysterically. "Let me see!"

He reacts by hiding it behind his back.

"It's over, Sandrine. Give it up," I say. "Either you tell Frédéric what happened or we do."

After a long, silent pause, she shocks me by beginning to weep, her jewelled hands flying up to her face to hide her tears. "I'm so sorry. I don't know what came over me," she says between sobs. "I didn't mean to do it. I'm so ashamed."

Ever the gentleman, Rikash hands her a tissue. "You should've thought of that before calling in the police, love."

"It's time for you to tell Frédéric the truth, Sandrine," I say, dialling his extension and asking him to come by my office, then crossing to the door to unlock it. I look into her eyes and see fear. She's cupping her hands between her knees like a child. I ask the million-dollar question: "Why go it alone, Sandrine? We could have done it together."

She sniffles. "Desperation, I guess. I really need a raise. Arnaud and I are in a tough place financially."

*Pauvre de moi.* Given her apartment in the city's poshest neighbourhood, it seems to me that "desperation" doesn't really apply to her situation. But then I remember Jeffrey's determination to maintain an excessive lifestyle, no matter what. After his company went public, he bought a yacht named *I Can't Get No Satisfaction* and a fleet of sports cars. For some people, enough is never enough.

Sandrine interrupts my musings. "After Arnaud lost his job and his shares became worthless, our debt grew. Now we owe more than the value of our assets." She looks down at her wedding band. "I didn't want to lose everything I inherited from my family, especially not my home." She looks away. "I figured our only way out was if I got a promotion. So when I found out what the two of you were up to, I thought it was my chance. I guess that was very childish of me." Her face is the picture of shame. "Please forgive me."

I try to feel sorry for her, but I can't. She has everything anyone could hope for. Save integrity.

"How did you figure out what we were doing?" Rikash asks.

She blows her nose before answering. "I overheard you talking about Le Furet one night and put two and two together. Coralie had caught him copying confidential information about our anti-counterfeiting efforts late one night when he still worked here. We learned he was sending it out to third parties. I fired him and we reported it to the police. He left right away for the south, so not that many people knew about it. I didn't realize he was still at it."

There's a knock on the door and Frédéric walks in. Seeing the look on Sandrine's face, his smile instantly changes to a frown. "Is something wrong?" he asks.

Rikash and I exchange glances. No matter what he thinks has happened, he certainly won't be prepared for this.

"Yes, Frédéric, there is," Sandrine replies flatly. "You'd better sit down."

# Chapter 41

"Dear Lord," Frédéric mutters. "What a day. And it's only just started." He looks exhausted. As Sandrine told her story, it was as though his world was crashing down. He's clearly as shocked as we are.

Now that Sandrine has gone back to her own office, Rikash shows Frédéric the video and plays the taped conversations. Frédéric watches and listens to it all without expression, then places his elbows on his knees, removes his glasses, and wipes them clean using his silk tie.

"To tell you the truth," he says, "I've had the feeling something was wrong for the longest time, but I just couldn't put my finger on it." He stares out at avenue Montaigne. "She wanted to know everything about your raids and was always asking for updates. She also tried to take credit for your idea about publicly destroying the seized goods, but I called her on that. Never in my wildest dreams did I think she would do something like this."

"I still can't believe the king of the Indian underworld was involved," Rikash says.

"Luckily, Rikash had the good sense to contact the police and the Indian embassy to let them know what he saw," I add. "The police managed to catch him, thanks to the lead provided by our video."

Frédéric looks at Rikash like he's just saved his life. "Thank god you handled this the way you did. Can you imagine the effect on our reputation if the Indian press found out a former Dior employee was collaborating with a Mumbai kingpin? We have four new stores opening in India in the next year." He stands up and leans against a bookshelf, looking tired. "You're very brave—both of you—and I commend you on your excellent work. I wish I had that kind of guts."

Rikash is beaming, and I'm flattered too. Despite our rocky professional start, I was sure that Frédéric would do the right thing and take our side.

"Your efforts will not go unnoticed, I assure you." He

walks toward the door. "I will see to it myself. I'm sorry I ever doubted you."

"No harm, no foul," Rikash replies jovially. "Besides, we've worked with worse jerks."

Frédéric laughs, thankfully, so Rikash and I do too.

"I want you two to accompany me to the president's office," Frédéric says. "He needs to see this video for himself. And I'm certainly not going to take credit for your hard work." He opens the door and politely signals for us to precede him out. I'm comforted by the fact that not all my colleagues are disloyal.

After a tense meeting with the company president that concluded with some admittedly satisfying accolades for our work, I collapse into my office chair. Rikash has run off to Paris Plage for his lunch break to show off his hip hop abs. Not even the drama of breaking up an international counterfeiting ring can dampen his enthusiasm for meeting handsome French men on a fake beach along the Seine.

I'm still having trouble understanding why Sandrine

took it upon herself to organize Le Furet's arrest alone. I guess we're all in danger of letting pride cloud our judgment.

A knock on the door pulls me out of my reverie. Sandrine walks in, pale and dejected. She looks like she's been crying again: traces of mascara line her cheeks. "I've just been demoted," she says softly, looking at the floor.

I wait for her to go on.

She fiddles with her Cartier tank watch and her glittering tennis bracelet. I once read an article about former Wall Street execs visiting pawn shops to exchange platinum Rolexes and heirloom diamond necklaces for cash after the financial meltdown. I wonder if Sandrine will have to sell off some of her baubles. I once again try to feel sorry for her.

"I got what I deserve," she continues, looking me straight in the eye. "Catherine, I'm sorry. I know I was supposed to be your mentor, and I ended up stabbing you in the back. I've let you down." She wipes a tear from her cheek. "To tell you the truth, I think that, deep down, I was worried you would take my place."

Really? Lately, I've felt like a puddle of insecurity riddled with self-doubt, thanks to my former colleagues at Edwards & White and Jeffrey's trial. So this is a surprise.

"It's probably too soon to ask, but I hope you'll find it in your heart to forgive me." She tilts her head sideways like a young child begging for her mother's approval.

"That *is* a lot to ask, Sandrine. Trust is the basis of all relationships, professional and otherwise. Once it's gone, it's very hard to get it back."

"I realize that." She looks away. "I can assure you it's costing me dearly. I'm no longer Dior's general counsel, and Arnaud is filing for divorce."

*Ah non.* No matter how reprehensible her behaviour has been, I feel a tiny wave of empathy for her. We all make mistakes, and the price we pay for them can indeed be steep. Karma is one tough lady.

"I'm very sorry to hear that," I murmur as she walks to the door.

My cellphone rings, and I look down and recognize Lisa's number.

"Lisa! Am I happy to hear your voice!"

"Me too, sweetie. I just heard the incredible news."

I freeze. What news? How can she know about the counterfeiting bust already?

"It was all over the financial news—Charles caught it first. You must be so relieved!"

Oh! Unbelievably, I've almost forgotten the trial. "You mean about Jeffrey?"

"*Yes!* What else? He's going to jail!" she shouts joyfully. I run a Google search and see that the verdict was rendered early this morning: *Guilty on all counts.*

A deep sense of peace washes over me. A major thorn in my side is gone, once and for all. I want to throw open my office windows and shout my happiness from the rooftops.

"Yes, I'm relieved. The corporate world is rid of one more thief," I say, thinking about Le Furet too.

"No kidding. Now you can focus on planning my wedding!" she adds. It's less than a month away now.

"You'll be thrilled," I assure her. "My mother picked out the most gorgeous decorations. It'll be exquisite."

Now my office phone rings, and to my astonishment, I see Wolfgang's name appear on the display. Lisa and I agree to talk and celebrate later, and I pick up.

"*Bonjour,* Mademoiselle Lambert."

"Hello, Monsieur de Vrees. How can I help you?" What could he want?

"Congratulations. A little bird told me that lawyers do come in handy, after all." He's his usual melodramatic self, but his tone isn't unfriendly.

"Thank you. I appreciate the compliment. I understand you don't give them out often."

"Hmm. That is incorrect. I don't give them out *ever.*"

"In that case, it means even more, doesn't it? Thank you." Is there a catch? I wonder.

"I'm not finished."

"Okay." Here it comes.

He clears his throat. "I wanted to say that I appreciated your honesty at the Crillon the other day."

I'm totally thrown now. I can't think of what to say.

"You see, legal and business details bore me to death. And not many people would have expressed their opinion like you did. Actually, I can't think of anyone else on this planet who would have said those things to me. You've got guts, *ma chère.* Bravo."

I have to smile—I helped crack a global counterfeiting ring and impressed one of the world's most revered designers, all in one day. Not bad.

My cellphone beeps with a text from Antoine: *Have u hrd the amzing news?*

Antoine must have been following Jeffrey's trial more closely than I thought. This is a win for both of us.

I jump on the line and call him. "Yes, Lisa just called. *Dieu merci!* I'm so relieved!"

"Your testimony and evidence were crucial. I'm so proud of you, Catou."

My eyes water. I'm still a little ashamed of what happened with Jeffrey, but Antoine always makes me feel appreciated.

"How did things go today?" he asks.

"I'll have to tell you later what Rikash did—it's a long story—but the upshot is, Sandrine admitted to taking credit for our work and got demoted. Oh, and her husband wants a divorce."

"Wow. Now that's what I call a rough day. It must've come as a shock to your colleagues."

"Yes. You should have seen Frédéric's face—he was staggered. We talked to the president of Dior, and he promoted Frédéric to general counsel on the spot."

"Sounds like a good move. Frédéric seems like a very smart man."

"Yes, he is," I say with a hint of glee. "And guess what? He wants you to be co-counsel on the eShop lawsuit."

"Really?" he asks, surprised. "I thought that was off the table."

"Not anymore. We need the extra help now that we're involved in this criminal investigation too."

"Thanks, Catou. You're the best. We'll celebrate tonight. I'll put some pink Champagne on ice when I get home."

Just as I'm about to slip outside for some much-needed fresh air, my cellphone rings again. I shrug and answer it without checking the display. This is one crazy day.

"Hello, Catherine."

It's the last voice I expected to hear.

"Hello, Jeffrey." My tone is controlled, but my knees are trembling and I want to gag into my office wastebasket. I put him on speakerphone and press Record. I've done it before; I'll do it again. Who knows what Jeffrey's capable of?

"You must be thrilled: you got what you wanted. I'm going to jail."

"It's what you deserve." There's a long, awkward silence. I can hear him breathing, and it revolts me.

"I'm just calling to let you know that I'm going to appeal the decision."

I knew things were too good to be true. Moments ago, I was sure I was finally going to be able to move on with my life, but it was foolish to think this was all behind me. I'm dealing with a wealthy man who can afford expensive lawyers. The words of Henry Ford come to mind: *Money doesn't change men, it merely unmasks them.*

"As you please, Jeffrey. Just remember that no lawyer can change the truth. Facts are stubborn things. It sounds to me like you're throwing good money after bad. Actually, I take that back. Your money isn't good, it's dirty."

"Goodbye, Catherine. See you in court," he snaps. The line goes dead, and my happiness seems to have died along with it.


Antoine and I sit in Le Restaurant, the acclaimed dining room of L'Hôtel, one of the city's most charming establishments. Nestled in the heart of Saint-Germain on rue des Beaux Arts, the hotel has been a hideaway for Parisians for two centuries. Oscar Wilde lived here, and the exclusive guest list is heavy on celebrities.

We're here for a gourmet candlelight meal and a private swim in the vaulted underground pool. Antoine's surprise was really thoughtful, so it's gut-wrenching to have to deliver the news about Jeffrey's appeal, but I figure it's best to get it out into the open before the Champagne arrives.

When I tell him, his eyes become as wide as saucers.

He places his serviette on his lap and opens his menu in silence. I've learned how Antoine deals with bad news: he needs a little time to process it. Still, my heart is pulled in a million different directions. I just want us to be done with this chapter of my past.

After reviewing the long wine list for what feels like an eternity, he finally says, "I'm not that surprised. On what grounds?"

"I have no idea. We didn't discuss his legal strategy. It was a pretty short conversation."

He puts the menu aside and smiles. "Okay, I'm having the frog legs—they're apparently to die for. I suggest you order the sea bass and we share the foie gras with candied rhubarb as an appetizer. How does that sound?"

Relieved, I reach for his hand. Antoine may not be the world's most relaxed guy, but he has a heart of gold and knows how to live in the moment. He also knows that there's a strong chance Jeffrey will lose his appeal.

"That sounds perfect." I lean across the table and kiss him.

"We better not eat too much, or we'll sink to the bottom of the pool," he adds, patting his stomach. "And that isn't what I had in mind when I booked it for just the two of us."

# Chapter 42

I'm meeting my mother and Yulia at Les Nuits des Thés, a quaint tea room on rue de Beaune, near our apartment. It has a feminine atmosphere: flowered vintage tablecloths, soft draperies, and a collection of lovely antiques. I've decided the best approach is to introduce Yulia to *maman* during a leisurely lunch without any pressure. Why not simply let my mother be seduced by Yulia's irresistible charm?

My mother appears in a long black dress and a cloche hat, her lips bright red. She's glued to her cellphone. She wouldn't have been caught dead with one a few years ago: proof that everything does change.

"Hello, *ma chérie,*" she says, kissing me on the side of the head.

"*Bonjour, maman.* You look beautiful today."

"Thank you." She peers at my ensemble: a psychedelic 1960s shift dress, a canary yellow J.Crew cardigan I picked up in New York, and a multitude of coloured bangles. I can tell she doesn't like it.

"Does Dior approve of you dressing like that?" she asks. "It's a bit loud, *non*?"

"You don't like my dress? It's vintage Pucci."

"Let's just say that it would make a lovely tablecloth."

I ignore her. My personal style may not always be in line with classic French taste, but I've come to embrace bright colours, and wearing them makes me happy.

"So how was New York? And the trial?"

"Everything went well," I answer. I'm not anxious to linger on the topic. "Speaking of work, I think I've found someone to help you out with your business. Her name is Yulia, and she's meeting us here in a few minutes."

She stares at me incredulously. "What are you talking about, *ma chérie*? I can't afford staff yet."

"Okay, then consider her an intern, not an employee. She's a student, so she can work for a small salary, and if it works out, you can pay her a commission. You'll find a solution—you always do."

She shakes her head, not entirely happy, I can tell. "I can't believe you did this. Where did you find this person?"

Just then, Yulia walks in, looking like she's straight out of a perfume ad. Every head in the room turns. She's wearing a light pink chiffon dress, tan leather sandals, and a matching belt. Her hair is in a high ponytail, and her cheeks look tan and healthy.

"*Bonjour, madame.*" She reaches for my mother's hand. *Maman* looks completely enthralled.

"Yulia has been modelling in Paris. We met at a Dior photo shoot," I say. "She was wearing an outfit that made her look like an X-rated Kermit the Frog, so I thought I'd better save her from that."

"Ah, you're a model. You're a real beauty, *ma chérie*. Where are you from?"

"Bulgaria. I've only been in Paris for a year."

I see from the expression on her face that it's been a long and difficult year. I hope this lunch will send her life in a different direction.

"And you're studying interior design?" my mother continues.

Yulia shoots me a look, unsure how to answer.

"Not exactly," I jump in. "Yulia is passionate about design

but hasn't taken any classes yet. She's looking into studying on a part-time basis. But she's done some impressive work on her agency apartment." I wink at Yulia conspiratorially.

"*Ah bon? Formidable.* What is it about interior design that you like?" my mother asks, turning this chat into an informal interview. I smile and take a sip of tea.

"I love spending time on the Internet, looking for accessories and original furniture. I also like browsing at flea markets." Yulia's eyes light up. She looks nothing like the vulnerable and fragile gamine I met just weeks ago. She's more like a businesswoman in training. No one would guess that she's only fifteen.

I nod at my mother, knowing this is exactly what she has little time for these days. They chat about the best places to find decor items and inspiration.

"So, Yulia, are you interested in making a career out of this?" my mother finally asks. "It's hard work, and the clients can be difficult. It's not just about buying things that you like; you need to consider your client's taste first. And it certainly won't pay as much as modelling for Dior."

"Yes, I know, but I'm a very hard worker. And I've had enough of modelling. I'm definitely looking for a new line of work."

"I understand." My mother pats Yulia's hand gently. "I modelled too, you know." This was back in her youth, when the industry wasn't as cutthroat and having hips and breasts was considered an asset, not a liability.

"*Non*, really? For who?"

My mother waves her hand dismissively. "Oh, a department store that no longer exists and Madame Grès."

"Madame Grès? *C'est incroyable!*" Yulia looks stunned.

"You know who she is? That's way before your time, *mon enfant.*"

"I saw an exhibit about her couture house last year. What an impressive woman she was."

I listen to the two of them gabbing like two old friends. It's a match made in heaven.

"Okay, then it's settled. You'll work for me," my mother announces as the waiter arrives with a new pot of tea. "We'll get you a new computer so you can work from home, and you can come to the south of France for meetings when needed."

"Really?" Yulia claps her hands gleefully.

"*Fantastique!*" I'm thrilled to be helping out two people I care so much about. "I'll have the paperwork drawn up for a student visa."

"Wonderful. I think we should order some food, *non?* I'll have a fruit salad," my mother announces.

"Me too," Yulia concurs.

"Suit yourselves, but I'm having the caramelized cheese tart, the house specialty," I say.

My mother starts to wag her finger in mock disapproval. But I'm past worrying what she thinks about my eating habits.

Yulia changes her mind. "You know what? I'm done modelling. I'll have that too!"

My mother gives in. "Ah, to hell with the diet. Make that three tarts."

Kate Moss said, *Nothing tastes as good as skinny feels,* but today we're proving her wrong. "And why don't you add a bottle of pink Champagne?" my mother tells the waiter.

I guess the apple doesn't fall far from the tree, after all.

# Chapter 43

"Catherine, that dress looks wonderful on you," Frédéric says as I enter his office. This is the first personal compliment I've received from him, and I accept it demurely.

"*Merci.*" I'm wearing a brocade jacket over a peach vintage sheath dress and a bow-shaped Valentino belt that belonged to my mother. She's recently cleaned out some closets, and I'm the lucky recipient of some very fashionable castoffs.

"How are you doing?" I ask. His workload has increased since he's taken over as general counsel.

"Just fine. Management's been supportive and everyone on the team is very understanding. By the way, the employees have been told that Sandrine has taken on a reduced work-load for personal reasons."

I nod. Keen as I am for Rikash and me to get credit for uncovering the truth, I can see how it's wise to keep the matter under wraps.

"Okay. I'll fill Chris in today," I say. "Are there any other developments I should know about?" I'm curious about the next steps in a big operation like this.

"Tons of counterfeit merchandise was seized in Pierre's apartment, along with other contraband and cash. The Parisian police, French customs, and the FBI are all investigating." He shakes his head in disbelief. "It's all surreal."

"And what about Sandrine? What will she be doing now?"

"Well, she's been taken off anything having to do with counterfeiting. She'll be handling administrative matters, negotiating our leases and the like."

"Ouch. That's a major demotion. What about eShop?"

"She won't be overseeing that case anymore, either. Antoine and I will take care of it."

"Oh good! You won't be disappointed, I promise."

"But I have something else I've been hoping to talk to you about." He turns his chair to face a map of the world on the wall. "You're a hard worker and a loyal employee, Catherine. We're thinking of offering you an opportunity to branch out from the law. Would that interest you?" Seeing my surprised expression, he continues, "As you know, Dior is looking to expand its brand globally, and there is a business development opportunity opening up in India." He turns to face me.

"India?" I travelled to Goa after university, but spending time on a beach doesn't teach you much about a country or its culture. I've learned a little about India from Rikash and would love to visit again, but could I really move there? I think back to Shanghai and how the runway shows were infused with an intoxicating Eastern influence. Maybe a new challenge is just what I need.

"The higher-ups here were impressed with how you and Rikash handled the fallout with Sandrine. And thanks to you, one of the most wanted men in India will be extradited back to his country to stand trial for murder and racketeering."

Our little amateur sleuthing mission now seems even more audacious.

"The consensus is that you have the skills for a business position abroad: you're resourceful and dedicated. You've also proven your loyalty." He sounds enthusiastic. "I think it could be a fantastic opportunity for you, Catherine. It will allow you to grow with the company and learn. Not to mention travel."

I begin to speak, but he anticipates my words. "Don't worry, Rikash is part of the package."

"That's good. I really couldn't manage anywhere without him."

But it's Antoine I'm most concerned about. After all, I moved to Paris to be with him, and we're only now starting to really feel in sync. Can I realistically spend time abroad, and so far away? I ask for some time to think about it.

"Sure, I understand. Won't Antoine be thrilled to spend time with you in India?"

Maybe, I think. Antoine always puts my needs ahead of his own. "He likely will, but we do need to talk it through."

I imagine store openings and fashion shows in the palaces of Jaipur and the deserts of Jaisalmer, places I've only read about in travel magazines. The idea is invigorating, I have to admit.

We call Rikash in—though I already know he'll be doing somersaults at the idea.

When he arrives, I waste no time in breaking the news. "How about a new job for Dior in India?"

He smiles and waves his index finger in the air. "Don't kid about things like that, dah-ling. You know how I feel about my homeland. I can make jokes about it all I want, but no one else can. It's off limits."

"Who says I'm joking?"

He looks like he's just seen the ghost of Mother Teresa.

"We're serious, Rikash," Frédéric says. "I've just offered Catherine an opportunity there. Nothing is set in stone yet, but it's a strong possibility."

"And, of course, you'd be part of the deal," I add with a wink.

"*Oh my god!* That's fantastic!" Rikash jumps up and down, moving in for a hug. "My prayers to Shiva have been answered!"

"You would be instrumental in making this work," I add, my voice serious now. "It wouldn't be a legal position but a business development one. I would need your help overcoming the cultural and language barriers, and who knows what else."

"That sounds perfect! And more fun than legal work

anyway! No offence, Frédéric." He starts dancing and breaks into a rendition of Madonna's "Like a Prayer."

Frédéric laughs before interrupting the show. "How about we send you both to Fashion Week in Mumbai? It's organized by a prominent Indian cosmetics brand. You can make up your minds when you get back."

We're elated. Outside Frédéric's office, Rikash grabs my hand and looks deep into my eyes. "It'll take some work, dahling, but I'll teach you everything you need to know about India, including how to look like Padma Lakshmi. Yoga and spicy food aren't the only things that are hot in my country."

I meet Yulia at a café in the 9th arrondissement. We're planning an apartment hunt today. I arrive out of breath, having run from the metro. I take off my hat and she greets me with two kisses. She looks like a breath of fresh air in her rolled-up boyfriend jeans, turquoise cashmere sweater, and pale ballet flats.

"I'm so happy you picked out this neighbourhood," I say as we sit down. "It's where I used to live. You'll just adore it. It's fun and unpretentious, and the rents are pretty affordable."

Her budget is modest, though she's now paid off all her debts to her agency. She earned a handsome fee for her work in Dior's latest show, so she's now set for a few months' rent and tuition.

"There are terrific restaurants and cafés. And great little shops, too. I'm sure you'll have a blast, *ma chérie!*" We've discovered a mutual admiration for all things vintage and sparkly. She grins and takes a sip of lemonade.

"I have good news and bad news," I tell her after ordering coffee. "Which do you want first?"

She looks at me anxiously. "What? Please don't tell me that your mother's changed her mind about me."

"Of course not. Are you kidding? My mother's completely smitten." I pull an envelope from my handbag. "The good news is that you look breathtaking." I have the pictures from Yulia's photo shoot with Jean-Michel. I show her the untouched photographs. "The bad news is that this is what you'll look like if you don't use our new face cream." I pull out the digitally enhanced photo and wait for her reaction.

She peers at the prints from behind her oversized hipster glasses and bursts out laughing. I'm glad she isn't taking this too seriously. "*Oh la la! Quelle horreur!*" she exclaims.

"Can you believe what they do to sell their products? It's complete bullshit, *non?*"

"Watch your mouth, young lady. This is my employer you're talking about here, so show some respect, *s'il vous plaît.*" I wag my finger in jest.

"Pfft, whatever." She's clearly over the whole modelling thing. "It's just shocking to see my face like this. I'm fifteen, remember?"

In the altered image, she looks at least fifty years older. The methods our industry uses to sell so-called magical potions are laughable, there's no way around it.

"I just hope the cute boys around here won't recognize me in this ad." She cringes.

"Oh, please. You're stunning. Did you look in the mirror this morning? Besides, it's what's on the inside that matters, right? But watch out for those Parisian boys, okay?" I say, my protective side kicking in again.

"Isn't your boyfriend Parisian?"

"Yes, he is. But we're together first and foremost because we respect each other's minds. It's not all about appearances. Whatever you do, go for the smart boys—they're the sexiest."

"Yes, *maman.*" She finishes her lemonade in one gulp

and grabs her bag. "Let's go. I can't wait to find an apartment and sign my new lease!"

We arrive at a tiny apartment, and as we open the door, Yulia gasps. "Wow!"

It's a fourth-floor walk-up, with tall windows overlooking a small courtyard and a school. It has a compact kitchen and a tidy bathroom. It's the perfect hideaway for our designer-in-training.

"This space has lots of potential," Yulia says, taking in every inch. "I would put my bed here, my desk there, and an armoire there." She points to a space next to the window. "And I would add bright silk curtains. What do you think, Catherine?" She twirls around, her ballet slippers barely touching the antique wooden floors.

"You don't need my approval—you've got it all figured out. And now you can take advantage of your designer discount when you're shopping."

We sign the lease and make our way back to the street. Yulia gives me a warm hug. She's deliriously happy. As I take her picture in front of her new building, a young man with dishevelled dirty blond hair and wearing dark skinny jeans walks by. He's carrying an easel and a tall stack of books. He can't take his eyes off Yulia and whispers "*Bonjour, mademoiselle*" before entering the building.

I wink before whisking her away. "I think we might have found a smart one."

A girlish smile lights up her face.

Mae West once said, *I never worry about diets. The only carrots that interest me are the number you get in a diamond.* The lady knew what she was talking about.

Today is the big day: I'm visiting the fine jewellery atelier. Until now, I've been too busy to take up Laetitia on her offer.

I meet her in the Dior lobby. She's stylish as usual in a black wool dress with puffy pink sleeves and a crystal necklace she's wearing as a belt.

"*Bonjour,* Catherine! So happy you could finally make it." She gives me a warm smile. "You will just die when you see this collection."

She leads me into a room hidden away behind massive

grey double doors that are flanked by two security guards. My jaw hits the floor as I take in the shimmering diamonds, pink sapphires, and pearls sparkling from every corner. "*C'est magnifique!*"

"Isn't it amazing? Our jewellery designers like to play with semi-precious stones and lacquered gold. Their inspiration comes from pop culture, floral motifs, and the cinema. This is the rose collection." She points to a dozen flowered pieces. "According to the designer, these pieces represent the union of jewellery and haute couture. And the rose was Mr. Dior's favourite flower."

She then shows me the love collection, made with diamonds and Burmese rubies, which cast rays of red light onto the wall behind us.

"This is absolutely breathtaking," I stammer, overwhelmed. I can only imagine the painstaking work involved in creating such magnificent pieces. "No fakes in here, I guess," I joke.

"Oh, no!" She shakes her pretty head. "Only the real thing."

I wonder who can afford such marvels. Clearly, only clients who can sample luxury's highest tier.

"These two pieces are made of pink gold, tourmaline,

and marquise-cut diamonds." She points to a set of bangles. "They were influenced by the colours and spirit of Bollywood," she goes on. "Several famous actresses have worn them in popular Hindi films. We're thrilled about that." She beams with pride.

I smile back, thinking about my upcoming trip to Mumbai. What an amazing time to be part of it all—the subcontinent is clearly influencing European designs.

After we leave the room, Laetitia puts a hand on my shoulder. "*Alors?* What did you think?"

"Can't you see the drool here?" I point to the corner of my mouth. "Seriously, it was divine. Thank you so much, Laetitia. I'm so grateful for the visit."

I put on my coat and head to the elevator. The doors open, revealing a tired-looking Sandrine. She's dressed in slim black cigarette pants, a camel-coloured trench, dark sunglasses, and flats. She looks at me as I walk in, then looks down.

I take a few seconds to collect myself, then carefully tell her what I've been wanting to say for the past few days: "Sandrine, you're forgiven."

She nods sombrely and whispers, "Thank you, Catherine. That means a lot."

I leave the office feeling lighthearted. Despite its flaws, this business is about making people dream. The exquisite gems, the stunning fabrics, the expensive advertisements, and the runway shows allow us to escape reality and envision a more beautiful world, however temporarily. It's something we all need. The French writer Stendhal summarized it perfectly: *Beauty is nothing other than the promise of happiness.*

# Chapter 44

Christian Dior believed that pink was the sweetest of colours, symbolizing joy and femininity. So it's fitting that my mother has chosen pink, along with other pastels, for Lisa's wedding.

It's a gorgeous day, without a cloud in the sky. Thanks to Yulia, flowered pillows dot the grounds so guests can lounge in style, and umbrellas of pink-and-white-striped canvas cater to those who prefer to sit in the shade. Some of my mother's beautiful antique furniture has been brought out onto the lawn. It's gracious and elegant, but not over the top.

My mother gazes at Lisa and Charles from across the garden, looking as though she just might believe in happily ever after. She's orchestrated the event with panache, and is now mingling and making sure that everyone is content. French women don't have a shelf life, it occurs to me. We admire the maturity and wisdom gained through experience. Here, femininity is something that endures. I look forward to happily growing older here.

Christophe, my stepfather, is a chef, and the hors d'oeuvres he has prepared have a pink and coral theme: salmon, trout, prawns, grapefruit, and watermelon. And, of course, there's pink Champagne by the caseload. A jazz quintet is having a blast playing standards from the Great American Songbook.

I'm wearing a vintage confection of cream lace and pink silk with a calf-length bouffant skirt. It's from a local shop: no designer frocks today. I did splurge a bit on an Olympia Le-Tan minaudière I'm using as a clutch, whimsically embroidered with a vintage cover of *The Great Gatsby*. For Antoine, I ordered a custom shirt from Charvet and a pink silk Dior pocket square.

My mother is beautiful in a pale yellow dress and matching hat, her happy face lighting up the garden. Yulia, who offered her assistance, is gorgeous in a blush-coloured dress to which she's added a handmade silk flower pin.

Rikash looks dashing in his seersucker jacket, Bermuda shorts, and pink gingham bow tie. He's decided to channel his inner prepster, and the look suits him to a T. He's also sporting a happy grin; knowing that we're soon to be flying to his native land has put a new spring in his step.

Lisa, unsurprisingly, looks divine in her white knee-length Pucci dress and long baby pink veil. Her Giuseppe Zanotti stilettos are embellished with crystals that shimmer in the sunlight.

After the tear-jerking ceremony, we're all enjoying cocktails on the lawn overlooking my mother's flower beds, while Cole Porter's "Let's Do It, Let's Fall in Love" plays in the background.

"What's this I hear about India?" My mother asks, replenishing my Champagne.

Seeing Rikash's face, I have an idea how she might have gotten wind of this. "Rikash and I may have an opportunity there," I say, sipping my drink. "It's only a possibility; nothing is confirmed yet."

I'm not sure how she'll react, so I look over at the newlyweds.

"That's great!" she says. This is a relief—it's not the time for a cross-examination. "I'd love to visit you there. I hear there are some fantastic yoga retreats. And now that I have Yulia, I can travel a bit."

"Things are working out with her, then?"

"*Absolument.* She's *une petite merveille.* My clients love her. They're all buying the silk flowers she makes. Aren't they lovely? I'm very grateful for her, *ma chérie.*"

Lisa's beside us now, offering hugs all around. "Thank you for everything! This is hands-down the best day of my life."

"It's our pleasure," my mother answers. "Friends are like family around here."

Rikash barges in on the group hug. "So happy to hear that, *maman!*" He kisses my mother on the cheek, and she chuckles.

"Okay, *mes enfants,* it's time to move on to the tent for dinner." She leads us to another area of the property.

The four-course dinner, with matching wines from a local vineyard, is divine. At one point, I clink my glass to indicate that I'll be saying a few words. I stand up and offer a heartfelt toast.

Afterward, Antoine leans over to embrace me softly. I run my fingers through his windblown hair, and we gaze into each other's eyes, taking in this special moment. "That was great, Catou." He kisses me again before we dig into our terrine. "I need to enjoy every second with you before you run off on your next crazy adventure." Antoine and I have discussed my job offer, and he's supportive of it, so long as Paris remains our home base. He's actually looking forward to discovering India and its treasures.

Looking around, a feeling of deep contentment comes over me. I'm surrounded by the people I love, and right now, life seems as perfect as it can be. During a quick phone conversation, Chris let me know that he'd be spending most of his time in the near future shuttling between L.A. and various cities in China, the major current counterfeiting hubs. It means that I will see very little of him for a while; I suspect it's for the best.

"Is there anything on this menu I should be worried about?" Rikash whispers into my ear.

I shake my head. "No, you're fine. There are no strange animal parts."

"Phew." He reaches for his glass of Champagne, then spends the evening entertaining Lisa's family and flirting with one of her California relatives. We eat and drink for hours before the dessert arrives: a divine *croquembouche*— a huge tower of profiteroles—in a rainbow of pastel colours with a tiny birdcage at its side. The guests take pictures of Lisa and Charles next to it, then my mother opens the cage's door and two lovebirds fly off into the night.

Later on, music plays as a disco ball throws flashes of light throughout the tent. Rikash jumps up from his seat and gets the party started by hopping around the dance floor to "Sexy and I Know It." Antoine follows suit, wrapping his tie around his forehead and grooving with my mother in the middle of the crowd.

When Grace Jones' upbeat rendition of "La Vie en rose" begins to play, Rikash grabs my arm and shakes his thing while the crowd merrily looks on. After a few minutes of showing off his moves à la *So You Think You Can Dance*, he twirls me around, then whispers, "Just wait until we get to India. Then I'll show you how to really dance."

"Now you're talking," I laugh between pirouettes.

We finish our routine with a dramatic dip, and Rikash giggles at me. "You, my dah-ling, are a star."

# *Acknowledgements*

Irst, a major *merci beaucoup* to my lovely editor, Lorissa
Sengara, for her invaluable wisdom, dedication and
impressive élan, which are as authentic as can be. Also, a
sincere and heartfelt thank-you to the entire HarperCollins
Canada team for their continued support and enthusiasm.

A special thank you to my agent, Peter Bernstein, and
his lovely wife, Amy, for their wise counsel and love of
everything French.

Thank you to all my dear friends for their ongoing
support. A special mention goes to Isabelle Rayle-Doiron
and Marie-Claude Germain for their precious feedback. It
means the world to me.

A major thank-you to all who provided me with a

glimpse into the coveted world of international glamour and haute couture, as well as Parisian chic: Heather McDonald, Corinne Champagner Katz, Jacques Lee Pelletier, Virginie Vincens, Christine Maestracci, Caroline Lemoine, Gerard Vannoote, Denis Boulianne, Pascale Bourbeau, Serge Jean Laviolette, Marie Geneviève Cyr, Carole Villoresi, Valerie Salembier, Jean-Pierre Lee, Frédéric Loury, Marc and Sophie Le Guillou, Haleigh Walsworth, Frankie Springer, Dana Thomas, and Emilie Higle.

Continuing love and gratitude to the Laflèche and Commune families. I am so blessed to me surrounded by your encouragement and panache.

Finally, I am beyond grateful to Patrice Commune for his immense generosity, patience, and unwavering support. You are the *éclair* to my *chocolat*.

Also available from

*Harper Weekend*

"A stylish and very entertaining debut."
—Isabel Wolff, author of *A Vintage Affair*